The Magnolia At Christmas

By

Dennis Roy Maynard

Book Eight
The Magnolia Series

Dionysus Publications
49 Via Del Rossi
Rancho Mirage, California 92270

Email Orders & Comments: Episkopols@aol.com
Telephone: 760.324.8589
ISBN 9781497414365

www.Episkopols.com

Dionysus Publications
Books for clergy and the people they serve.

FOR SPECIAL OFFERS
AND
VOLUME DISCOUNTS,
ORDER DOCTOR MAYNARD'S BOOKS
AT:

www.Episkopols.com

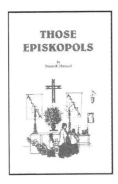

Those Episkopols

Forgive & Get Your Life Back

The Magnolia Series (8 Books)

When Sheep Attack

Preventing A Sheep Attack

Healing For Pastors and People Following a Sheep Attack

COVER DESIGN

I am grateful to Chris Koonce of Fort Worth, Texas, for designing the cover for this book. He is a very talented young artist. Chris earned a Bachelor of Fine Arts degree in 1991 from the University of North Texas. I encourage you to visit his website to view his portfolio of artwork. There are several opportunities for personalized gifts for yourself and others. He can also be a great resource for fundraising opportunities for your organization, parish, or school. Please visit his website at:

www.kcfunart.com

ALSO
ON YOU TUBE AT KCFUNART

DEDICATION

This book is for my grandchildren.
I now have three, but I remain hopeful.
I am grateful for
Jonathan David, Emory Madeleine and Bennett Greyson.
You give me three more reasons
to thank God for giving me
another day
on planet earth.

Postscript:
Just as this book goes through the final editing process
before release,
we've learned that grandchild number four is on the way.
Happy. Happy. Happy.

Forward

When I finished *The Changing Magnolia* two years ago, I believed the voices from Falls City, Georgia, had grown silent. About six months ago (at this writing), one lone voice spoke to me from her prison cell. Virginia Mudd continued to reveal her ongoing saga. Soon, others joined the conversation. Some of the old timers such as Almeda, Stone, and Chief Sparks spoke most clearly. The volume increased even further as the newer residents to the Falls City drama began to make their voices known. Pastor Melvin and Rose MacClaren, Bishop Sean Evans and his lover, Jim Vernon, added to the chorus. When I began to hear Ned Boone speak to me from the grave, I knew that another book in *The Magnolia Series* was inevitable.

I am grateful to my family, friends, and readers. You have encouraged me to allow their voices to speak and record their stories between the covers of an eighth book. For me, the most exciting part of this process is that I don't know what these characters are going to do until the final chapter is written.

My wife, Nancy, has read and re-read my manuscripts and made multiple suggestions that have greatly improved this work. In a very real way, she has helped me breathe life into the colorful characters that call Falls City, Georgia, home. Much of the excellence in this book is due to her many contributions.

I am also grateful to the dynamic congregation of Saint Jude in Ocean View, Hawaii. They not only provided my wife and me with wonderful *Aloha Hospitality*, but with a reclusive month to finish this book. Being in their presence renewed my spirit, touched my soul, and filled me with hope for the Church's greater mission to the poor.

I am indebted, in particular, to all the fans of *The Magnolia Series*. You have promoted this series through your bookstores, Facebook, various social media pages, your churches, and your book clubs. Thanks, as well, for the positive reviews you've written about the books on Amazon.com. The faithful members of First Church would have ceased to speak long ago had it not been for your encouragement. Because you have learned to love them, and you have loved to hate some of them, this volume is possible.

Will there be a ninth *Magnolia Book*? I honestly don't know. It's totally dependent on the good citizens at Historic First Church in Falls City, Georgia. As of this date, however, they have once again chosen to be silent.

In spite of multiple proofreads, revisions, and editorial services, a few little gremlins always seem to creep into the final copy of any book. For this, I ask your understanding and forgiveness.

Now... do you smell the incense? The bell is ringing in the First Church steeple. Do you see the choir and acolytes forming the procession? The organist is bringing the prelude to a grand crescendo. God is calling the community of faith to worship. We need to hurry. Every seat in the nave is filled with worshippers. Once again, the Holy Mysteries will be celebrated. The ancient but ever new story will be repeated. Prayers will be offered for the sick, the poor, and the dying. The Risen Christ will make Himself present with us in the Holy Sacrament. We will leave this place forgiven and renewed to carry His love and grace into the world. It's a good thing we are about to do.

Come. All is in readiness. The service is about to begin. Welcome to Historic First Church in Falls City, Georgia. I'm so glad you're here.

Dennis Maynard, D. Min.
Autumn, 2014

Primary Character Review

Falls City, Georgia

This is a fictional town in South Georgia. It's just the kind of place most all of us would like to call home. If our ancestors were white Europeans, certain privileges would belong to us. If we inherited their land and money, life would even be better. Many of the historic buildings and homes still stand along the tree-lined streets with manicured lawns.

Historic First Church (Episcopal)

It is the parish of the socially elite. This is the parish to join after you've been accepted into membership at the country club. Serving on the First Church Vestry is a plus for young attorneys seeking partnership in their law firms. The Church, all denominations, plays a major role in the lives of the citizens of this community. The fact is, if you don't attend a church on Sunday, you'd better hide your car in the garage.

The Reverend and Mrs. Steele Austin

Steele and Randi are a most unlikely couple to be called as the rector and spouse of Historic First Church. Father Austin's understanding of the Gospel continually clashes with the unwritten membership standards of the parish. His inclusive mission is an affront to the way of life the current members and their ancestors fought to maintain. Still, as rector of one of the most prestigious congregations in Georgia, he wields tremendous influence on the affairs of the community and the state.

Almeda Alexander Drummond

She is the grand dame of First Church. Almeda is a powerbroker that few dare to cross. Her arrogant spirit finds its origin in the life of poverty she lived before marrying wealth. That same strong spirit led to her remarkable recovery from a debilitating stroke.

Chadsworth Purcell Alexander

His ancestors left him a fortune that he continues to further enrich. He was seduced into marrying Almeda after she and her mother managed to put him in a drunken stupor. He lived a double life in Falls City as a closeted gay man. When his secret was about to be discovered, he faked his suicide. He disappeared and took the identity of his dead lover, Earle Lafitte. He arranged that a sizeable trust fund for the needy be set up for the rector of First Church to administer.

Doctor Horace Drummond

He is the African-American priest called by Father Austin to be the senior associate at First Church. The widowed Almeda Alexander shocked the entire community by marrying him.

Mary Alice Smythe

She is the undisputed head of the politically powerful First Church Altar Guild. She has been president of the Guild for decades. No one dares challenge her for the position.

Stone Clemons

Stone is a wise attorney and counselor to Father Austin. He is one of Father Austin's strongest advocates and defenders.

Chief Joe Sparks

He is known simply as *the Chief.* He's a close boyhood friend with Stone Clemons. He is the Falls City Chief of Police. Along with Stone, they are Steele's closest friends and defenders in the parish.

Ned Boone

Before he was killed in a horrific car accident, Ned had a history of attacking and removing any director, school head, or college president he could not control. He resorted to underhanded methods to attack Father Austin. Once his antics had been exposed, he left First Church to join Saint Andrew's Presbyterian Church. There he continued his devious deeds.

Virginia Mudd

She is one of the most dysfunctional personalities in Falls City. At one time, she was a powerbroker at First Church. Her addiction to drugs and sex destroyed her marriage and reputation. Her complete lack of a superego ultimately lands her in prison.

Henry Mudd

He is a leading attorney in Falls City, and a strong friend and supporter of the rector. Once he divorced Virginia and took custody of their two daughters, he married the beautiful Delilah. They are expecting their first child together.

Howard and Martha Dexter

Howard is the keeper of the treasury at First Church. He is a constant critic of the rector's financial management of the parish. His own greed and stinginess leaves his wife, Martha, to resort to begging for food at every social occasion. Martha Dexter is Mary Alice Smythe's constant companion.

Colonel Mitchell

He is not a real Colonel. His first name is *Colonel.* He is a non-recovering alcoholic with incredible control needs. His dry drunk behavior is acted out frequently and maliciously. His envy and jealousy of Steele Austin's popularity and success keeps him seething.

Gary Hendricks

Gary is a very uptight and immaculately dressed attorney. He demands perfection of himself and the rector. As a former chair of the school board, and strong supporter of the school, he believes the only way to gain the school's independence is to rid the parish of Steele Austin.

Tom Barnhardt

It is commonly accepted that Tom, and the partners in his law firm, have made their fortune by stealing from the widows and orphans. Tom's only investment in First Church is separating the parish and the school. He believes the only way he can achieve his goal is to destroy the rector's integrity and credibility.

Elmer and Judith Idle

This is one of the most disgustingly pious couples at First Church. Their fundamentalism causes them to continually clash with the rector. Ultimately they leave the parish to follow Ned Boone to unite with Saint Andrew's Presbyterian.

The Right Reverend Sean Evans

Sean had always wanted to be a bishop. Now he is bishop of one of the most conservative dioceses in the Episcopal Church. He must keep his homosexuality and his relationship with his lover, Jim Vernon, a highly guarded secret.

The Reverend Melvin MacClaren and his wife, Rose

Pastor MacClaren is Ned Boone's handpicked pastor. He embodies all that Ned believes a pastor should exemplify. The pastor is homophobic, chauvinistic, and rules over his wife and children with a firm hand. Rose, his longsuffering wife, grows her own marijuana plants in order to cope and survive.

The resemblance of any character in this novel to any person, living or dead, is not intended. The characters, events, and locations are completely fictional.

However, since we all have a dark side, each of us just might see ourselves in one or more of the people that reside in the fictional community of Falls City, Georgia.

Being a pastor is like death by a thousand paper cuts.
You're scrutinized and criticized from top to bottom, stem to
stern. You work for an invisible, perfect Boss, and you're
supposed to lead a rag tag gaggle of volunteers towards
God's coming future. It's like herding cats, only harder.
The Reverend Doctor Ken Fong, Program Director
Fuller Theological Seminary
Pasadena, California

Chapter 1

The Reverend Melvin MacClaren, the senior pastor at Saint Andrew's Presbyterian Church in Falls City, Georgia, was presiding over his family's breakfast. Pastor MacClaren believed with all his heart that God had ordained him to rule his family with a strong hand. The world is full of too many temptations. Satan could lead even clergy children astray. The evils of drink, smoke, drugs, dancing, and worse were all around. He was fully aware that clergy spouses could also fall victim to the Devil's wiles. He was not about to allow such shame to fall on his household. For that reason alone, he began each morning at the breakfast table with a family devotional. Before any member of his family partook of one bite of food, he would instruct them in the way of the Lord. This included a reading he'd chosen from sacred scripture and a teaching. His wife and each of his children were assigned a Bible verse to memorize. They were expected to recite it from memory the following morning at breakfast.

This particular morning, he wanted to reinforce in his family the danger that comes from associating with heathen. He knew his wife confined her relationships to members of the congregation. His children, however, attended a public school. The Devil and his minions were all around them. He was particularly concerned about his oldest son. The boy was coming into his teen years. He'd walked past his son's open bedroom door and he'd seen that the sleeping boy was aroused. As the boy's reproductive urge increased, Melvin knew he must correspondingly intensify his instructions. Pastor MacClaren was not going to allow one of his son's female classmates and their short skirts to lead his boy into the eternal fires of hell.

Melvin's face glistened with perspiration as he gave this morning's instruction. "Those that associate with whores, queers, drunkards, fornicators, and adulterers will be cast into the eternal fires of hell. There will be gnashing of teeth.

They will pray for mercy and forgiveness, but it will be too late. There will be no mercy. There will be no forgiveness. Not one drop of water will be offered to douse the flames burning their tortured bodies. Their flesh will burn, but it will not be consumed. It will just burn and burn and burn. It is their reward for but a moment's pleasure. I ask you wife... I ask you, my children, is one drink of whiskey worth burning in hell for all of eternity? Is one minute of illicit pleasure of the flesh worth being cast into a lake of fire that never goes out?"

Rose MacClaren knew all too well the answer she was to give her husband. "No, my husband."

Pastor MacClaren pointed at each of his three children. "And what say you?"

"No, Papa." Each one answered in turn.

"Do any of you doubt my teaching this morning? For if you do..." Pastor MacClaren turned red in the face with emotion. He grabbed the tattered Bible from the breakfast table and held it before them. "It's right here in God's Holy Word. God Himself has decreed the punishment. Do you believe that God would lie?" He pointed at his wife with the Bible.

"No, my husband. God does not lie. The words of the Bible are true. Your words are true."

Each of the children repeated when his eyes met theirs, "No, papa."

Pastor MacClaren wiped the sweat from his face with his breakfast napkin. "Fine, then. Let us join hands and give thanks to the Lord for our breakfast."

John Calvin, the youngest of the three children, was seated next to his mother. He whispered to her, "Mommy, I'm really hungry."

She patted him. "We'll eat after Papa has said grace."

Pastor MacClaren glared at the seven-year old. "Boy, would you eat without first thanking the Lord?"

John Calvin slid down in his seat and leaned against his mother for protection. "No, Papa."

. Melvin MacClaren raised his voice. "Boy, you listen to me. You know the only people that eat without first thanking the Lord?"

"No, Papa."

"No?" He shouted.

"I mean... yes." John Calvin whispered.

"Well, which is it?" The boy shrank even closer toward his mother. "Your mother is not going to protect you. Now let me tell you, boy. The only things that eat without first thanking the Lord are pigs, donkeys, cats, dogs, and heathen. Are you a pig?"

"No." The boy whispered meekly.

"No, what?" Pastor MacClaren shouted.

"No, sir."

"That's better. Now, let's join hands and close our eyes for prayer." All at the table did as instructed. "Almighty God, I come to you this new day, giving you thanks for your clear word of instruction. You have given us caution not to succumb to the temptations of alcohol, or the pleasures of the flesh. You have shown us just how we might be able to stand innocent before you on that Great Day of Judgment, when all secrets will be revealed. Nothing done in secret is kept from you, because you know all things and you see all things. On that great and wonderful Day of Judgment, the heathen will be exposed. Those that have disobeyed your commandments will be cast into the lake of fire. And all your blessed children, who have been obedient to your Holy Word, will rejoice at the sight of the unbeliever's eternal damnation. It will be a glorious day to finally see all the whores, drunks, adulterers, fornicators, and homosexuals set ablaze in the devil's dominion. I give you thanks that my wife and children, along with me, will be welcomed into the Gates of Heaven and not driven into damnation. I know this because each one of them has heard and understands my instructions. Now bless this food. Amen."

Rose MacClaren rose from the table. In the kitchen she retrieved the breakfast from the oven. She'd hoped her husband would not have gone on so long. The food was warm, but dry. She feared the children would not eat it. As for her husband, he was devoid of any taste buds. He ate anything and everything she placed before him. The stomach that seemed to grow daily over his belt was true testimony to that observation.

The family ate in silence. Pastor MacClaren was lost in the conversation that he'd recently had with Judith Idle. At one time, she had been one of the most devout members of First Church. Since leaving the Episcopal Church and joining Saint Andrew's Presbyterian, she had been meeting with him each week. Her standing appointment was for spiritual guidance. Judith had not missed a single session. Pastor MacClaren looked forward to their meetings. He enjoyed the stimulating conversation they shared. He found his time with her to be so inspiring, he hated to see it end. She had told him that she had been mistreated at the Episcopal Church. They spent many hours asking God to heal her memories surrounding that horrible experience. It was gratifying for him to know that she was in need of his counsel.

Judith had shared with him that she and her husband, Elmer, wanted to consecrate their marriage bed to God. She told him about going on a marriage retreat led by a couple that were a part of the Charismatic Movement in the Roman Catholic Church. The couple had reported that they had placed Stations of the Cross around their house. These fourteen crosses depict the trial, suffering, and crucifixion of Jesus. The couple believed that their marriage bed had become a spiritual experience. Before joining their bodies in the act of love, they would recite the Stations of the Cross together. The procession around the house ended at their bed where their Biblical love was consummated.

Pastor MacClaren told Judith that he would have difficulty engaging in a devotional that was clearly sanctioned by the Pope in Rome. However, he was not so sure that he shouldn't find a substitute. He really liked trying to redeem and sanctify the necessary, but lascivious, marital duty. He could see that it would be a way to keep the marriage bed pure. It would also be a method to keep the devil from planting erotic thoughts about others in the minds of a couple while they were engaging in the physical act of love. Perhaps he could devise a more scriptural, yes, a Presbyterian form of the devotional that his members could practice. He would teach them... no, as their pastor, he would insist that every married couple use the devotional before engaging in the carnal act. He resolved to begin work on it when he got to the office.

Rose MacClaren was lost in her thoughts as well. She needed to harvest the marijuana plants that she had been secretly growing. Her business partner from Florida was going to drive up later this morning to take most of the current harvest back to their customers there. Rose was still in the process of building a customer base around Falls City. Progress had been slow. She was looking forward to seeing her old friend. She was the woman that had introduced her to this secret but exciting part of her life. They always enjoyed sharing a smoke when they got together.

The children had their thoughts as well, but they were filled with anxiety. They knew what was coming next, and it had to be done to perfection.

Pastor MacClaren handed his empty plate to his wife to take to the kitchen. "All right, children, let's hear you recite your assigned Bible verses. Rose, you go first." Rose and the two oldest children did so without error. When it came to seven-year old John Calvin, however, he kept forgetting. "John Calvin," a red-faced Pastor MacClaren shouted. "Memorizing the passages I assign you from God's Holy Word is the most important thing you have to do; nothing else matters. Now, I am going to give you one more attempt. If you fail, you know what your punishment will be."

Once again, John Calvin leaned into his mother's side, seeking protection. "Rose, leave the table!" Melvin barked. "Go to the kitchen. You two children go to your rooms and prepare to leave for school."

Rose hated to leave her son. He had already started whimpering. The tears were streaming down his face. The little boy pleaded, "No, Papa. Please, no. I'll try to do better."

Rose knew she had no choice. She'd tried to interfere when the boy was younger, only to be slapped severely. She'd tried to explain to her husband that the school counselor thought the boy had a learning disability; he had a hard time focusing. His schoolwork also suffered. He had a difficult time with memorization.

Her husband had almost broken her arm as he shoved her away. "I'll not have some quack school psychologist put a label on that boy. The only disability he has is laziness. The Devil is after that boy's soul. This is a battle between God and Satan. If I have to beat the tar out of that boy every day, he's going to learn the Bible."

Rose stood silently in the kitchen, twisting a towel in her hands. She tried to prepare herself to block out what had now become the familiar screams of her son. She knew there was nothing she could do to stop her husband.

"John Calvin, this is your last chance." The boy began to sob so severely he could not speak. "You were warned. You will start memorizing the assigned Bible passages or I will beat them into you." Pastor Melvin MacClaren stood and yanked his belt off. The little boy began to scream. Pastor MacClaren grabbed him and pulled the boy's pants down to his knees. The sound of the belt on his buttocks and back could be heard throughout the house. Rose held two potholders over her ears in an effort to block out the blood-curdling screams of her young son.

The Magnolia Series

Dennis R. Maynard

Chapter 2

Virginia Mudd is a survivor. As a guest of the Stone Mountain Federal Correctional Facility in Atlanta, Georgia, Virginia learned quickly just what she needed to do to survive. Inmate Mudd pled *no contest* to a murder for hire scheme. She was recorded trying to get an undercover federal agent to murder her lover's wife. Her lover and attorney, Thackston Willoughby, had come to her aid. Her defense fell apart when it became public knowledge that she had been having an affair with her defense attorney. Her murder for hire target was his wife. Once Virginia's affair with him became public knowledge, Mrs. Willoughby immediately filed for divorce against her husband. Her petition included a restraining order against her husband and Virginia. She feared for her life. Although he was not implicated in Virginia's story, Mrs. Willoughby did not want her soon to be ex-husband near her or their children. Virginia could not have planned it better. This sent Thackston running back to Virginia's bed. He now belonged to her.

Thackston used all of his influence as an attorney, and as one of the more elite citizens of Falls City, to negotiate Virginia's case. True to the *good ole boy system,* he was able to pull in several favors. The lead prosecutor had once been an intern in his law firm. The judge had been one of his card-playing buddies for years. Virginia could have easily been sentenced up to ten years for her crime. Thackston negotiated a plea deal with his former intern. Virginia would plead *no contest* and receive a sentence of four to six years. With good behavior, she could be out on parole in eighteen months to two years.

Keeping Virginia out of the state prison system was his next challenge. The two women's correctional facilities in Georgia were nothing less than hellholes. That is where women who had successfully killed another person were sent. The prisoner-on-prisoner physical abuse was rampant. The guards were not the least bit reluctant to use that same abuse to maintain discipline and order. Thackston was determined that Virginia not be subjected to such an environment. He appealed to his card-playing buddy to send her to the one federal correctional facility for women in the state. It would not be a country club, and it would not be easy for her, but she would be better off there than in a state facility. The judge agreed.

"Hey girl, what's your name?" Adrianna Garcia lit a cigarette. She was sitting on one of the two bunks in the cell that she and Virginia would share.

"My name is Mrs. Henry Mudd the Third." Virginia used her most sophisticated, deep-throated voice. She wanted to communicate to the Mexican that she was a lady of class and distinction. Lest there be any doubt, she also stood in an upright stance, head up, eyes looking downward. That was a posture she'd been taught in the classes preparing her for her debutante ball.

"Listen, bitch. I'm your first and only hope to survive this place, so don't give me any attitude. You're not at one of your society meetings. This place is dangerous, and you don't want to begin by pissing me off. You do realize that I could strangle you in your sleep any night I choose."

Virginia sank down on the cot that was to be hers. She stared at the Hispanic woman seated across from her. "I'm sorry. This is all really scary. I don't know who to trust. I've just gone through the most humiliating experience of my life."

Adrianna laughed. "So you've never had your cavities examined before?"

"Well, by a doctor, but that was different."

"You can say that again. Now, listen to me. We are going to be roommates, so let's get a few things straight. I will have your back if you have mine. Okay?"

Virginia nodded and lit a cigarette.

"Let me make something else real clear to you. I'm not a *fem*. I'm not interested in having sex with you or any woman."

Virginia nodded again.

"So, let's begin again. My name is Adrianna, Adrianna Garcia." She extended her hand for Virginia to shake. "I do hope we can be friends. I was a friend with the last woman that slept on that cot, but it was a little easier with her. She was a member of my tribe."

"Tribe?" Virginia asked, while shaking Adrianna's hand.

"Yeah, this place is organized around tribes. It's not a bigot thing; it's just the way it is. You're going to want to stay with your own kind at meals, in the yard, and in the day room."

"So... how can we be friends? I don't understand." Virginia was confused.

"Oh, me. I'm a *coconut* and so was my previous roomie."

"A what?"

"My mom was Anglo and my Dad was Cuban. They call me a *coconut*. The Latinos really don't want me, so I hang with the Anglos. So how's about it ... friends?"

"I'd like that." Virginia exhaled the smoke from her cigarette through her nose.

The two women sat studying each other. "You look like you might have been well maintained."

"I don't understand."

"You do a white collar crime? How much did you steal?"

A surprised look washed over Virginia's face. "I didn't steal anything."

"Then drugs? Were you a *mule*? Did you use? If so, you'll have plenty of company in here. In fact, that's about all some of these broads can talk about. They miss their fix."

"No, I wasn't selling drugs."

"Then what? You got me curious, girl. What did you do?"

For the first time in the entire process, Virginia actually felt a twinge of guilt. "They accused me of trying to have my lover's wife murdered."

"Whoa! You did what?" Adrianna roared. "Why aren't you in State? That's where murderers go."

"I was falsely accused, but they had a witness that testified against me. I was framed. The woman's alive and well. No one was killed. My attorney believed me. I was innocent, but he advised me not to go to trial. He made a plea deal for me. My attorney is also my fiancé. He pulled in some favors."

"Shh! Don't say that too loudly." Adrianna moved from her bunk to sit next to Virginia. "Keep your voice down. If word gets out that you have influence on the outside, you'll become a target."

"What kind of target?"

"Listen, most of the women in here had to settle for a pimply faced public defender. A lot of them were right out of school, and they didn't know the first damn thing about defending a case. You claim you're innocent. This place is filled with women saying they didn't do the crime. Hell, I honestly believe that some of the poor saps in here are innocent. They just didn't stand a chance in the system."

"What's that got to do with me?"

"They'll be all over you for favors. They'll threaten you and even harm you if you don't follow through for them. You're going to need a protector."

"A what?"

"Someone to protect you. As soon as the word gets out, and believe me, it will..."

"What word?" Virginia interrupted.

"The word is that you have a boyfriend that knows how to work the system. As soon as that word gets around, your ass is going to belong to someone. You've got to choose."

"Choose?"

Adrianna lit another cigarette off the one she'd been smoking. She studied Virginia from top to bottom. "You a *dyke*?"

"A what?"

"You know, a *dyke*. Do you like having sex with women?"

"No! I just told you that my lover was a married man."

"Okay, don't get your panties in a bunch. It's something you might consider. Some of the best protectors in this place are the *stud broads*."

"The what?"

"You know, the *bulldaggers*."

Virginia shook her head.

"Are you really that dense? *The butches* are the women lesbians that like to be the man."

"No." Virginia shook her head again. "No, no, no."

"Well listen, you may have to consider it unless you want to get your ass kicked on a regular basis."

Virginia's hands were shaking as she followed Adrianna's lead and lit a new cigarette off the one she had been smoking. "You really think I'm going to need a protector?"

Adrianna nodded. "I've been studying you. You're real pretty and you've got a great body. My guess is that you're a college girl. You may have even been one of those society bitches. You know, with the big house and a bunch of Mexicans or blacks running around waiting on you. If that's so, it's just a matter of time until someone looks you up on the computer in the library."

"I don't understand. Why would that matter?"

"Did you get a chance to see the women that are in here?"

"Not really. Just the ones that were on the bus with me."

"And?"

"And what?"

"Not only do you need a protector, but girl, you've lived a pretty sheltered life. Most of the women on the bus were either black or Hispanic. Correct?"

"I guess so."

"Well, *Miss College Graduate*, did it strike you that they were also poor? Most of them are in here for selling drugs, prostitution, or being used in some white-collar crime by their bosses. Like you, they were probably sleeping with the guys that got them sent here. Hell, their lovers were probably beating them. Did your lawyer lover beat you up?"

"No. He loves me."

"Exactly."

"Exactly what?"

"Virginia, girl, am I going to have to explain everything to you? The women in here are filled with hatred and disgust. They believe the system has screwed them over. They've had rough lives. Now, just how do you think they are going to feel about an inmate that has lived the dream? This is no castle, and you don't get to be a princess in here."

A tear ran down Virginia's cheek. "You're really scaring me."

"Good. You need to be scared. Now, we need to find you a protector, and we need to do it quick."

"I don't want a lesbian by whatever name you call them."

"Then your only alternative is one of the male guards."

"But most of them are Negroes!" Virginia blurted.

"So you are an uppity white woman. I thought as much."

"I... I mean...uh..."

"Oh, forget it. There are a few white guards that work in the *bubble*."

"The *bubble*?"

"Yeah, the control booth at the end of the corridor. It would be good if you hooked up with one of them. They can always keep an eye on you, and make sure the other guards protect their property."

"What will I have to do for him?"

"Not him, them."

"Them?"

"There are three shifts. You'll need a guard on each shift to protect you."

"You're kidding."

"I don't kid about being safe in here. You either have protection, or your time in here is going to be a living nightmare."

"Do you have a protector?"

"I do."

"Guards?"

"Yes. That brings me to my next question. Would you be interested in sharing?"

"Sharing?"

"God, girl, you are going to put me in lockup with your innocence. Share my guards with me. If we both have the same protectors, it will be less work for each of us."

"What will I have to do for them?"

"Don't worry. They aren't going to ask you to do anything painful or kinky. It will just be sex. Nothing more. Just sex."

"How do you know they'll want me?"

"Oh, they're going to want you. You're plenty hot. I'll arrange everything. By the way, one of them is black."

Virginia shuddered.

Adrianna chuckled. "Oh, he's not so bad. He's actually well built, and pretty good looking."

Virginia looked down at the floor.

"Cheer up, girl. You know what they always say about black men and size?"

Virginia nodded.

Adrianna laughed, "Well, don't worry about it. At least in his case, it's not true."

The darkness of her prison cell enveloped Virginia with an eerie chill that first night. Her thoughts went back to the big house she had shared with Henry and her two daughters on River Street. Yes, she had been a society lady. As Mrs. Henry Mudd, she'd been a member of all the exclusive clubs in the city. She and Henry were local celebrities of sorts. They were also leading members of the organizations open only to the community's elite. The Governor's Mansion flashed before her eyes. On more than one occasion, she had sat with the governor in his dining room. Henry had taken her to Washington, D.C., for the inauguration of the previous president. They had danced the night away at one of his inaugural balls. The beautiful gowns and jewelry that Henry had bought her for those events were now gone. She'd had to sell all of them. This entire experience had forced her to come to terms with certain truths. First, Henry had really loved her. Second, she'd not returned his love. Further, he'd been really good to her. She'd failed to be faithful and had violated his trust at every turn. She'd returned his trust and fidelity with lies and half-truths. Then Virginia thought of her daughters. They no longer wanted anything to do with her. They refused to respond to her letters or talk to her on the telephone. She'd had a wonderful life until... Virginia Mudd buried her face in the one lifeless pillow on her cot. Her entire body shook as the fear, regret, and grief poured out of her.

The Magnolia Series

Dennis R. Maynard

Chapter 3

Henry Mudd sat silently next to the hospital bassinette holding his newborn son. His wife, Dee, was sleeping in the adjacent bed. Henry's life had been next to perfect since Dee had entered it. He loved her with every fiber of his being. She had proven to be a wonderful wife and homemaker. The aristocracy at First Church had not only accepted her, but they had made it known that they approved of her. His two daughters were devoted to her. She was a wonderful friend and stepmother to them.

There was a time that he had deceived himself into believing that he was living a charmed life. His marriage to Virginia had appeared to be perfect. They had two beautiful daughters. They were leading members in all the exclusive societies in Falls City. He was a respected leader at First Church and a close friend and confidante of the current rector. His wife, Virginia, had been a beautiful woman. She was a gracious hostess. His only mistake had been to trust her. There were so many signs that he'd ignored. Their marriage bed had not been a happy one for years. Virginia was continually reluctant to make love to him. She would often delay the act itself until he had already fallen asleep. Their infrequent sex life seldom included foreplay. She did not respond to his lovemaking. She would simply close her eyes and lie still until he was finished.

Henry shook his head. He felt like such a fool for not coming to terms with her lies sooner. There were all those days she would park their daughters with the maid and disappear. Henry did not know where she was, and neither did the maid. When he questioned her she always had an answer, but Henry recalled the feeling in the pit of his stomach. He knew she was lying to him. There were the trips that she claimed were to visit friends at the beach. Again, he had ignored his instincts. She continually disappeared at parties and social events. He often searched for her, but she was nowhere to be seen. He thought about her inability to hold her alcohol, often coming to bed inebriated. On occasion, her hair would smell of marijuana. But the most telling indication of her infidelity was when he had actually smelled the hints of men's cologne on her. Henry was disgusted with her, and with himself, that he'd not confronted her secrets sooner. Now he was just thankful to be rid of her.

Dee was making little sleeping noises. He stood and walked over to her bed and pulled the blanket up to cover her shoulders. He leaned down and kissed her on the forehead. Back in his chair, his thoughts went again to Virginia. She'd gone through the inheritance her parents had left her. She did not have a single cent left. The real tragedy was that he had no idea where it had gone. She had been in and out of substance abuse programs. It hurt Henry to recall how the schoolboys had teased their daughters. They were without mercy with their taunting when their mother's adultery became fodder for the town gossips. "Hey, your mom's giving it away, how about you? Like mother like daughters."

All of their humiliation became complete when Virginia was charged and subsequently sentenced in a murder for hire scheme. She had actually tried to have the wife of her current lover, a prominent Falls City attorney, murdered. She tried to fight the charges by inventing another one of her stories. Henry knew it was exactly that. It was a product of Virginia's twisted imagination; it was pure fantasy. In short, it was another one of her lies. He couldn't recount the number of times he'd said to her, "Virginia, you can lie to me and you can lie to others, but for God's sake, stop lying to yourself." Now she was in prison. Henry's daughters removed their mother's photos from their rooms. They tore up the letters Virginia wrote them without even opening them. They never spoke of their mother. Dee had become their mother. They were even calling her *Momma Dee*.

Henry again looked at the sleeping miracle wrapped in the blue hospital blanket. During his disastrous marriage to Virginia, he'd had a vasectomy. He'd thought he was sterile when he married Dee. But the doctors failed to advise him that there was always a remote chance the vasectomy could reverse itself. Now he and Dee had a child together. Henry smiled as he looked at his son, a love baby. Still, everything was not perfect. Something was eating at him. His son's face and hair possessed some features that he simply didn't understand. The baby's hair was black, but so was his. That didn't bother him. He was disturbed by just how tightly the curls were woven to the baby's scalp. He might have been able to look beyond that, but there was his little nose... and his lips. They didn't look like his or Dee's. Henry shook his head. He didn't want to go there, but he had promised himself, after Virginia, that no woman would ever make a fool out of him again.

Henry had been in the delivery room. He'd seen this baby born. There had been no hospital mix-up. This was definitely the child that Dee had delivered. His doubts returned. Henry's skin was white. Virginia used to describe him as *pasty white*. It was impossible for him to tan. In the sun, he would turn red and then peel. Dee could tan. Her skin often glowed with a beautiful brown tone. That was one of the things he found so sexy about her. The skin pigmentation of the baby lying next to her was much darker. The baby's skin was more the color of a cup of coffee with cream. That's not possible, Henry argued with himself. Something was not right. He did not want to believe that Dee had been... He couldn't even finish the thought, but then there was a time he didn't want to believe that Virginia had betrayed him either.

Henry stood and began pacing around the room. He glanced at Dee and then at the baby. He walked to the window and looked out. He'd made sure that Dee had a nice room with a view of the park below. He didn't want her to have a room looking out at the parking garage. His doubts rose to a crescendo. He'd had a vasectomy. He'd never questioned Dee's report that it's possible for a vasectomy to reverse itself. He believed her. His own physician had confirmed that it could happen. He believed that by some miracle or freak of nature, he'd fathered this child. The only thing he knew for sure was that these doubts were tearing him apart. He needed to find out. Not to do so would eat at his love for her like a slow growing cancer. He could not live with a cloud of doubt hanging over their marriage. He refused to pretend. He'd done that once. He resolved never to live like that again. But then, if she had been untrue ... if she had conceived this child with another man... Just then there was a light knock at the door. Henry opened it. His family doctor gestured for him to come into the hallway.

"Are you sure you want to do this?"

"I have to. It's eating me up. I have to know."

"Okay. Open your mouth." The doctor inserted a cotton swab and scraped some of the cells from Henry's cheek.

The Magnolia Series

Dennis R. Maynard

Chapter 4

The sins of Ned Boone were on the verge of being exposed for all of Falls City to see. He'd employed a handsome and muscular young man to pose for suggestive photos with the unsuspecting rector's wife. The photographer was able to capture a picture of them just as the young hunk shocked Steele Austin's wife by untying her bikini top while she was sunbathing at the swimming pool. The photo made her look both suspicious and guilty. Ned wanted to use the photos to destroy the rector's marriage. He thought that would be a way he could get rid of Father Steele Austin.

He'd successfully rid Saint Andrew's Presbyterian of a pastor he didn't like. He hired that same blonde Adonis to plant child pornography on the pastor's office computer. He then orchestrated its discovery. His scheming was exposed when he'd attempted to do the same to the diocesan bishop. Ned was spared criminal charges and public humiliation when he was killed in a fiery automobile crash. In a strange act of *Karma*, the coroner believed that Ned was burned alive in the crash.

The pastor and people in his new church home were mourning his death. He was given the primary credit for securing the new and very popular senior pastor for Saint Andrew's Presbyterian, The Reverend Melvin MacClaren. Since Ned's sins were unknown to the people of that parish, it was anticipated that his funeral would be one of the largest ever attended.

As expected, on the day of Ned Boone's funeral, the cavernous worship space of Saint Andrew's Presbyterian Church was filled to overflowing. The huge congregation had gathered to give thanks to the Almighty for the life of Ned Boone. The mourners that crowded into every pew did little to mirror those that would have assembled for a prominent member of neighboring First Church. Had Ned Boone been an honored member of First Church, then all of the community leaders of note, as well as the important representatives from city, county, and state government would have been in attendance. At a First Church funeral for a prestigious member, it was not unusual to have the governor, the congressional representative, and one, if not both, of Georgia's senators in attendance.

Many of those that gathered at Saint Andrew's could best be described as *wannabes.* They were worker bees in the community that desperately sought a higher station in life. Due to their poor choice of birth parents, no such notoriety would ever be theirs. Some might ultimately distinguish themselves professionally. In so doing, they would find themselves comfortable members of prestigious First Church. Until such time, they were forced to be content as members of Saint Andrew's.

One only had to observe the dress of the various mourners. At First Church, the ladies in attendance would be wearing labels purchased at Saks, Neiman Marcus, or an exclusive designer shop in Atlanta. The ladies at Saint Andrew's might be adorned with the same label, but it was purchased at Marshall's, the outlet mall, or a local consignment shop. Most, however, wore clothes purchased at one of the department stores in the local mall.

The overwhelming majority of the membership at First Church would not even consider being seen at Ned's memorial service. The only faces in attendance, once familiar at First Church, were those of Elmer and Judith Idle. They sat front and center. Colonel Mitchell, Howard Dexter, and Tom Barnhardt also attended to express their condolences. Ned's attacks on Father Austin had become public knowledge. Even some of those at First Church that disapproved of Steele's leadership style were offended by the personal and slanderous attacks on their rector. Judith, Elmer, and Ned had all been ostracized from the social circles in that parish.

The Reverend Melvin MacClaren, the senior pastor at Saint Andrew's, had asked Judith Idle to help him select the music for the service. "I hope you won't mind if we devote your appointment time this week to planning Ned's funeral."

"Whatever you want, Pastor MacClaren." Judith smiled. "I'm just so honored you asked me to help."

"You knew him longer than I have known him." Pastor MacClaren invoked. "I know you agree with me that he was a fine man and an exemplary Christian. He is deserving of a triumphant service."

"Amen. Praise be the name of Jesus. Ned's life mirrored our highest Christian values. He stood up against all those that wanted to destroy Christian marriage. It's the primary reason we chose to leave First Church. His message and ministry were rejected by that rector and the leaders over there."

"That's my understanding. Ned Boone led the fight at First Church and here at Saint Andrew's against the godless sin of homosexuality. For that reason alone, we simply must celebrate his life with a service befitting a saint."

"True. He was clear about homosexuality being a sin, but he had so many other virtues."

"Yes, he was one of the finest Christians I've known in my pastorate. His life ended long before his good work on earth was completed. It falls to you and me to make sure he receives the tribute in death that he was never afforded in life."

"What about his wife?" Judith inquired. "Surely she would like to select the music."

"To the contrary," Pastor MacClaren shrugged. "I probably should not be sharing this with you, but his wife did not want to have a service. I had to convince her otherwise."

"What?" Judith heard herself screech.

"Do you know the woman?"

"Actually, I don't. She was never around. Ned seldom spoke of her. I don't ever recall her coming to worship with him."

"Did he explain her absence?"

Judith cast her eyes downward. After a moment of silence, she met Pastor MacClaren's gaze. She leaned forward and whispered, "I heard rumors about her having a drinking problem."

"Well, that would explain it. If it's true, it just adds to the rich holiness of the man. Just think of the terrible life and marriage he has endured with such a woman. Yet, he never complained about her, or worse yet, divorced her. I am convinced the man was a saint."

"Will his wife attend the service?"

"My understanding is that she will, but their son will not."

"Son?" Judith could not disguise the confused look on her face. "Ned never mentioned having a son. I just assumed they were childless."

"No. He has a son. He lives in San Francisco. Did I mention that he's not married? He won't be in attendance." Pastor MacClaren stared at Judith, looking for a reaction. Finally he broke the silence. Clearly, they were both thinking the same thing. "Well, I think we should sing some of the old Gospel favorites at Ned's funeral."

"Yes, I agree. Let's start out with a rousing hymn such as *Stand Up, Stand Up for Jesus.*"

"Judith, I could not agree more. If there was ever a man that stood up for the teachings of Jesus, it was Ned Boone. In fact, I think I will use that as my sermon theme. He stood up for Jesus and against Satan's efforts to destroy the family. I simply must exhort the congregation to follow his example and stand up to the false prophets in the Church. I'll not make it my total tribute to him, but his work against those that would bless the perverted lifestyle simply must be recognized."

Judith closed her eyes in prayer. Her lips uttered thanksgivings to God for the ministry of Pastor MacClaren and the life of her friend, Ned Boone. When she was finished, she opened her eyes and smiled piously at her pastor. "Do you know that wonderful song titled *Jesus, Lord of All?*" She began singing it.

"Isn't that melody the same as the *Co-Cola Jingle*?"

"Yes, don't you see? That's what will make it so wonderful. The congregation will immediately recognize it. We can sing it over and over again until every person present is caught up in the praise of the Lord."

Pastor MacClaren's eyes lit up. "Judith, I knew I'd chosen the right person to help me with this service. Ned is smiling down from heaven. He is well pleased with you right now."

"Thank you, Pastor. Have you thought about any other music?"

"There's only one song that the Lord continually calls my mind to rehearse. I think it should be the closing hymn. Let's have the entire congregation stand and sing *Onward Christian Soldiers* as we carry Ned's body from the Church."

"Oh, thank you, Jesus. Praise be the name of Jesus." Judith once again lifted her hands. "Don't you feel the Lord's presence here with us, Pastor MacClaren? The Holy Spirit is filling this room as we plan this service. I think Ned is here with us as well."

"Judith, you are a fine woman. I am so pleased that you and Elmer are members of Saint Andrew's. Our gain is First Church's loss. You never belonged over there. This is your home."

"It is now," Judith smiled. "First Church was such a different place before Steele Austin arrived." A shudder ran over Judith's body. "You just won't believe what he's done to that congregation."

"So I've heard," Pastor MacClaren nodded in agreement. "One day he will have to stand before the judgment seat of God and explain just why he led so many of the Lord's precious sheep away from righteousness and into sin."

"I couldn't agree more."

"There's one surprise that I will be announcing at the service for Ned."

"Oh?"

"Now, I am only going to share this with you because you are helping me plan his service. I don't want you to repeat it to anyone."

"Not even my husband?"

"Well, I suppose you should tell your husband. It's not right for a wife to keep secrets from her husband. That's disrespectful. It's your duty to keep him informed of all your activities. So yes, do advise your husband. The husband is the head of the wife, and the wife is to submit to her husband in all things."

"Amen." Judith smiled. "It's so refreshing to have a pastor that knows the Bible."

"Now, about the surprise. I have met with the session and they have agreed. I'm going to announce at the funeral that we are naming our chapel in honor of Ned. It will now be known as the *Ned Boone Memorial Chapel*."

On hearing this, Judith immediately dropped from her chair to her knees. She threw her hands in the air and began shouting a chorus of phrases, thanking God and praising His name for the life of Ned Boone.

The Magnolia Series

Dennis R. Maynard

Chapter 5

The reflection staring back at him from his bathroom mirror filled The Right Reverend Sean Evans with disgust. He leaned in closer to study the double layers of tissue. The once crisp chin and muscular jaws were now covered with fleshy, drooping jowls. Even his arms that once exploded with dark blue blood vessels were now smooth and without any hint of muscular fiber. His disgust flashed with anger as he turned so that he could look at his profile. His muscular midsection was now covered with ugly belly fat. He relaxed his stomach. It protruded even further. Most any woman in her last month of pregnancy would have a smaller bump. He was further sickened as he studied the thick layer of fatty tissue now hanging over his upper thighs.

Sean turned from the mirror. In his dressing closet, he opened a drawer to retrieve a pair of boxer shorts. He paused as the row of sexy jockey briefs he once wore caught his eye. Before he'd allowed this job to destroy his body, he would have worn one of them. Now he was only comfortable in baggy boxer shorts, size XX-Large. Even at that, the waistband often folded over on him. He resolved that he would not buy a larger size.

He'd moved the trim fitting suits and shirts he used to wear to a closet in the extra guest room. He'd even stopped wearing a belt with his suit pants and had resorted to suspenders. They held his pants in place. He didn't have to concern himself with a belt cutting off his circulation. Sean's breathing became labored as he sat down in the chair to put on his socks and shoes. He leaned against the chair back and drew in a deep breath. The reflection of the fat man mocked him in his dressing room mirror.

He had been unable to maintain his exercise program. Most every day of the week he had to leave for his office by 6:30 in the morning. One morning each week he was the celebrant at the 7:00 o'clock *Bishop's Mass* at the Cathedral. The other days he alternated between the staff meeting, the executive committee meeting with the diocesan leaders, the finance committee, or one of the many board meetings he was required to attend. Breakfast was invariably served either before or after each of those events. By the time he got to his office, his first appointment and a stack of telephone calls were waiting on him. Lunch was often consumed with another meeting. His afternoon would be equally power packed with e-mails, telephone calls, and appointments. Most every evening he was required to meet with various clergy and parish leaders from around the diocese. Food and more food would be served. When was he supposed to exercise?

Sean was breathless as he stood after getting fully dressed. He buttoned his suit jacket and, once again, studied his reflection. The dark suits he now wore were somewhat trimming, but he knew he was only kidding himself. He resolved to do something about it; he wanted his body back.

The unmade bed caught his eye as he stopped at the side table to put on his watch. The bedchamber that had once brought him such delight had become a lonely place. Jim Vernon, his longtime lover, was now sleeping in one of the guest rooms. Sean recalled their last argument about the new sleeping arrangement. Jim had tried to reassure him, "Sean, it's not that I don't love you. It's just... well, you know..."

"Out with it, Jim. Why do you feel the need to sleep in a separate room?" Sean thought he knew. "It's because you no longer find me attractive, isn't it? You think I've gotten fat and ugly."

"No, Honey. That's not it at all. Yes, I wish you'd do something to take better care of yourself. I'm afraid this damn job we both wanted for you is going to kill you. Neither of us wants that."

"Then what is it? I miss you. I miss sleeping with you. I want to wake up holding you in my arms."

Jim hesitated. He realized he would have to tell Sean something. "I can't sleep with you right now."

Sean felt himself to be on the verge of tears. "So, it's because you're repulsed by me?"

Jim shouted. "No, Sean! You snore! Since you've gotten so fat, you've started snoring. You sound like a friggin' freight train. It's impossible for me to get a decent night's sleep."

"Well, why didn't you say so sooner? I could get one of those sleep apnea machines."

"Sean, listen to me. You don't have sleep apnea. You snore because you've gotten so heavy. Get back in shape and you'll stop snoring."

Bishop Evans stood quietly looking around his bedroom. Recalling that argument had only made him more disgusted with himself. He then muttered, "My snoring doesn't explain why we haven't made love in months." Sean made his way into the kitchen. His butler and cook, Clarence, handed him a glass of orange juice. Sean started to reach for it and then stopped himself. "Clarence, do we have a smaller glass?"

"Yes'sa, Bishop. We got juice glasses."

"From now on I will limit myself to one serving of orange juice at breakfast in one of those glasses."

Clarence's eyes widened. "You not feeling well, Bishop?"

"No, Clarence." Sean slapped his stomach. "It's time to do something about this."

Clarence chuckled. "Yes'sa. You's da boss. Is you gonna go on a diet?"

"No, I just think I need to cut back and lose some weight. I don't think diets work."

"Huh-uh. I know that. Where would you like to eat yo' breakfast?"

"Is Jim up yet? If so, we'll eat in the dining room."

"Oh, Misturh Jim already gone. He left for da exercise club over an hour ago."

Sean nodded. "Well, I have some work to look over, so I'll have my breakfast at the desk in my study."

"If'n you say so."

"After I eat, I have to leave for a meeting over at Saint Michael's."

"I'sa gonna bring it right to you. You want bacon and sausage with your pancakes and eggs?"

Sean caught himself in mid-nod. "No pancakes, no sausage or bacon. Just a couple of eggs and some fruit. Toast, but no butter or jelly."

Clarence chuckled. "Sounds like you's be serious 'bout cuttin' back."

"I'm as serious as I can be."

Sean sat down at his desk. He reviewed the notes from his visitation to Saint Mark's in Graniteville yesterday. This job was just not what he thought it would be. Saint Mark's was a mirror image of so many of the churches in his diocese. At one time it had been a thriving congregation. Past leaders had built a church that would seat two hundred and fifty people with room for an overflow. Now, no more than thirty-five worshippers spread themselves over the empty pews. They struggled to pay a part-time priest. Their Sunday organist was the only other paid employee. The building and grounds were falling into disrepair. Sean admitted that he felt foolish processing down the aisle of the empty nave. He shook his head. Bishop Rufus Petersen, his predecessor, had called such visitations *necrophilia*. Sean chuckled, "that may be closer to truth than fiction." The average age of the congregants in these churches had to be late 70s to early 80s. Unless things changed soon, he would have to close one third of the congregations in his diocese. Sean made himself a note. He would have Jim send a letter to every priest in the diocese. He would advise them to purchase automated external defibrillators. The clergy should have the ushers trained to use them should they be needed.

Sean quickly swallowed the breakfast that Clarence brought him. He stood to leave when a yellow *Post-It Note* on a file on his desk caught his eye. It was in Jim's handwriting. *You aren't going to believe this!* Sean opened the file. It was the parish report from First Church in Falls City. Jim had highlighted one line in the annual budget titled *Rector's Compensation.* Sean gasped. He couldn't believe it. Steele Austin's salary was now thirty percent larger than his own. How did that happen? Sean liked Steele. He liked what he was doing at First Church, but this? How did this happen? Sean felt himself growing angry. Having one of his clergy receiving that amount of compensation was totally out of line. It simply could not be justified. Sean's hands began to shake as he tucked the file into his briefcase. He mumbled, "No priest in this, or any diocese, should be paid more than their bishop. I'm going to do something about this."

The Magnolia Series

Dennis R. Maynard

Chapter 6

Stone Clemons stood at the door in the law enforcement center leading into Chief Joe Sparks' office. He watched the Chief chewing on his signature unlit cigar. He was shuffling through a stack of papers spread across his desk. "Shouldn't you be out chasing the bad guys? I don't think the taxpayers are paying you to sit on your ass in your air conditioned office and play paper charades."

The Chief glanced up. His eyes followed the sound of the familiar voice. "I thought I'd be hearing from you today."

"It's a damn mess. That's what it is."

"Well, I certainly never figured on such a strange turn of events."

"Come on in and sit down. I'll bring you up to date." Stone pulled a chair out and was just about to be seated. "Whoa! Stop right there."

Stone froze. "What?"

"Have you checked your zipper, you old fool?" Stone glanced down at his pants trousers. "Your barn door is standing wide open."

A big grin spread across Stone's face. "Hell, it doesn't matter if the barn door stands open when the horse is dead."

Both men roared with laughter. "I hope that's not the case," the Chief chided. "You know they make little blue pills for that sort of thing."

"It'll take more than a blue pill to resurrect this horse. It's completely worn out."

"I don't doubt it. You wore it out when we were both young bucks."

"Me? If I recollect correctly, you didn't go to your marriage bed innocent."

"Just zip up before one of my officers walks in here and sees you."

"Hmm, you afraid of what they might think?"

"Exactly. Now zip it."

"Okay, okay. Check your homophobia. You're not my type."

"Well, after all our overnight hunting and fishing trips together, it's reassuring to know that I didn't have to worry about you molesting me in my sleep."

"Enough of this. What do you know?"

"Since Ned Boone is dead, the solicitor can't move forward with any kind of charges. Obviously, he's not here to defend himself."

"I know that." Stone pulled on his lower lip. "Have you heard that Saint Andrew's Presbyterian is naming their chapel after him?"

"I did hear that."

"It just doesn't seem right. The man destroyed the lives of so many people and he came close to destroying the lives of so many more. I'll never forgive him for what he tried to do to Steele and Randi, let alone his attempts on the bishop."

"Don't forget the former senior pastor at Saint Andrew's."

"Naming a chapel after the man is a sacrilege."

"You know about the statue?"

"What statue?"

"He left instructions to have a statue of himself erected in the park near his house."

"What? Isn't that a city owned park?"

"That's what I asked the mayor. It seems that park was a part of the original Boone Plantation owned by Ned's great-grandfather. Pieces of the plantation have been sold off through the years for housing development. The Boone family still owns the park."

"But the city's been maintaining it."

"True. It's part of some screwball arrangement Ned made with the city council. Something about the land being given to the city on permanent loan, whatever the hell that means. Having a statue erected of himself after his death was a part of the deal."

"Permanent loan? I've never heard of such. I'm going to have my legal beavers down at the firm look into it."

"That's all well and good, but in the meantime, there's nothing we can do about the statue."

"What about Tom Barnhardt and Gary Hendricks?"

"Here again, the solicitor doesn't feel like he can move forward since our blonde Adonis has skipped bail. He can't be found. Without his testimony, the solicitor feels like the grand jury won't indict."

"So you're not going to search for him?"

"The most we have on him is breaking and entering the bishop's office up in Savannah. He didn't steal anything. He did skip bail, but I doubt any agency will devote their resources to looking for him."

"Who bailed him out?"

"Tom Barnhardt had one of the flunkies from his office come down and bail both him and Hendricks out. We had to let them go."

"Were you able to run him through the system?"

"His name is Bruce Chance. He's been in and out of trouble since he was a teen. He even did a short stint in juvenile. His expertise seems to be breaking and entering. He was arrested a couple of times for male prostitution."

"That's all in keeping with the purposes for which Ned, Tom, and Gary employed him. I wonder if they knew he was a gay boy?"

"That question is filled with irony."

"Where's Hendricks?"

"Interesting. He's disappeared as well."

"What? I hadn't heard that."

"He's gone. He closed up his law practice, sold his house, and sold all of his possessions. He's simply disappeared. Absolutely no one associated with him has a clue."

"Barnhardt?"

"He swears he doesn't know. He's also out the bail money he put up for Chance."

"Man, that just doesn't sound like the Gary Hendricks I've observed. He's the most buttoned-down guy in Falls City. He was always perfectly dressed. He never wore anything but a white shirt and a bow tie with his custom tailored suits. I never saw so much as a wrinkle in his shirt or suit. I used to think he was just about as anal retentive as his appearance. Are you looking for him?"

"We have a bulletin out on him, but honestly, without the witness to testify and absent an indictment, we can't classify him as more than a missing person."

"And Tom Barnhardt gets off as well."

"I'm not so sure. I had a visit from a couple of members of the state bar association up in Atlanta. They asked me some pretty pointed questions about him and about Gary."

"I'd almost forgotten that Barnhardt had a law license. To my knowledge he never used it."

"That's where you're wrong. He didn't use it formally, but he used his legal expertise continually."

"You're right," Stone nodded. "That's exactly how he was able to put together all his crooked deals without actually violating the letter of the law."

"We investigated some of his dealings, but he was careful not to actually cross the legal line."

"The man has left a trail of bankrupted widows all over this town. It's a regular trail of tears." Stone frowned and shrugged. "Even if the state bar should revoke his license, my hunch is it wouldn't matter much to him. I don't guess it would mean anything to Gary either, since he's disappeared. I guess we'll just have to see where all that goes."

The Chief sighed, "Don't hold your breath."

Stone squirmed in his chair. He shook his head, "Sometimes I long for the day that we could turn the *Klan* on guys like this. The men in the hoods could give them a good horsewhipping."

"I fear those days are gone." The Chief closed the file in front of him and tossed it to the corner of his desk. "On another subject, what are all these rumors I hear about the rector?"

"Some folks out in Texas are trying to get him to run for bishop. My sources down at the church tell me that he's also gotten some letters from other parishes, and a big cathedral wanting him to throw his hat in the ring as well."

"Didn't we just go through all this? I thought after his sabbatical he recommitted to staying at First Church."

"He did. You can't blame the boy for considering other options. He's still young and his future is bright. I think we're foolish to believe that we'll be able to keep him here. There are too many folks in this place that believe they've been called by the Almighty to make the boy's life miserable. I wouldn't blame him if he left for greener pastures. Of course, I want to keep him here as long as we can. He's the best preacher that's ever graced our pulpit. And just look at all he's been able to accomplish. The parish and the school have never been in better shape."

"Can't we do something to persuade him to stay?"

"I met with the finance committee a couple of months ago. I brought them a study of what other congregations of similar size to First Church pay their pastors. The truth is, we were underpaying him. The finance committee agreed with me that we needed to put the golden handcuffs on our rector. We boosted his salary to better compare to rectors of a similar size parish. We are all hoping that will give him pause and hopefully keep him in Falls City."

"Sounds good to me, but we both know just how restless young men can become."

Stone allowed a slow grin to light up his eyes.

"Okay, what bright idea has painted that look on your face?" Chief Sparks recognized the devilish look on Stone's face.

"You know, I was just thinking about that statue of Ned in the park."

"And?"

"Oh, I just might find some satisfaction in visiting that park once the statue is up."

"How's that?"

"I think it will become my life's work to spread a lot of birdseed at the base."

"You're going to do what? Why?"

"Just think about it. Birdseed brings birds. Birds poop. Seeing Ned's likeness continually covered in bird dung just might make a lot of folks in this town real happy. I know it'll please me."

The Magnolia Series

Dennis R. Maynard

Chapter 7

"How's it going?" Randi walked up behind her husband, Father Steele Austin, and wrapped her arms around his neck. He'd been sitting at the desk in his home study for most of the morning.

"I think I'm finished."

"Good. Remember, you promised Travis that you would take Mandy and him to the park this afternoon."

"I remember. I've already loaded her stroller in the car. It probably won't do any good. Since she's started walking, she'd rather push the stroller than ride in it."

Randi smiled. She turned to sit on the edge of his desk and picked up the papers he'd been working on. "You want me to review these for you?"

"I wish you would. Where are the children right now?"

"Mandy is stirring. She's waking up from her nap. Travis is watching cartoons."

"I'll make a picnic for us."

"Do you want me to go with you?"

"That would be nice, but I thought the entire idea was for you to have some time to yourself."

"It was, and I really do appreciate it. I think I'll get my nails done."

"You enjoy yourself, and I'll make sure that Travis and Mandy have a fun afternoon with dad."

"Speaking of that, Steele, please make Travis choose between cotton candy, a snow cone, and a box of *Skittles*. Don't buy him all three. He'll come home all hopped up on sugar."

"How about two of the three?"

"Oh, you're as bad as he is. Please be the adult and don't let him overdo the sweets at the snack bar in the park."

"Okay, message received, Mother."

Randi chuckled and gently pushed Steele on the shoulder, "And please, don't start calling me *Mother* for at least another fifty years."

Steele smiled. "Okay, Mommy. We'll not have too much fun at the snack bar."

Randi began thumbing through the pages she'd picked up from the desk. "Are you satisfied with your answers?"

"They're pretty much the standard questions I've seen other search committees ask their candidates for bishop. You know, tell us about your spiritual journey. What is your vision for our diocese? What is a mistake or failure you've made in your ministry and what did you learn from it? All the typical questions."

"Any of them bother you?"

"The one about homosexuality. I'm not sure the Diocese of San Antonio is going to like my answer."

"How do you feel right now about being a bishop?"

"I have the same concerns that you and I have discussed. The big one is moving. I guess if we are going to move Travis and Mandy, we should do it while they're young."

"Even at that, I hate the thought. Travis really likes his school, and he does have his friends."

"I know. I'm just not sure about the job. It would mean that I'd need to be on the road most every weekend. There are some long stretches of highway between the congregations in that diocese. I just don't know if I want to leave you and the kids every weekend for the next twenty years."

"I agree. That part of the job really sucks. But Steele, you realize that if a parish is in trouble, you may have to make trips out during the week as well."

"That's just it. There will be meetings and gatherings all over the diocese, not to mention the travel I would have to do with the House of Bishops."

"Have you also thought about what you'll miss in the parish?"

"That's major. I love being a part of a community. I like making things happen. I really enjoy being a pastor. I'm afraid I don't know too many bishops that get to be a pastor. Most are so busy with meetings and travel they rarely have time to pastor anyone, especially the clergy."

"What about Bishop Powers in Oklahoma?"

"I think he's the exception. I also think that has come at great expense to his wife and children. I fear he's neglected them in order to have time to pastor his priests."

"Steele, why do I get the impression that there's something even greater bothering you?"

Steele took Randi's hand in his, "And why is it so eerie that you can read my mind?"

She placed her other hand on top of his and squeezed. "My advice is that you not ever forget that. I can read you like a book."

Steele nodded. "Let me show you something else." He opened a manila folder and handed it to her. "I don't think I'm supposed to have this at this point in the process, but I convinced Charles Gerard to send it to me. As chair of the search committee, he counseled me that it was for my eyes only. I don't think he'd mind if I shared it with you."

"What is it?"

"It's a copy of the diocesan budget. I also have copies of all the congregation's parochial reports for the past three years."

"So, what did you find?"

"There are quite a few things that really bother me."

"Go on."

"The first thing that bothers me is the amount that the congregations have to send to the diocese. Over twenty percent of their receipts have to be forwarded to the diocese."

"That seems high."

"I think it is."

"Do you think the diocese administers them well?"

"Oh, that's a subjective question. Do I see things that seem incongruent? Yes."

"For example?"

"Well, that required me to go to the parochial reports. First, there are mission congregations averaging only twenty or thirty people a week, with little or no hope for demographic growth. The diocese puts thousands of dollars into those congregations every year."

"Don't most dioceses do that?"

"This one does. Here's the other side of that coin. They are taking the money from congregations that are growing and prospering to prop up dying ones."

"Isn't that the way it's supposed to be?"

"That's what we've all come to accept. Consider this. If those growing congregations could keep more of their money to employ a youth minister, a full-time music minister, perhaps another priest, or even expand their facilities, would they grow even faster?"

"I'm sure you're not the first priest to ask that question. So what's really bothering you?"

"This!" Steele opened his desk drawer. He pulled out a legal tablet. "I went through the compensation for all the clergy in the diocese over the last three years. Randi, most of the clergy have not received even a small cost of living increase. Some have actually had to have their salaries reduced. A few of the clergy in the most rapidly growing congregations have also had no salary increase, and a couple of them had their salaries reduced."

"Steele, Honey, if there's no money in the congregations to increase their salaries, then they can't be increased."

Steele became agitated. He stood and started pacing his study. "Randi, listen to me. The diocese is taking twenty percent plus from these congregations, and the growing ones are being stifled by it."

"That's your opinion."

"Okay, it's conjecture on my part, but it makes sense."

"That's not all, is it?"

"No, back to the stipends. The diocesan bureaucracy is being built on the backs of the clergy."

"Get to it, Steele. What's really set you off?"

Steele collapsed in his chair and stared up at his wife. He uttered softly, "Randi, while most of the clergy have seen their salaries stagnate, or even shrink, the bishop and his staff have received between a five and eight percent increase each and every year."

"Wow. Now I understand."

"It's even worse than that. Last year, the bishop's staff all got new computers. The bishop even put new carpet throughout the diocesan office. And look at this..." Steele pointed to an expense line item. "The entire staff went on a retreat at an expensive resort on Padre Island last year. But the final straw for me was when I saw the size of the expense accounts for the bishop and each of his staff. In the meantime, clergy throughout the diocese are being forced to take a cut in pay. They have less money to provide for their families. I'm sorry, it's just not right."

They were both silent. "If you were elected, could you change that?"

"I'd like to think so, but I have an even larger issue bothering me."

"Tell me."

"Randi, do bishops build successful congregations, or do rectors?"

"What are you asking me?"

"I guess I'm trying to decide just what bishops have to do with building up growing and vibrant congregations. For the most part, a congregation only sees their bishop once a year. I've got a feeling that the majority of the members of a parish don't even know their bishop's name."

"Your point is?"

"I'm not sure. I just know that a gifted rector can increase attendance, strengthen the congregation's ministry, attract new members, and all that goes with it. What role does the bishop play in any of it?"

"Steele, are you questioning whether or not we even need bishops?"

"No, I know that we need them. But do we need them to be taking twenty cents or more out of every dollar given to a parish to prop up dying congregations? Do we need them to run programs that do little, if anything, to build up a local parish?"

"So you're reconsidering whether or not you even want to be a bishop?"

"I just think I'd better come up with some answers to these fundamental questions. I know what I can do with gifted and committed leaders in a congregation. I just don't know if that can be transferred to a diocese without sacrificing the clergy and the growing congregations in it."

"Why not?"

"Just look at the transformation here at First Church. Bishop Peterson had nothing to do with any of it. Remember, we had to do it in spite of him and his interference. He did nothing to help and did a great deal to make the entire process more difficult. Even though our current bishop is supportive of my ministry, he really doesn't contribute anything to it. First Church is the biggest contributor to the diocese. His vision for the diocese has absolutely nothing to do with building up the ministry of First Church. Yet, we're supposed to sacrifice ministry locally in order to fund his vision. At the very best, it's nothing more than some sort of misplaced loyalty."

"Are you going to submit your questionnaire?"

"This is what I'm thinking. I'll return the questionnaire, and I'll go through the telephone interview if they ask me. But I really need an answer to my questions. I don't want to trade a ministry where I can see the results for one that appears to me, at this point, to be nothing more than that of a robber baron."

"Steele, that's harsh!" She reprimanded.

"Randi, it's just the way I feel after reviewing this budget and the parochial reports. Something's not right about this system. I just don't see what funding a big staff in a centralized diocesan house has to do with growing the local congregation. I really don't understand keeping dying congregations on life support at the expense of the clergy. And I positively can't justify inhibiting dynamic congregations that have potential for growth. I just don't know if it can be fixed."

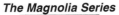

The Magnolia Series

Dennis R. Maynard

Chapter 8

"Momma Dee! Momma Dee!" Henry's two daughters ran to Dee's bedside in her hospital room. "We have a little brother!" Henry's longtime housekeeper, Shady, had brought them to see Dee and the baby.

Dee reached over and put her arms around both of them. She kissed each of them on the cheeks. "Yes, you do. Are you happy?"

"We're so excited. We can't wait to see him," the girls clamored at the same time.

"Well, come over here and meet your brother." Dee rose from the bed and led the girls the few steps to the bassinette. The girls moved cautiously to its side and looked down at the sleeping infant. The youngest girl observed, "Momma Dee, his hair is the same as daddy's, except he has more curls."

"That's right." Dee smiled.

The older girl stood staring. "Momma Dee, why is he so dark? His skin is a lot darker than ours."

Dee glanced at Shady. Shady's eyes widened with a knowing look. "Well, some babies just have darker skin. He may be a bit jaundiced. I'm going to ask the pediatrician about that when he comes in."

"What's jaundiced mean?" The youngest asked.

"It's not a big problem, and most babies just grow out of it in a few days. It's just that some are born that way."

"Oh."

"Would you like to hold him?"

The girls nodded.

"After you sit down, I'll have Shady bring him to you. The most important thing is that you make sure you keep his head in the crevice of your arm."

After each of the girls had held their little brother, Dee suggested, "I'm going to give you some money. I'd like for you to go to the gift shop in the lobby. Please pick me up a couple of magazines and buy a treat for yourselves."

When the girls left, Shady stood next to the bassinette with the baby in her arms. She shook her head, "Miss Dee, is you'n shore you got the right baby?"

"Why do you ask?"

"Suppose it ain't my place to say so, but this baby look more like my family than you'ns."

Tears welled up in Dee's eyes. "Shady, I promise you that's the child I delivered. I just thought all babies are born with darker skin, and then it will lighten up."

"Miss Dee, I'sa could be wrong, but I don't think this baby's skin gonna lighten. If'n anything, it gonna get darker."

"What are you saying?"

"I'sa just dunno. Somethin's jus' not right here. This baby shore look to me like he got some my people's blood."

"Shady, that's just not possible."

"Then the only explainin' here is you got the wrong baby. This hospital done gone and switched on you."

Dee wiped at the tears now streaming down her face. "Shady, I promise you, that's my baby."

Shady's eyes widened. "Well, I hear say you white folks got a 'spression about a woodpile. I thinks you'd better find that woodpile and see just who's in it."

"Does Henry have any ancestors that are black?"

"I'sa can't say for sure, but Mister Henry one of the whitest men I ever seen. Miss Dee, one time I saw him in swim shorts, and I thought I'sa gonna have to put on dark glasses." Shady chuckled. "That man's white as those sheets you lying on."

"All my people are white too. My skin is darker than Henry's for sure, and if I get out in the sun I can get real dark, but my people are all white. You met my parents...."

Before she could finish, Henry walked in with his daughters. "Look who I found down at the gift shop. And it's a good thing. I saw two young men that had their eyes on them. I had to scare those boys away."

"Oh, Daddy, there were no boys down there."

"That's because I scared them away before you saw them."

The girls giggled and handed Dee her magazines. "Daddy, you're so silly."

"Did you get to hold the baby?"

Both girls exclaimed at the same time, "Yes, can we do it again?"

"You can hold him when we bring him home tomorrow. We'll also expect you to change his diapers, and take your turns at feeding him in the middle of the night."

A surprised look crossed the girls' faces. Then they started giggling again. "Daddy, you don't mean it. You're just kidding."

"Well, we'll see about that." Henry smiled. "Shady, how about you take the girls back home. Dee needs to get some rest."

When Shady and the girls had left, Henry sat down on the side of the bed next to his wife. He took her hand in his. "Dee, you know that I love you."

"And I love you, Henry Mudd."

"I have a confession to make, and I hope it won't upset you. Please don't be mad at me."

Tears once again welled up in Dee's eyes and slid down her cheeks. "I know what you want to confess. I need to make the same confession."

The two sat in silence holding hands and staring at the baby. Dee broke the silence. "Henry, I know that baby is ours, but I just don't understand how..."

"I don't either," he interrupted. "But that's what I have to confess. Have you ever heard of something called Ancestor and Genealogical DNA Testing?"

"No, what is it?"

"It's a way that they can trace our ancestry back as much as a thousand years."

"And you want to do that with our baby?"

"Yes."

"And you think that will explain why he's so dark..." She paused. "And his hair and... "

"Yes."

"I'd like to know. Will the test hurt him?"

"No, it won't hurt him at all."

"Are you just going to do my ancestors?"

"No, they'll do a DNA history for both of our families."

"Let's do it. I really want to know."

"I was hoping you'd say that."

Henry kissed her. "I'll pick the both of you up in the morning. Now just try to get some rest." As Henry drove home, he felt a twinge of guilt for not telling Dee everything he'd done. The paternity test that he'd paid extra to rush came back positive. He could still hear the doctor.

"Henry, you're definitely the father. The analysis is 95% certain. That child is yours."

"But how do you explain his features?"

"Henry, clearly either you or Dee has one or more ancestors with those DNA markings."

"I don't believe it."

"Well, there's a way we can find out."

"Oh?" The doctor then explained the Ancestor and Genealogical DNA Testing. Henry had told him to do it immediately.

"It will probably take a week to ten days to get the results."

"I'll pay extra to get them sooner."

"It will depend on how busy the lab is; I'll check."

Henry was satisfied that the baby was, in fact, his. What he didn't know was how he was going to explain the baby's features to Falls City society.

The Magnolia Series

Dennis R. Maynard

Chapter 9

The industrial park on the south side of Falls City includes several large warehouses and distribution centers. The small side streets host smaller complexes that have been divided into multiple units. They each are twenty-five feet wide and fifty feet deep with twenty-foot ceilings. The complex that Rose MacClaren had chosen contained five units. An independent printer rented the corner unit entering the driveway. He was there most every day and many evenings. He printed everything from business cards to wedding invitations to catalogs for the local businesses. Conveniently located next to him was a bulk mailing facility. The third unit had a sign over the door that read simply *Mexican Imports*. Rose had never seen anyone there. Then came her unit. On the other side of her space was the other corner unit rented by a church. The sign above their door read *Iglesias de Cristo*. While Rose did not speak Spanish, she understood they only had one service on Sunday mornings at 10:00 a.m. She'd never seen anyone there during the week. Each unit had two doors. There was a large door that could be raised for loading and unloading large shipments, and a smaller door leading into an office, with another door leading into the warehouse. All of the doors appeared very solid and were windowless. Each unit also had running water and a toilet facility. Each could be individually climate controlled.

Rose chose the unit between the church and Mexican Imports for her garden unit. Rose wanted to deter unwanted visitors. She placed a sign over her door that read, *Stockage Privé,* which translates into *Private Storage* in French. She'd looked the phrase up in an *English to French Dictionary* in the library. She was counting on the fact that very few, if any, of the people that would wander past her facility would be able to speak French. All others would be so confused by the sign they'd simply pass her by.

The industrial park was over eight miles from the Saint Andrew's Manse where Rose lived with Pastor MacClaren and their three children. Each time she went to the warehouse, it was a sixteen mile round trip. Pastor MacClaren regularly checked the odometer on Rose's car. She'd had to find other excuses that he would deem acceptable for driving so far. To her credit, she'd found a small farm nearby that sold eggs and seasonal vegetables. She'd also discovered a small grocer that had day-old bread and dented canned goods that were priced lower than the super market. She always stopped at both as an explanation for her mileage. Pastor MacClaren was well pleased when she saved money on groceries.

As she drove to the warehouse, Rose remembered the first time that she met Gloria Ramos. It was late at night in a public laundromat near her home in Florida. Her own washing machine was in need of repair. Pastor MacClaren did not want to spend the money to buy her a new one or repair the old one. She was left with no alternative but to take the family laundry there. It was late at night. Her husband had insisted that his dinner be served and the kitchen cleaned before she could do the laundry. Further, she needed to help the children with their homework and to memorize their Bible verses. Once all that was done, and the children and her husband were in bed, she was free to take the laundry.

No one was in the laundromat that night but Gloria and Rose. They began talking. As they talked, they discovered they had so much in common. Both had controlling and abusive husbands, the only difference being that Gloria had left hers. She put a restraining order on him, filed for divorce, and moved her two children to another city. Rose opened up to Gloria in a way that she'd never done with another woman. The bond between the two of them grew strong in just a couple of hours. Then Gloria introduced Rose to something she'd never experienced in her life. Gloria invited Rose to go out to her car with her.

Once they were in the car, she lit a marijuana cigarette. She taught Rose how to pull the smoke into her lungs and hold it there before exhaling. A wonderful, peaceful feeling washed over Rose. She couldn't remember the last time she'd felt so relaxed. Rose started giggling.

"What's funny?" Gloria asked.

"My husband would be so upset if he knew I was doing this."

"And that's funny?"

Now Rose was laughing uncontrollably. It became contagious, and Gloria started laughing as well. "Why are we laughing?"

"Oh, the good stuff just does that to you. Everything gets funny," an amused Gloria explained.

Suddenly Rose sat forward. "Is he going to smell this on me?"

"Who?"

"Melvin."

A giggling Gloria asked, "Who's Melvin?"

Rose filled with more laughter, "Melvin. You know Melvin."

"I don't know anyone named Melvin. Melvin who?"

Rose fought to gain control through the fog that had enveloped her. "Melvin is my husband. Is he going to smell this on me?"

"No. Just take a shower when you get home and spray on some perfume."

That caused the laughter to pour out of Rose. She held her stomach, she was laughing so hard. "Perfume! He doesn't let me wear perfume. Look at my face. He forbids me to wear any cosmetics. I can't wear makeup, lipstick, or any of it."

"What are you talking about?"

"Just that. He says only whores wear all that stuff. He refuses to let me look like a prostitute."

Both women were bent over with laughter. "But that's not funny." Gloria sputtered. "That's just sad."

Rose began sobering up. "How am I going to keep him from knowing what I've been doing?"

Gloria sensed the seriousness of her question. "Do you have any lilac soap?"

"No, he insists that we only have *Ivory Soap* in the house."

"Well, that'll have to do. When you get home, take a shower and wash your hair. Soak the clothes you have on in the sink and then hang them outside to dry."

"That ought to work. He sleeps soundly. Once he's out, he's out. I could run the vacuum in the bedroom and it wouldn't wake him."

Gloria opened her glove compartment and brought out a bag of *Hershey's Kisses.* "You hungry?"

"I'm famished."

As the two women swallowed the chocolate as fast as they could open it, Gloria asked, "Rose, do you think you'd like to smoke this stuff again?"

"Yes, I was going to ask you if I could have some."

"Sure, I'll give you what's left in this little bag. How'd you like to learn how to grow your own?"

"I could do that?"

"Not only can I teach you how to grow it, but I can help you grow enough to make some extra money."

"How much?"

"Well, what's left in this bag would sell for around fifty dollars."

Rose's eyes grew big. "How many plants would I have to grow?"

"That's up to you."

That was the beginning of the best friendship Rose had ever had with another woman. It was also the beginning of her clandestine, not to mention, very profitable business. Rose pulled into the drive leading to her warehouse. There were a couple of cars in front of the printer's unit and one in front of the bulk mailing office, but no more. The street was clear. She would wait in her office on Gloria to arrive.

Looking around to make sure no one was watching, Rose opened the door, entered her office, and locked it behind her. She went into the warehouse to inspect the crop she'd most recently planted. Currently there were only a couple dozen plants. Gloria had provided the startup money to buy the additional grow lights and other equipment she'd needed. They were now partners. Their plan was to gradually expand the operation out of each of their profits. She counted, once again, the harvest that Gloria was going to pick up.

Returning to her office, she opened her desk drawer. She took out the tin containing some of the leaves she'd been saving for Gloria and her to share. She put a small amount in a cigarette paper and rolled it. Her lighter was on top of the desk. She would just relax until Gloria arrived. A couple of puffs would be enough. Then she'd share the rest with her friend. Rose enjoyed more than just a couple of puffs. She smoked the entire joint. It was just what she needed. Listening to Melvin whip young John Calvin this morning was something she just could not get used to. His screams were still echoing in her ears. The smoke from her joint filled the little office. The haze brought her some comfort. The colors in the painting on the wall above her desk were more brilliant than ever. There was a knock at the door. Gloria had arrived, Rose was so excited. She stood and walked to the door. Rose opened the door, "Hey, I've..."

Gloria was not staring back at her. Rose was looking into the sun-glassed face of one of Falls City's finest. "Lady, what's that smell? Have you been smoking marijuana in here?"

Rose panicked. She tried to shut the door on him, but he forced his way past her. In one swift move, he pushed her up against the office wall and turned her around. She squealed in pain as he grabbed her arms and pulled them behind her back. In an instant, Rose MacClaren, the wife of the senior pastor at Saint Andrew's Presbyterian Church, was in handcuffs. She heard him shout into the microphone on his lapel. "I'm at unit seventeen in the industrial district. I need the drug dog and a search warrant. I've walked in on a pot smoker. I think she's a grower, and this is her garden."

As Rose was being led to the squad car, she glimpsed Gloria's car enter the driveway. When Gloria saw the activity in front of Rose's unit, she pulled into a parking space in front of the bulk mailing office. The occupants were standing in front of their unit watching the scene. Gloria asked, "What's going on?"

The Magnolia Series

Dennis R. Maynard

Chapter 10

Bishop Sean Evans dreaded the drive to Mount Stater in the lower part of his diocese. It was one of those small dying towns replicated in every state. Most of the young people had left to follow their dreams. The only residents remaining were older and settled. They had their burial plots reserved in the city cemetery next to their ancestors before them. At one time, there were three or four industries that brought middle class prosperity to the community. The younger generation followed them out of town. The town square had once been the center of thriving businesses. There were a couple of department stores, dress shops, men's stores, and children's clothing stores. Multiple restaurants and two movie theatres brought folks to the square in the evenings. Now the movie theatres were boarded up. The department stores sat empty. The specialty clothing stores had been converted into resale stores and antique shops. Most sat idle.

When the town was prospering, the local faithful had built a picturesque Episcopal Church. It contained stained glass memorialized to many of the faithful departed at the time. A parish hall, nursery, and Sunday school classrooms stood adjacent. The pipe organ that was once masterfully played by a full-time music minister was now pounded by a Sunday supply. The nursery was seldom used and the classrooms stored memories of better times.

Sean pulled into the parking lot thirty minutes before the service was to begin. An elderly woman wearing an embroidered smock with the words *Altar Guild* on it greeted him. Her hands were shaking as she went about showing Sean where he could hang his vestments. Sean examined the attendance book. Consistently, it recorded thirty-nine to forty-five in attendance. He flipped the pages to look back at the Easter attendance. Seventy-eight worshippers had been present for the service. Curiosity got the best of him as he turned the few pages back to examine attendance at last year's Christmas service. He was amused to see that ninety-four people had come to celebrate the birth of Jesus but only seventy-eight were present to celebrate his resurrection.

The vicar arrived. He was a late vocation priest, having been ordained in his mid-fifties. Sean knew that this would most likely be the largest congregation he would ever serve. He was not without gifts, but his lack of experience would keep the larger congregations from considering him.

The organist brought the service music for Sean to review. The service leaflet listed the hymns. "Can the congregation sing these hymns?" Sean asked.

"Oh, yes, Bishop. This congregation loves to sing. We sing most everything."

Sean opened his vestment case. He contemplated not wearing his cope and mitre for such a small congregation. The vicar, sensing that may be what Sean was thinking, explained that some of the worshippers would be bringing their protestant friends. They wanted to show their friends what a bishop wears. Sean relented.

The organist started the prelude. The vicar led Sean to the back of the nave. An elderly man dressed in a red acolyte's robe was holding the processional cross. Behind him stood another elderly man and woman dressed in cassock and surplice, holding processional candles. They would be the servers and would read the scriptures. They would also be leading the prayers of the people. Sean looked out at the congregation. The nave had a seating capacity of two hundred people. An usher whispered to Sean, "We have a full house for you, Bishop. There are sixty people here." Sean surveyed the sea of thinning white hair. The average age was as he expected. He thought seventy-eight years would be on the low side. To his surprise, there was a younger Hispanic couple with two teenage children sitting on the back pew.

The organist announced the opening hymn. Sean couldn't believe it. It was one of the most difficult in the hymnal. He alternated between anger with the organist, and sympathy for the congregation struggling to sing the hymn. When the service was over, Sean would have a word with the organist. No, that wouldn't be enough. He was going to send a letter to every organist in his diocese. He would insist that they choose music appropriate to the ability of the congregation.

After the service, one of the ladies brought him a plate filled with baked goods and small sandwiches. "The ladies of the Church made these in your honor." She stood smiling at him, anticipating he would take the plate and eat. Sean did not have the heart to refuse. At the same time, he was disgusted with himself for doing so. It was the very reason that he'd grown so large.

In the sacristy with the Vicar, Sean shut the door. "Sit down, Father. Let's talk awhile." Sean continued. "How are you doing? How's your family?"

Sean listened carefully to the man report on his wife, children, and his grandchildren.

"I don't think I've ever met your children. Do they live here in Mount Stater?"

"Only my daughter, but she doesn't attend church very often. She did come last Christmas, but she's in the process of moving to Atlanta. She's got a job up there."

"Well, hopefully, she'll find a church to unite with in Atlanta."

The priest shrugged. "My wife and I are struggling financially. We were hoping that you could help me find a new spot. We don't need a lot more money, but we've not had an increase since I came here four years ago."

"I'll keep you in mind as vacancies occur. Have you been able to increase the stewardship here?"

"Bishop, I've tried, but the people in this congregation live on fixed incomes. Their own resources have not increased, so they have very little more to give. In the meantime, their expenses are going up. As you are aware, the government says the cost of living is only increasing one or two percent a year. That's all the increase they get on their pensions and social security checks. In the meantime, groceries, gasoline, medicine, utilities, and most everything else that the government refuses to include in the cost of living index is in the process of doubling in price. These folks just can't keep up with all that."

Sean nodded. "I know. We also see it in the analysis of the average annual pledge to the parishes in the diocese. We just aren't seeing the necessary increase in financial giving each year to keep up with parish operations." Sean paused. "Have you done any baptisms this year?"

"No."

"Are you preparing anyone for confirmation?"

"Did you see the two teenagers on the back pew?"

"The Hispanic family, right?"

"Yes. I'd like to think I'll get to prepare them, but the family is still learning English." The priest was silent for a minute. "Bishop, this town is dying. This church is dying. I just don't know how it's going to survive but maybe another ten years."

"Are there any new people moving into this community?"

"The Hispanics are moving in, but since most of them speak very little English, they don't come here."

"Is there a Hispanic Church in Mount Stater?"

"Not that I know about."

"If you offered a Mass in Spanish, would they come?"

"I hadn't thought about it. I guess that's because I don't speak Spanish."

"Is there a Roman Catholic Church here?"

"No, the bishop closed it and boarded up the property about ten years ago."

Sean asked thoughtfully, "Do you think there is a possibility that we could reach out to the Latinos? Most of them have been raised as Roman Catholics."

"Bishop, this Church doesn't have the money needed to bring them in. It'll take more than just putting up a sign. It will take real legwork. It's all I can do to take care of this congregation. There aren't many of them, but do you have any idea how much time I have to spend visiting them? A few of them are seriously ill every week. You realize I also have to sell insurance just to make ends meet. That requires me to make calls in the towns around us."

Sean nodded. "I understand. I really do. I just don't want us to miss an opportunity." Sean stood to leave.

The vicar extended his hand. "So you'll keep me in mind for another position?"

Sean nodded. As he turned his car onto the freeway leading back to Savannah, he considered the resources the diocese was already pouring into the dying congregation. He contemplated moving forward with dissolving the little church and selling the property. If he closed them down, he could redirect the money to congregations that were growing. But then, who would buy a church in a dying town? He thought about putting even more money into it for a Hispanic ministry. Reaching out to the Hispanics moving into the town had real potential. Reality hit him. The diocesan budget was already stretched to the limit. There simply wasn't any more money to put into Mount Stater. He had to make a choice. Either he would close it or he would have to find money to put into it, but where would he find the money? The budget of First Church in Falls City flashed before him. He fixated on the rector's compensation. Anger rose up in him. Steele Austin would be getting a piece of his mind and he'd be getting it in the next couple of days.

The Magnolia Series

Dennis R. Maynard

Chapter 11

The annual appreciation luncheon for the Altar Guild of Historic First Church is one of the most envied social events of the autumn season. Not all one hundred fifty members of the Guild are invited to the luncheon. Attendance is limited to the chairs of the various committees on the Guild itself. These sought after positions are limited to the dozen ladies that have actually been trained in the fine art of *setting up services*. The chairs and co-chairs of the subsidiary Guilds that set up the chapel and school services are also included. The young women that have successfully completed Junior League training, and have been admitted to the Guild, will have to wait decades for their opportunity to attend. For over two hundred years, the privilege of *setting up services* has been limited to those that have paid their dues. Every new member began, as a young woman in the chapel, polishing the followers on the altar candlesticks. The generation of women above them will literally have to die before they will be able to move to one of the cherished positions. Then, and only then, will they be allowed to touch the gold and silver vessels used on the altar of First Church.

Almeda Alexander Drummond would be hosting this year's luncheon. Almeda spent weeks preparing. She sat with her houseboy and chef, hour after hour, going over every detail of the menu. Additional tables needed to be rented and placed in the spacious living room in her mansion on River Street. Arrangements had to be made for valet parking for those in attendance. Flower arrangements had to be carefully selected. She lay awake multiple nights wrestling with a color scheme. One morning at breakfast, she informed her husband, The Reverend Doctor Horace Drummond, the senior associate at First Church, that she was not going to be predictable in her choice of colors. "Just because it's the beginning of autumn, I know that I will be expected to utilize fall colors. But Horace, orange, yellow, and rust just do not complement the decor in my living and dining room. Can you imagine those colors in our house?"

Horace had learned early on in their marriage not to have a contrary opinion when it came to such things. He simply nodded and smiled. "My Darling, your taste in these matters is impeccable. I trust you completely. Whatever you choose will both complement our home, and it will be a feast for the eyes."

Almeda so loved her husband. He always knew just the right thing to say. "Well, I've thought on this subject for several nights now. I believe I have decided on the ideal flowers for the arrangements. I'm going to use white calla lilies and white hydrangeas. For color, I am going to have them add cymbidium orchards. Do you think I should use magnolia leaves or assorted greens for the fill?"

"I think either one would be lovely. As usual, you have put together an arrangement of flowers that will be just spectacular."

Almeda smiled. "You are a wonderful husband."

The menu was as carefully chosen as were the flowers, tablecloths, and serving napkins. "I want to loosen this group up a bit so we can all have a nice time," Almeda told her chef. "So, let's start by marinating some canned peach halves for a couple of days in a generous portion of *Southern Comfort*. Right before my guests arrive, put the peach halves in the large wine goblets. Smother them with some additional *Southern Comfort* and then pour chilled champagne on top of it all. It will make a lovely drink and should insure that everyone will have a joyful time."

Her chef raised his eyebrows. "Oh, I think that will do the trick. And the hors d' oeuvres?"

Almeda wrinkled her forehead. "Oh, dear, that could be a problem."

"Problem?"

"Yes, our rector's wife, who, mind you, I just adore, is insisting on bringing her stuffed mushrooms. They really don't go with my menu. She's just such a sweet girl; I can't find it within myself to refuse her."

"Are they not any good?"

"To the contrary, every time I've seen her serve them, they are the hit of the party. They actually are quite delicious, but then those in attendance tend to ignore the other offerings."

"Well then, how do you want me to serve them?"

"I have thought on that subject at some length. This is what I want you to do. Just place a couple of trays on the buffet table over there. Let the ladies discover them on their own, but I don't want you to leave them out very long. After all, I don't want my guests filling up on mushrooms. They need to save themselves for my luncheon."

The menu Almeda had chosen was ever so predictable for a gathering of southern ladies. Equally predictable was that she would add her own unique touch to each item. The tomato aspic would include the usual ingredients. She would have the chef omit the minced onion and replace it with some finely grated lemon zest. She would also have him add some finely chopped green bell pepper in addition to the chopped celery ribs. Her secret ingredient was to add a generous helping of vodka to the tomato juice. Almeda had also special ordered her own ramekins to put the aspic in to chill. She had them molded in the shape of a magnolia flower. She instructed that the aspic, once chilled and removed from the ramekins, be strategically arranged on a bed of fresh spinach leaves on a large silver tray. She could not believe that some women actually served their aspic on iceberg lettuce. "Tacky. Just tacky." She shook her head. She instructed that each serving of aspic was to be topped off with a teaspoon of *Duke's Mayonnaise. "Now,* you will use *Duke's* and nothing else. Dust the mayonnaise with just enough paprika to add some color." As a final touch, she wanted the tray to have asparagus vinaigrette and thinly sliced boiled eggs added so they could be served on the salad plates with the aspic.

She ordered the country ham for her biscuit sandwiches from a smokehouse over in Macon. The pimento cheese sandwiches would, once again, be her own recipe. She instructed that the crust be trimmed from the bread and that only *Sunbeam* white bread be used. The third item on the plate would be her secret recipe for Cha-Cha Chicken Salad. Dessert would be Chocolate Roulage.

As anticipated, the very first to arrive was the longtime chair of the Altar Guild, Mary Alice Smythe, and her ever present sidekick, Martha Dexter. Martha quickly consumed her first glass of champagne and started looking for a spoon so she could eat the peach. Then she spotted the mushrooms. Mary Alice came up behind her, "Martha, you've got to slow down. You know that Almeda is infamous for spiking her food. I don't want to have to carry you to the car."

"Oh, everything she does is so delicious."

"Well, just be cautious. Please don't embarrass yourself."

When Mary Alice had walked away, Martha quickly wrapped some of the stuffed mushrooms in a napkin and slid them into her purse. She then made her way back to the bar. "May I have another one of those peach drinks?"

When all had gathered, the chatter centered on the arrest of the pastor's wife at Saint Andrew's Presbyterian Church. The group's speculations fluctuated between her involvements with a drug cartel out of Miami to running prostitutes. "She was not only selling drugs, but she had several young women working for her as prostitutes. You know, she was a madam. I have that on the highest authority."

Almeda wanted to turn the conversation to a happier topic. "Has anyone been to see the new Mudd baby?"

"No, but I just think it's wonderful that Henry now has a son. And that precious wife of his is so darlin'."

"Well, that other wife he had is just a disgrace. Does anyone know anything about her?"

"She's in the women's prison up in Atlanta. She's getting everything she deserves."

"Oh, I don't know. I hear she may be eligible to get out in just a couple of years."

"That's disgraceful. After all she's done. Horrible!"

As the lunch progressed, Martha Dexter quickly consumed her first plate and returned for a second. With pimento cheese clinging to her lower lip, she approached Almeda. "How do you make this pimento cheese? It's just delicious."

Almeda smiled. "It's my own recipe."

Mary Alice signaled for Martha to wipe her lip. "Yes, Almeda, it's just wonderful. Will you share your recipe with us?"

Almeda smiled, "Well, that all depends. How do you feel about *Velveeta*?"

"*Velveeta*? You don't! You mean to say you use *Velveeta*?"

"I do."

"How do you get it to come out so smooth?"

"You just put it in the bowl with the other cheeses, pimentos, and *Duke's Mayonnaise.* Then you just *beat the tar* out of it." Almeda chuckled.

"Well, it's delicious."

"If I could have everyone's attention for just a moment." Almeda stood in the center of the room. She was leaning on her walking cane with one hand, but her other was free to gesture. "First, I want to thank you ladies for coming. This is such a wonderful occasion. I received a telephone call from a reporter at the newspaper this morning. They came over and took photos of me with the flower arrangements. They intend to put a report of our luncheon on the society pages this Sunday." Her announcement was met with approving nods and coos around the room.

"What about *Falls City Magazine*?" Martha Dexter asked.

That question caused Almeda to stand even more erect. She put her free hand on her waist and pounded her walking cane on the floor several times in anger. "I am absolutely disgusted with that magazine!" She spit the words out of her mouth. "Did any of you see last month's edition?"

"I glanced through it." Mary Alice admitted.

"And did you notice anything missing?"

"I can't say that I did."

"With your eye for detail, Mary Alice, I just don't know how you could have missed it."

"What did I miss, Almeda?"

"I counted thirty-eight photos of the various social events around Falls City. There was not a single prominent member of First Church featured in any one of those photos!"

A collective gasp rose up in the room. "I guess that's the reason the issue didn't keep my attention." Mary Alice apologized.

"Ladies, it's an outrage. They did not photograph a single person of importance at any of the events they covered. Well, I'll have you know that I called that editor. By the way, she's a member of our congregation. Of course, she would never qualify to be on the Altar Guild, but nonetheless, she is a member of First Church and should know better. I gave her a firm talking to. I reminded her that the people in this town that matter have a long history here. They have buildings and streets named in their family's honor. I scolded her for printing photos of the newcomers and upstarts in Falls City. Her readers have no interest whatsoever in seeing pictures of the middle class. The reason that people purchase her little tabloid is to see what events the outstanding citizens in this town are attending. They want to see what we are wearing, and noting the various organizations we belong to and support."

"Well, good for you, Almeda." Martha Dexter cooed, while popping another sandwich into her mouth.

"Another thing that I found absolutely objectionable was the house they chose to feature. It was not even one of our beautiful historic homes here on River Street, or any other neighborhood of distinction."

"Where was it?" Martha asked, spraying food into her lap.

"Can you believe they chose to feature one of those awful houses out on the north side of town? You know, out there where they are building those new monstrosities for the social climbers. I don't think anyone is buying them but those noisy and ill-mannered Yankees that are moving down here for the climate."

"I, for one, appreciate you drawing this to our attention." Martha Dexter was standing to fill her plate for the third time.

"Thank you, Martha. I suggest that every one of you go home after this lunch and telephone that editor. If she doesn't answer the phone, then flood her answering machine with our complaints. I also told her exactly what would happen if she ever published another issue that did not feature the leading members of First Church."

"What did you say?" Mary Alice queried.

Almeda's eyes were filled with fire. "I told her I will see that all the businesses in my acquaintance that purchase advertisements in her magazine will stop doing so."

"That ought to do it." Martha agreed. "I know my Howard buys a full page ad every month. I'll remind her of that when I call."

"Well, I don't think she heard me. She told me she'd have a photographer and reporter present to take pictures of our Altar Guild tea. Do you see such anywhere in this room?"

Sounds of disgust were whispered around the room.

"Then we are all in agreement." Almeda continued to stand. "I do have just one bit of business. I'd like to bring this up before dessert and coffee are served. Since my unfortunate illness, and the necessity that I walk with this cane, I've become more conscious of the arrangement of our altar rail in the church. It's most difficult for me to climb the three steps to get up to the rail. I also find it impossible to kneel once I arrive." Almeda could imagine what she looked like, leaning heavily on her cane and dragging her lame foot up those stairs. She could feel the critical eyes of the entire congregation mocking her. Maybe their eyes were filled with pity. She didn't want either look. It was not an image she wanted to portray, or have others observe. She vowed to fix the problem, and fix it she would.

"But it's such an inspiration to see you climb those steps each Sunday." Mary Alice uttered.

"I appreciate that, but I have an idea that I've not even discussed with my husband, the rector, or anyone else. I wanted to bring it to you ladies first. I would like to see us bring the altar rail down to the level of the nave floor. We could also move the altar forward. We could then place the choir against the back wall so they could be heard better."

"I can't believe you're saying this, Almeda." Martha Dexter almost shouted. "When Misturh Austin arrived, he brought all this up. You were one of the first to reject it."

"I know, but my situation has now given me a different opinion on the subject."

Shaking her head, Mary Alice joined the objections. "Almeda, we usually agree on most things, but on this I must hold a contrary opinion. The altar and the altar rail have been in their current location since the church was constructed. I was taught in confirmation class that the three steps leading to the altar are there for a reason. They represent faith, hope, and love. We're each supposed to silently recite those words when we climb the stairs to communion."

"I understand all that. It's just that it's so difficult for people in my condition to climb those stairs. The same is true for a great many of our members. Have you even noticed how difficult it is for some of the elderly to make it to the rail?"

"Almeda, this has been a very nice lunch, and we all really thank you for it." Mary Alice tightened her lips. "But I don't believe you'll have our support if you pursue moving the altar rail."

Almeda silently looked around the room. For the first time in her life at First Church, she could see disapproving looks on the faces of her fellow Altar Guild members. "Well, let's just leave it there for now. I do wish you would each give it some consideration." She reached down and rang the little silver bell sitting next to her plate. The servers entered with dessert plates and a silver coffee service. Almeda ate her dessert, oblivious to the conversation around her. Her thoughts focused on a plan for moving the altar rail. She smiled to herself. I guess it's a good thing I didn't mention turning the priest's sacristy into a handicapped bathroom.

The Magnolia Series

Dennis R. Maynard

Chapter 12

Chief Sparks had agreed to meet Stone Clemons in the downstairs bar at The Magnolia Club. "An afternoon libation will put us both in a good mood," Stone told him on the telephone. "When I tell you what I want to do with those investigation files, it just may make your day, if not your week. Bring them with you. I'll sign for them."

The Chief was waiting on Stone at a corner table. It was as far from the bar and other ears as he could get. Stone walked up behind him and slapped him on the back. "Did you hear about the little boy that brought his report card home? He'd flunked every course he was taking."

"No, I don't think I've heard that one."

"Well, as you might suspect, his parents weren't too happy with him. So his daddy asked, 'What do you have to say for yourself?' But the little boy showed that he was no dummy. He countered, 'Pop, I think you're the one that needs to give me an explanation.' 'How's that?' his dad responded. 'Mom, Dad, I need to know. Do you attribute my report card to heredity or environment'?"

"That's a good one. Reminds me of the little boy that came home from church. His daddy asked him what the preacher had talked about. He answered, 'Sin'. 'Well, what did the preacher say about sin, son?' The little boy just shrugged his shoulders, 'He said he was against it'."

"What's the latest on Tom Barnhardt?" Stone asked.

"We don't have anything we can charge him with. Our star witness can't be found. The only thing we have is the statement he gave us. Tom would demand the right to face his accuser if we were to pursue this."

Stone nodded knowingly. "Well, he's not getting off completely. I know that he's been summoned before the state bar. He'll most likely lose his license to practice law in the state of Georgia."

"Yeah, I know. They asked for a copy of the statement that blonde boy, Chance, made."

"Anything on Gary Hendricks?"

"Now that's one for the books. He has just completely dropped off the face of the earth. No one, and I do mean no one, has a clue as to his whereabouts. It's the damndest thing I've ever seen in all my years of law enforcement. It's as though he vanished into thin air. There's no record of any travel documents. Gary canceled all his credit cards. Kaboom! He's gone."

"Misturh Clemons, do you want your usual?" The bartender was standing at their table.

"What's that he's drinking?"

"Chief Sparks be havn' a Rusty Nail."

"A what?"

The Chief chuckled, "It's a drink I learned about while I was at the national chiefs' meeting out in Texas last month. A lot of the Texans drink it."

"What's in it?"

"Equal parts of *Drambuie* and scotch over ice."

Stone twisted his mouth and shook his head. "Sounds like a drink to put you in an early grave."

"It'll put a little hair on your chest and lead in your pipe."

"Don't you be concerning yourself about the lead in my pipe," Stone chuckled. "And as for hair on my chest, I've got you beat there too."

The Chief snorted, "You wish."

"Just bring me my usual. A bourbon and branch will do nicely."

"Sounds to me like the perfect epitaph for your tombstone."

"I wouldn't mind if it were. In fact, I'd like to think my last drink on this earth might just be some of Kentucky's finest. I wouldn't mind if *Jim Beam* himself showed up to fix it for me."

"What do you plan to do with these statements?"

"I'm only interested in the part about the former pastor at the Presbyterian Church."

"Oh."

"We're going to file a civil lawsuit against Ned Boone's estate."

"Who's we?"

"That's the part you're going to enjoy. It took some doing, but I got one of my investigators to locate that pastor."

"And?"

"He found him out in Nebraska. The man had moved his family in with his parents on their farm. He couldn't find a preaching job anywhere. That accusation that he'd had child pornography on his office computer was hanging over his head. No church would touch him. The only thing left for him to do was help his dad work the family farm."

"He was actually living with his parents?"

"That's the tragedy of it all. He couldn't even get a job in a convenience store. The man has literally been through hell. Anyway, with Chance's statement that Ned Boone had employed him to plant the *kiddie porn* on the pastor's computer, we think we have a civil case."

"You think you can win it without Chance being here to testify?"

"We don't have to win it. They're going to want to settle with us, and they're going to want to do it as quickly and quietly as possible."

"Who will be representing Boone's estate?"

A big grin crossed Stone's face as he brought the bourbon and branch to his lips. "Oh, that's where it just gets so good you'll want to dance in the aisle at First Church."

"Come on, out with it."

"The law firm of Tom Barnhardt!" Neither man could contain his laughter.

"Didn't I just read in the newspaper that Saint Andrew's Presbyterian had dedicated their chapel to Ned's memory?"

"You did. Have you been by the park in front of his house?"

"Not recently."

"His statue is already in place."

"What? How? That was quick."

"Seems the old egotistical fool had already had it sculpted. It's just been sitting in one of his warehouses, waiting for him to die. They had that statue up before his bony ass could turn cold."

"So you're pretty confident that you'll get some money for the preacher."

"I'm more than confident. That poor man has had his ministry destroyed. His family has been shamed and subjected to humiliation. His very livelihood has been destroyed. He will never be able to get another church. And all of it was the doing of Ned Boone and his pack of lies. You bet we're going to get some money out of that SOB's estate. Pain and suffering are for the civil courts. There is no way that Barnhardt's firm is going to let this go before a jury. There is always a chance that his own secret will be exposed."

The Chief held his glass up to click it against Stone's. "Congratulations, my friend. I'm proud of you. You're doing the right thing."

"If you could just see that pastor and his family. They are so injured they couldn't even bring themselves to get on a plane and fly out here to Falls City at my firm's expense. We had to send our attorneys to them to take their statements. The very thought of being in this town was too much for them. He was the successful pastor of one of the largest Presbyterian churches in the South. Then overnight, he had it all taken from him by one devious man filled with deceit, jealousy, and hatred. No, they'll settle with us, and they'll settle for some mighty big money."

The Chief waved for the bartender to bring two more drinks to their table. "It's just too bad that it all has to be done behind the scenes. This would make a great front-page story. That pastor needs to be vindicated. The only way that can happen is if the news people here in Falls City find out about your suit."

A Cheshire cat grin lit up Stone's face. "I don't remember saying that that the news reporters won't find out about it." Stone's smile grew even larger. "You say Ned's statue is already set up?"

"I saw it for myself. It makes him look like a great statesman, or even a saint."

"Hmmm... wonder where I can find some birdseed this time of the day?"

The Magnolia Series

Dennis R. Maynard

Chapter 13

"Father Austin, I am here with five members of the bishop's search committee for the Diocese of San Antonio." The voice of Charles Gerard came through the speakerphone on Steele's desk. Charles had chaired the search committee that had tried to bring Steele to a parish in that diocese. Now, as Chair of the committee looking for a new bishop, Charles had contacted Steele once again. To be chosen as a candidate for bishop is flattering. Steele was fully aware of that feeling. He also felt like he owed it to Charles to go through the process. He continued to have a twinge of guilt about previously turning Charles and the parish committee down when they asked him to be their rector. "We have been selected by the larger committee for this telephone interview. The people in this room represent the diversity in our diocese. This interview is the next phase in our discernment process. Are you available to answer our questions?"

Charles' secretary had actually called Steele earlier in the week to set an appointment time. "Yes, I've cleared my calendar and asked my secretary to hold all my calls. I've looked forward to this conversation with you."

"First, let me assure you that we are pleased that you have agreed to walk this journey with us. The committee has been most impressed by your work history and your many accomplishments there at First Church."

"Thank you, but I need to make it clear, none of our ministry accomplishments could have been realized without the wonderful lay leadership here, and the supportive ministries of the people in this congregation."

"We are aware of that. It's one of the attributes we are seeking in our next bishop. We are looking for a candidate that has demonstrated the ability to bring diverse people together to achieve common ministry goals."

"Whoa! Charles. I don't want you or the committee to be misled. We were not able to achieve any of those ministry goals without some very strong opposition. There are people in this congregation, given the opportunity, who would happily dismantle some of the projects we've undertaken."

"Father Austin, we've done our homework. We interviewed folks that strongly support your ministry, but we've also spoken with those... well... let's just say they'd not be opposed to having you relocate to Texas."

Steele chuckled. "I appreciate that. I just didn't want you to think that our ministry accomplishments are the product of some harmonious love fest. I am fully aware that there are folks here at First Church that would be happy to see me move on. I'd like to think that they are in the minority. So far they've chosen to tolerate me, but I am also aware that, given the chance, they'd do whatever it would take to get rid of me."

"Father Austin, the Diocese of San Antonio is not looking for a passive people pleaser. We are looking for a leader that has the ability and creativity to get things done. It's more than a cliché. A leader cannot please everyone."

"Well, I can assure you that when it comes to pleasing everyone at First Church, I've failed miserably."

"The committee has reviewed your answers to the questionnaire that we mailed to all the candidates. Each person in the room has prepared an additional question to ask you. We are limiting each member to one question. They will be allowed a follow-up question based on your answer. Our hope is that the particular concerns of each person in the room here with me can be addressed. Is this agreeable?"

"It sounds like a good plan to me."

"Great. Now I will ask each person to introduce themselves in turn. So let's get started. We're going to start with the person on my right and then go around the table. Let's begin. Charlotte, you go first."

"Father Austin, my name is Charlotte De Paul. I am also president of the church women of the diocese."

"It's nice to meet you and to hear your voice."

"And yours, Father Austin. From what I can gather, your current parish has very specific roles for women. There are none on the vestry, and none have been elected a delegate to convention. We have a few congregations in this diocese that follow that same pattern. We did notice you have a woman priest and a woman deacon on your staff. What would you do, as bishop, to encourage the congregations in this diocese to expand the role of women, including accepting women clergy?"

"That's a good question. If I had my way, I would change things here at First Church. It's my hope, with teaching and persistence, I'll be able to do so. But as you know, I don't get to appoint the vestry or convention delegates. In this congregation, I don't even get to nominate them. They are nominated by congregational ballot and elected by congregational vote. I have tried to expand the ministry of women by opening it to include female acolytes, layreaders, chalicebearers, and, as you noted, women clergy. Those things are under my control."

"We only have one woman rector in this diocese. How would you change that?"

"Again, as a bishop, I wouldn't get to choose rectors. I would actively try to make sure that each vestry did give serious consideration to qualified women candidates."

"That's all good. Let's move on." Charles Gerard interjected. "Eduardo, you're next."

"I am Father Eduardo Flores, I noticed you do not have a Spanish service in your Church. Do you speak Spanish? Do you plan to start a Spanish service?"

"Thanks for the question, Father. No, I don't speak Spanish. It's a language I've wanted to learn but just haven't done so. There are Spanish-speaking people in Falls City, but none of them attend services at First Church. Quite honestly, it's just not a need that has come to my attention."

"But Father Austin, there are a great many Spanish-speaking people in the Diocese of San Antonio. Surely you must have thought of that. We also have several Spanish-speaking congregations. Just how could you be their bishop?"

"If it's God's will, I will try to be the bishop to all the people in the diocese. I can promise you that I will learn to speak Spanish if elected."

"Father Wright, you're next." Charles cleared his throat.

"I am Father DeMarcus Wright. We have three African-American congregations in this diocese. I'd like to know what you're going to do for us if you become our bishop?"

Steele was stunned by the question. His mind went blank.

"Father Austin, are you still there?" Charles asked.

"Uh, yes, I'm here. Father Wright, I'm not sure how to answer you. I guess I'd have to begin by asking what you need. What do you need the bishop to do for you?"

"Our congregations are poor. We struggle just to pay the light bill."

"Do you receive subsidies from the diocese?"

"We do, but they're not sufficient."

"I guess the only thing that I can suggest is that if I were to become your bishop, I would meet with all the congregations in the diocese that are receiving diocesan assistance. I would want to evaluate each of their needs and the resources the diocese has to assist them. I would try to make sure they were administered accordingly."

"Father Austin, Cindy Howard is our youth representative. She has a question."

"Father Austin, would you be willing to come to our summer camps?"

"Cindy, I am a big believer in Church camp. I serve as a counselor each summer for the fifth and sixth grade boys. I think it's very important that the bishop of the diocese visit each camp during its session. Yes, I'd be happy to do so."

"Fred, we'll end with your question."

"Mister Austin, I'm Fred Hoffman. I am the senior warden at Saint Boniface Parish in Bruno, Texas. We are a conservative congregation composed primarily of farmers and ranchers. One of my ancestors fought at the Alamo. I had family that fought for Southern Independence in the War of Northern Aggression. Which side of that war did your ancestors fight on?"

Once again, Steele was caught off guard. "I don't think I know."

"Then I'll just assume you come from Yankee stock. Now, I have to tell you, your answer to one of the questions is quite bothersome. If I read your answer correctly, you appear to have no problem whatsoever with homosexual clergy. Do I understand that you would find a homosexual rector acceptable?"

"Mister Hoffman, I can understand why my answer may disturb you. I realize that not all Episcopalians share my view. I try to be sensitive to those that hold a contrary understanding. I do not believe that a man or woman chooses to be homosexual. I believe they're born with that orientation. I also believe that, as Christians, we are to welcome everyone into the full membership and ministry of the Church. I believe there should be no outcasts."

"Yes, that's what's you said in your questionnaire." Steele detected hostility in the man's voice. "Charles has already told me I only get one follow-up question, so here it is. Father Austin, should I conclude from your answer that you do not believe that homosexuality is both a perversion and a sin?" Steele was now certain the man's voice sounded combative.

"My assumption from your question is that you do?"

"I damn sure do, as do all the people at Saint Boniface Parish. We will have a difficult time with a bishop that believes otherwise."

"Mister Hoffman, let me answer your question this way. Obviously, you and I have differing views on gay and lesbian people. I seriously doubt if we will be able to change each other's minds. As your bishop, I would not try to force my viewpoint on you, but I won't apologize for it either."

"So you would try to force us to take a queer rector?"

Steele answered calmly, "I don't believe it's the bishop's prerogative to force any candidate on a congregation. I would want to be a part of the discernment process, and I would reserve the right to veto a candidate, but I'd like to think the vestry in each parish will make their own choice."

"We are going to let that be the final word," Charles Gerard concluded. "Father Austin, we thank you for your time. We will be conducting this same type of interview with each of the clergy on our list. The next step will be to take the names of eight candidates to the full committee. We will then be sending representatives to visit each of those candidates. The final four will be brought to San Antonio for a visit and tour of the diocese. I will be contacting each candidate we have interviewed in about two weeks to advise them of their status in our process. Is that agreeable with you?"

"It sounds like a good discernment process. I appreciate being considered. I'll keep your committee in my prayers." Steele pushed the button on the phone cradle to end the call. That queasy feeling moved from his stomach to his chest and into his legs. It was a familiar sensation. He knew it was one he needed to listen to.

The Magnolia Series

Dennis R. Maynard

Chapter 14

"How'd your Texas interview go?" Stone Clemons was standing at the open door leading into the rector's office. Stone was one of the long-standing patriarchs at First Church. Few folks were willing to challenge him. He was a close friend and strong advocate for Steele Austin. His knowledge of The Episcopal Church, First Church, and canon law were a major plus.

"Come on in, Stone. I really need to show you something."

Steele walked from behind his desk to shake Stone's hand. "Let's sit over here." Steele led him to two leather wingback chairs in his office that were facing one another. "The Texas questions were interesting."

"How's that?"

"They had put together a representation of the various segments of the diocese. You know, a young person, the president of the women, a Hispanic, a conservative... the usual mix."

"Sounds about right. *The Republican Party at Prayer* has now given way to political correctness."

"Well, as you can imagine, each questioner presented his or her particular case. The bottom line is that each wanted to know what I would do for their constituency if they elected me their bishop."

Stone rubbed his chin. He was lost in thought. He then pointed his finger for emphasis. "John Kennedy's words have been lost. Remember, he tried to pull the people of this country out of looking to the government to do something for them, and to start thinking about what they could do for the country. I fear that too many in the Church today approach it from the standpoint of what the Church can do for them. I just wonder if it ever crosses their minds to ask what they might be able to do for their Church."

Steele nodded. "I'm not sure that a message of servanthood will appeal to those obsessing over their own needs and point of view. It was as though the only way they could see themselves or their supporters voting for me was if I would tell them what they wanted to hear."

"I don't have to tell you that we see it right here at First Church. Too many in attendance think that the money they put in the plate is *club dues*. In this parish, they sit back and demand that their every wish be met. And God forbid that one of the clergy express an opinion that disagrees with theirs."

"That pretty much sums it up. The problem is that I've examined the finances of the Diocese of San Antonio. The bishop doesn't have a lot of money to hand out. He's basically taking the money from the growing and successful congregations and giving it to the ones that are on life support. Beyond that, there's very little left to do anything with."

"I imagine that's the story in most every diocese."

"I think some of the larger dioceses that have been around for awhile probably have built up some pretty hefty endowments they can draw on."

Stone agreed. "I'm sure that's true, but not for the majority. Look at this diocese. It's been here for almost three hundred years, but the endowments are miniscule. Few congregants leave their money to the diocese when they die. If they leave any at all to the Church, they leave it to their parish. Hell, Steele, that's the only way some of those parishes up there in Savannah have been able to survive. They just keep living off the dead people's money. The living don't give enough, or aren't able to give enough, so they just sit around waiting for the next bequest. What they don't realize is that it's just a matter of time until they run out of dead little old ladies' money to sustain them."

"So then tell me this, Stone, why would anyone want to be the bishop of such a diocese?"

Stone Clemons stood and walked over to the windows in Steele's office, looking out on the churchyard. After a few minutes, he broke the silence between them. "Did you realize I can see my future resting place from your office?"

"Well, let's not have you move in any time soon." Steele rose from his chair and walked to the window to stand beside him. "You didn't answer my question."

Stone continued to stare out the window. "I'm torn. We need priests like you to lead the Episcopal Church. I'm not very optimistic about our future. I'm afraid most of the ones wearing the purple shirts don't give me much reason to be."

"So you think I should continue in the process."

"We need you here at First Church. We've come through so much to get to this point. I really feel like you're just now getting started. Most of those that were against you have left or been silenced."

"Most?"

"Father, you're never going to have them all. Remember, the Lord handpicked each of his disciples and one of them still betrayed Him. All the rest, except for John, ran away when He needed them the most."

"So what are you telling me?"

Stone chuckled, "I guess I'd like to believe that we can leave it all in God's hands, but I've been at my share of conventions that elected a bishop."

"And?"

"I'm not sure God had anything to do with any of them. The politics before and during the balloting was nothing more than that. They were just politics and more often than not lacked charity. A few times they were downright ugly."

"So you're not going to advise me one way or another?"

Stone shrugged, "No, this time I'd just really like to think it's in God's hands."

Steele opened a manila folder on his desk. "I need to show you this. It came in the morning mail." He handed Stone a letter. "It came from the bishop."

Dear Father Austin,

This is a most difficult letter to write, but as your bishop, I feel compelled to do so. Let me begin by noting that your many accomplishments at First Church and First Church School have not gone unnoticed by your bishop. The increase in membership, worship attendance, ministry programs and stewardship in the parish since you became rector is nothing less than remarkable. I am fully aware that First Church School was in decline, both financially and with enrollment. You and the headmaster deserve recognition for turning it around and putting it on a self-sustaining basis.

I want to also note my admiration for the work you have done in the community. The soup kitchen, free medical clinic, and housing for homeless gay teens deserve particular mention. I know that your ministry outreach has not been limited to these good works.

My predecessor, Bishop Peterson, gave me a full accounting of the opposition you encountered at First Church. He believed that from the beginning those who opposed you began organizing even before your arrival. It was his opinion that the fact that you were able to survive multiple attacks on your character and ministry was nothing less than a miracle.

Having noted all of the above, I must now proceed with the most difficult part of this letter. Your compensation package at First Church has been called to my attention. Father Austin, are you even aware that the total of your compensation package and fringe benefits is greater than the total operating budgets of half the congregations in this diocese? Further, your total is larger than that of your bishop's by several thousands of dollars. It grieves me to have to point out to you that your remuneration outstrips that of the vast majority of the bishops in this Church?

On a daily basis, I am forced to make decisions about diocesan program expenditures. Many of them must be *curtailed because of a lack of funds. I am even being forced to consider closing more than one of our struggling mission congregations for the same reason. As I said, it grieves me to know that these decisions must be made, while one of my own clergy is being granted what, to most of us, would be considered a luxurious lifestyle.*

Clearly it is the vestry of First Church and not you that sets your compensation package. As a priest of the Church, you do not have to accept it. I would like to counsel you to restrict your income from the parish and direct that the excess be sent to my office to assist with the diocesan program.

As I stated at the beginning, this has been a most difficult letter to write, but as your bishop, I have been compelled to do so. I trust you will receive it in the spirit in which it was written.

Faithfully,

+Sean Evans, Bishop

"What the hell!" Stone raised his voice. "That pious little twerp. Just who does he think he is?"

Steele retrieved the letter from Stone's shaking hand. "I believe he thinks he's the bishop."

"He's not going to tell First Church what they can or cannot pay their rector. That's our decision. And Steele, you won't do us any favor to accept a lower salary. We need to keep the rector's compensation competitive. It embarrasses me to tell you this, but we've already done some poking around. If you were to leave, we'd most likely have to pay your successor more than we're paying you."

"How do I respond to this?"

"You don't. I will. That bishop needs to be given a lesson in clergy recruitment. There just aren't that many priests out there with your gifts that this vestry would want to call. As I said, we've already discovered that any priest we would consider would cost us more than we're paying you. No, you leave the response to me." Stone snapped his fingers. "Hell, do you think he's jealous?"

"Jealous?"

"Well, I'll find out. If he thinks he should be making more money, he needs to take that up with the diocesan council. The answer is not to cut your salary but to raise his."

"I'd like to think this is not about jealousy. I really like the guy. I choose to take him at his word. I know he's having to deal with a lot of struggling congregations that can hardly make ends meet."

"Well, killing off First Church isn't the answer. If he forces us to call a less competent rector because our compensation package is not competitive, that's exactly what will happen."

Stone turned to walk toward the door. "Let me take that letter with me."

"Okay."

"Don't you concern yourself about it any further." Stone opened the door and then turned back to look at Steele. "I'm curious, would you have to take a cut in salary to be the bishop of San Antonio?"

Steele nodded.

"A big one?"

"Significant."

"You have a wife and two children to think about. You are not committing a sin to provide for them. Wasn't it Saint Paul that said something about a worker earning his pay?"

Steele smiled and waved at Stone. He closed the door behind him.

The Magnolia Series

Dennis R. Maynard

Chapter 15

Virginia Mudd had adapted to the routine of prison life. Her cell was the third one down the left corridor from the bubble. The day room was at the other end of the parallel corridors. She was thankful that the cells didn't have bars. Instead, there were solid doors that had been painted with bright colors. Each door had a small glass observation panel. The guards electronically controlled the doors from the bubble. The doors gave Virginia a sense of privacy when she was in what she'd now learned to call her *cage*.

Most of her time was spent in the day room. The one television in the room was often tuned to a soap opera. A very large *butch* controlled the television. The room watched whatever she said they were going to watch. On occasion, her choice included a sporting event. Virginia had never cared for athletics. When she was married to Henry, college football season meant several Saturday trips to the University of Georgia. Virginia tolerated those because it gave her an opportunity to show off a new outfit. Choosing just the right outfit to wear to a *Bulldog* tailgating party was not taken lightly. *Dress to impress* was her motto.

Virginia found one other woman in the day room that knew how to play bridge. Together they taught two others. Now she could pass her time with the one card game she truly loved. The food was edible but fell short of the delicious meals her housekeeper, Shady, prepared. The one saving grace for some of the inmates was that there was plenty of it. In just a few weeks, Virginia had watched the women that came in around the same time she did grow larger and larger. She speculated that they were substituting food for whatever drugs or booze they'd been absorbing on the outside.

Adrianna Garcia was never far from Virginia. Not only were they cellmates, but they had actually become good friends. Virginia was also aware that Adrianna had an ulterior motive. She was hoping that Thackston would file an appeal on her behalf. She didn't blame Adrianna. In her situation, she'd do the same thing.

The other prisoners called Virginia a *short-timer*. Most realized that with good behavior, she could be paroled in less than two years. Adrianna was filled with advice on just how she'd seen other inmates shorten their time. "Are you a church woman?" Adrianna had asked.

"I grew up in The Episcopal Church. I used to go to church every Sunday."

"Do they teach the Bible?"

"Every Sunday we would have three Bible readings and a Psalm."

"No, that's not what I mean. Do they have Bible groups? You know, to study the Bible."

"Yes, I belonged to a women's Bible study group."

"Then you should teach it in here."

"What?"

"If you start a Bible study group and teach it, that will help you when you go before the parole board."

"Really?"

"Yeah, they're really impressed by that stuff."

"What else?"

"Volunteer to help down in sick call. That's what I do."

"No, I don't like being around sick people."

"Then help in the library. The parole board loves that."

"You could also take a course. You know, better your education."

"Do they teach a Spanish course?"

"I think so. That would be great. I never learned the language. My mom didn't speak Spanish, and my dad never taught me. We could take the course together."

"Anything else?"

"Oh, you know the rest. Keep a low profile. Stay out of trouble. Be respectful to the guards."

Virginia rolled her eyes. "I think you and I are giving three of them about all the respect they can handle."

Adrianna giggled. "Well, since you showed up, they've bothered me a lot less."

"Men! They're all the same. Always looking for a new piece to nail, and then they move on as soon as another one shows up."

"My old man did that to me. I was the only thing he could think about until he grew tired of me."

"My Thackston is different. He really loves me."

"I hope you're right about that. The time you're in here is really going to test that. I didn't lead you wrong about our protectors though."

"No, at least I don't think so."

"Has anyone tried to mess with you?"

"No."

"And they won't as long as you have them to watch your back."

"You didn't tell me that they were all going to be *quick draw*."

Adrianna chuckled. "These guys just want to get their rocks off. They're bored with their wives and are looking for variety. They're in and out."

"Sometimes they come to me so excited that we don't even get that far."

"Like I said, they just want to get off. As soon as a new piece of meat arrives, they'll move on."

"Will they continue to protect us?"

"Sure. They'll still want some variety."

Virginia raised her eyebrows. "Have you ever heard this expression? *For every beautiful woman there is a man that has grown tired of doing her.*"

Adrianna's eyes widened. "Now, that's scary. I hope it's not true. I guess I still want to believe in love."

"Me too!"

"Yard time." The guard from the bubble made the announcement through the sound system. Adrianna and Virginia walked down the stairs and out into the bright Georgia sunshine. They chose a picnic table to sit on and smoke a cigarette. Some of the inmates quickly organized a softball game. Others headed for the basketball court. Most just gathered in groups to gossip and smoke cigarettes.

"It's nice to be outside, isn't it?" Adrianna asked, blowing the smoke out through her nostrils.

"I needed some fresh air." Virginia agreed, pulling the cigarette smoke deep into her lungs. Then she noticed a group of women that had gathered in one of the corners of the yard up against the building. "What's going on over there?"

"You don't want to know."

"But I do."

"They're smoking weed."

"They're what? Where'd they get it?"

"That big guard standing in front of them with his back to them. That's Javiar. He brings it in."

"Can anyone get it from him?"

"I suppose, but Virginia, you don't want to get messed up with him. He's one mean man. He's the one man that really runs this place. Even the other guards are afraid of him. There are rumors that's he's connected to a big drug cartel. Girl, you're a short timer. He'll screw that up."

Virginia watched the girls huddled together. They were laughing and passing the joint around.

"Virginia, don't!" Adrianna shouted after her as she walked toward Javiar. "Please, Virginia, listen to me. You don't want to go there. Please, Virginia. I'm begging you."

A few minutes later, Virginia was standing with the small group. She pulled the smoke deep into her lungs. "God, I've missed this."

The Magnolia Series

Dennis R. Maynard

Chapter 16

Normally, the health of The Reverend Doctor Horace Drummond would be Almeda's first priority. During his last physical checkup, his doctor warned him that his cholesterol and triglycerides were too high. Beyond that, his glucose reading suggested that he was about to become borderline diabetic. Since then, she had instructed her chef to put both of them on the Mediterranean Diet. "Almeda, I like fish as much as the next guy, but can't we have it fried every now and then?"

"You heard what the doctor said to you. No fried foods. Fried foods are a thing of the past."

"And what about salad dressings? Can't we have something besides vinegar and olive oil?"

Once again, Almeda was firm. "I had all those creamy dressings taken over to the soup kitchen."

"So, it's okay to kill off the homeless with decent tasting salad dressings, but you torture your husband with greasy lettuce."

"Oh, it's not as bad as all that."

"And what about lard? Almeda, I grew up with foods fried in *Crisco*."

"Yes, and all that lard has taken up permanent residence in your arteries."

Almeda watched his diet as closely as she could when he was at home. She kept a food diary of each day's meals. Her suspicion, however, was that he was sneaking off to the local greasy spoon cafe on a daily basis. Tonight she needed him to be on her side. She knew that the best way to bring him around would be with one of his favorite meals and then... well, she knew exactly what she'd be wearing out of her dressing closet into their bedroom.

"My oh my, woman. What's this all about?" Horace rubbed his hands together as he sat down at the dining room table. His eyes widened as the houseboy placed Horace's dinner plate in front of him.

Almeda smiled. "We're not going to make a habit of this, so don't get used to it. I talked to the doctor, and he said that one meal like this from time to time won't kill you."

"When is the last time I told you just how much I love you?"

"When you got home from the office thirty minutes ago, but I never tire of hearing it."

"Almeda, this is wonderful. Fried chicken, cheese grits, fried okra, and what's this on my salad? It can't be blue cheese salad dressing with real blue cheese crumbles, or is it?"

"Enjoy it all, my Darling. You've earned it."

Horace quickly grabbed his fork and dipped it into his salad. He closed his eyes as he began to chew. "Oh baby, I've missed you," he uttered. Then his eyes opened wide, and he glanced at his wife. The smile on her face was undeniable. He put his fork down and leaned back in his chair. He folded his arms across his chest. "Okay, Almeda, what do you want?"

"Whatever do you mean, Horace? Can't a wife do something nice for her husband without falling under suspicion?"

"Normally, yes, but I know you too well. Come on. Out with it."

"Horace, I need your help with a project I want to undertake down at the church."

Horace held up his hand. "Stop right there, Almeda. I've already heard about the Altar Guild luncheon. It seems to me you have stirred up a hornet's nest. If not the nest, you've certainly angered some of the hornets."

"So, you've heard?"

"I think the entire town has heard. I've been expecting to read it in the *New York Times*."

Almeda put her hand over her mouth. "Oh, I had no idea."

"I have to admit I'm a bit surprised. Of all the people at First Church, you are the last person that I think would want to rearrange the sanctuary."

"What have you heard?"

"I heard you wanted to rip out the altar rail and tear up the altar."

"Now, you know that's not right."

"I know, but that's the way it's being passed around. Gossip is never accurate. You tell me what you said."

"I think we should make the altar rail more accommodating to those of us with walking problems. It's difficult for me to climb the steps to the rail, but I've noticed I'm not the only one."

"Almeda, I'm not saying it's not needed, but I think you're in for a battle."

"I realize that now, but I was hoping that you and Steele would back me."

"You know I will, but let's think this through."

"What do you suggest?"

"First, you need to find the best historical church architect in the country. Have them draw up a visual of what you want the church to look like once it has been remodeled."

"That makes sense. Do you know one?"

"I do, but he's expensive, and I don't think the vestry will approve his fee."

"I'll pay it."

"Okay. What would you think of leaving the current altar where it is? Have a new movable one built to sit closer to the front. I also think you'd be better off to leave the current altar rail in place. Make the new one portable, like the new altar. That way it can be removed and the church can be set up like it is now for weddings and funerals. You know how important it is for some of these people to have the church look just like it did when their grandparents got married."

"So I take it from all this you'll help me?"

"Of course. I know Steele will get behind it as well."

"What about the handicapped bathroom?" She asked.

"I hadn't heard anything about it."

"Oh, I didn't mention it at the luncheon. I want to take the priest's sacristy and turn it into a handicapped bathroom. We can convert the north hall entrance in the back of the church into the priest's sacristy."

"Actually, that makes a lot of sense. But you do have a battle on your hands. Mary Alice Smythe and some of those guardians of tradition here at First Church are going to put up a fight."

"I have to admit that caught me off guard. It's the first time Mary Alice and I have been on opposite sides."

"Well, you know who she'll turn to. This is already out on the gossip circuit. They're not the type to just roll over. My darling wife, if I remember correctly, in past causes you were on the lead horse with that group right behind you."

Almeda nodded. "But this time it's different. This time it just makes sense."

Horace rose from his chair and walked around the table to his wife sitting at the opposite end. He took her hand in his, "Honey, right now it only makes sense to you."

The Magnolia Series

Dennis R. Maynard

Chapter 17

Pastor Melvin MacClaren had requested and been granted a one month leave of absence. Saint Andrew's Presbyterian Church had been shaken to her very foundation. The senior pastor's wife had been arrested and charged with the possession of an illegal substance. That story filled one half of the front page of the Sunday newspaper. Further charges against her were pending evidence that she might actually have been growing the marijuana to sell to others. Federal authorities were conducting a separate investigation to determine if she had been growing the illegal drug to transport across state lines.

The other side of the Sunday paper included the news of a civil lawsuit. The former Senior Pastor of Saint Andrew's Presbyterian Church filed that lawsuit. The estate of one of the leading members of the congregation, Mister Ned Boone, was named as the respondent. The timing of this lawsuit could not have been more fortuitous. Just a few weeks ago, the chapel of Saint Andrew's Church had been renamed to honor Ned Boone. The lawsuit alleged that Ned Boone had employed a man to plant child pornography on the pastor's computer. That plot had subsequently led to the pastor's dismissal. The lawsuit also named each member of the session of Saint Andrew's Presbyterian at the time. It held that the board corporately and individually was liable. The suit alleged that the members failed to carry out their fiduciary responsibility to fully investigate the case against their pastor. It stated they had rushed to judgment, and failed to provide their pastor with an opportunity to respond to the allegations against him. The suit for ten million dollars was for loss of income and retirement benefits, past and future. The uncontested allegations had made the pastor virtually unemployable and had ended his ministry. The suit also demanded that the pastor and each member of his family be compensated for pain and suffering. The members of the session were being individually charged with reimbursing the pastor and the members of his immediate family for the medical and psychiatric expenses they had incurred because of the event.

Saint Andrew's was literally standing room only for the one service that Pastor MacClaren would address when he resumed his pulpit duties. Pastor MacClaren chose not to enter the sanctuary until the last verse of the sermon hymn. The whispers could be heard throughout the congregation. "Where is he?" Each questioner was met with a shrug. As the sermon hymn drew to a close, a disheveled Pastor MacClaren entered the sanctuary through a side door and walked to the pulpit. He was not wearing a preaching gown. His suit suggested that he'd slept in it. The pastor's hair was unkempt and his face was covered with at least a week's worth of bearded growth. The senior pastor looked more like a homeless vagrant than the spiritual leader of one of Falls City's largest Christian congregations.

When the hymn concluded, the silence hanging over the anxious congregation was deafening. Melvin MacClaren motioned for the congregation to be seated. The people were used to his opening sentences being spoken with depth and clarity. Many in the crowded church had to lean forward to hear Pastor MacClaren's first words. His voice broke and his eyes were moist with tears. "This morning the only words I have for you are the words of Holy Scripture. There is nothing more I can add. The Word of God will have to speak for me. I am going to begin with some familiar words from the Book of Proverbs."

His voice quivered as he began to read. *"Who can find a wife with a strong character? She is worth far more than jewels. Her husband trusts her with all his heart, and he does not lack anything good. She helps him and never harms him all the days of her life."*

The tears were streaming down the Pastor's cheeks. He reached in his pants pockets for a handkerchief to wipe his tears away. He had none. The assistant pastor sitting in one of the pulpit chairs walked to him and offered him his.

Pastor MacClaren struggled to maintain his composure. Judith and Elmer Idle were sitting on the front pew. Tears streamed down their respective faces. As the pastor continued to compose himself, Judith threw her hands in the air. Her lips moved with prayer for the pastor. Others in the congregation wiped at their own tears.

The pastor cleared his throat. His voice was now a bit stronger. "I'm going to continue with these words from the Book of Proverbs, the thirty-first chapter. They speak for themselves. *She seeks out wool and linen with care and works with willing hands. She is like merchant ships. She brings her food from far away. She wakes up while it is still dark and gives food to her family and portions of food to her female slaves. She picks out a field and buys it. She plants a vineyard from the profits she has earned. She puts on strength like a belt and goes to work with energy. She sees that she is making a good profit. Her lamp burns late at night. She puts her hands on the distaff, and her fingers hold a spindle. She opens her hands to oppressed people and stretches them out to needy people. She does not fear for her family when it snows because her whole family has a double layer of clothing. She makes quilts for herself. Her clothes are made of linen and purple cloth. Her husband is known at the city gates when he sits with the leaders of the land. She makes linen garments and sells them and delivers belts to the merchants. She dresses with strength and nobility, and she smiles at the future. She speaks with wisdom, and on her tongue there is tender instruction.*"

He then looked down at his three children sitting on the front pew. They were sobbing uncontrollably. The members of the congregation sitting with them tried in vain to console them. The pastor buried his face in the handkerchief and laid his head on the pulpit. His entire body was shaking with sobs. The two assistant pastors walked to him and put their hands on his shoulders. They wiped at the tears on their own faces. Several minutes passed before the pastor could continue. "*She keeps a close eye on the conduct of* her family, and she does not eat the bread of idleness. Her children and her husband stand up and bless her."

His voice was shaking with grief. His tear-stained face was red with emotion, but he continued to recite the concluding words from the scripture he had chosen. *"He sings her praises by saying, 'Many women have done noble work, but you have surpassed them all!' Charm is deceptive, and beauty evaporates, but a woman who has the fear of the LORD should be praised. Reward her for what she has done, and let her achievements praise her at the city gates."*

Once again, the pastor struggled to compose himself. Then, in an instant, as if a newfound strength entered his body, he picked up his Bible and held it in the air. He now shouted into the microphone. His voice was strong and clear. "I had always believed that the *King James Version* of this Holy Book contained all the wisdom that I ever needed. Last night, as I was on my knees in prayer, I heard a voice tell me to look in the *Catholic Bible.* I believe that little voice was the Holy Spirit. There is a book in the Catholic's Bible that we Presbyterians don't have. I drove to the library and found a copy of their Bible. My fingers were led to the *Book of Ecclesiasticus.* Now, that's not the same as our sacred *Book of Ecclesiastes.* In the fifteenth chapter, the Lord led me to the following words that He wants me to share with you this morning." Pastor MacClaren leaned over the top of the pulpit and pointed his finger at the congregation. "Hear these the words of the Lord thy God."

His voice thundered through the sound system. *"Do not say it was the Lord's doing that you fell away!"* He continued to shout with particular emphasis on any reference to the Almighty. *"For He does not do what **He** hates. Do not say it was **He** who led you astray for **He** has no need of the sinful. The **Lord** hates all abominations. Such things are not loved by those who fear **Him**. It was **He** who created humankind in the beginning and **He** left them to their own free will."*

The pastor grabbed the pulpit microphone from the stand. He held it in his hand and walked back and forth on the platform. He continued to shout. *"If you choose..."* He stopped and pointed his finger from side to side at the congregation. His eyes were filled with fire as he tried to make eye contact with every person present. *"If you choose you can keep the commandments. Acting faithfully is a matter of your own choice. **He** has placed before you fire and water. Stretch out your hand for whatever you choose. Before each person are life and death, and whichever one chooses they will be given."*

He stopped and wiped his face with the handkerchief the associate pastor had given him. He lowered his voice. *"For great is the wisdom of the **Lord**. **He** is mighty in power and sees everything. **His** eyes are on those who fear **Him**, and **He** knows every human action."*

With that, Pastor MacClaren walked to the front of the pulpit. He leaned forward. It appeared as if he was about to leap off the platform. And then, in a whisper heard clearly by all present, he concluded the passage from Ecclesiasticus. *"**GOD ALMIGHTY** has not commanded anyone to be wicked."* His voice then wailed, *"And **God** has not given anyone permission to sin."* The congregation watched in stunned silence as their pastor folded in on himself and dropped to his knees. He threw his hands in the air as a fresh flood of tears streamed down his face. It was as if a star quarterback had just scored the winning touchdown in the final seconds of the big game. The congregation rose to their feet, clapping their hands, stomping their feet on the floor, and shouting love and support for their pastor.

The Magnolia Series

Dennis R. Maynard

Chapter 18

"Have you gotten the results back, Henry?"

"I called the doctor this morning. They said it would probably be another week."

"We're going to have to come up with something to tell folks. Henry, is there any doubt in your mind that this baby is yours?"

"No, Dee. I believe you. We've been through all that. I know you've been faithful to me. Our love is strong. Besides, I just don't think you're the kind of woman that would do that sort of thing. You're too much of a lady."

"Not to mention that I'm madly in love with you. I thank God every day for sending you into my life."

Henry took her in his arms and held her. He kissed her on the lips. He then looked into her eyes. "Uh, how many more weeks?"

Dee gently slapped him on the arm. "I saw your calendar. You have the date circled in red."

"Has anyone tried to see you?"

"Mary Alice Smythe and that Dexter woman came by yesterday. Shady told them that I was sleeping, and she didn't want to disturb us."

"I know those two. They'll be back. We've got to come up with an explanation."

"Clearly, Henry, the explanation is with one of our ancestors. Have you ever heard anything about your heritage?"

"Dee, my family came to this country from England. To hear my mother tell the story, you'd believe they booked first class passage with Christopher Columbus. My great grandparents held slaves. There's no denying that. But as far as I know, they were never a part of our family lineage. For God's sake, Honey, you've seen me naked."

"You're definitely a white boy."

"I don't think I could get dark in one of those booths that paints the tan on."

"That's never been a problem for me. As you know, I can get a pretty good tan."

"I know. That's one of the things that attracted me to you. Are you sure there's nothing? Did you ever hear any rumors?"

Dee thought for a moment. "You know, Henry, my mother did tell me that we have some Indian Blood. I think my grandmother or great grandmother was Creek, or maybe she was Navajo. That's something we can ask my mom next week."

"Are they still insisting on driving?"

"You know my dad. He loves to drive that house on wheels."

"When you talk to them, remind them that my offer to fly them is still good."

"I will, but I don't think they'll change their minds."

Henry's eyes lit up. "Dee, why don't we use your Indian blood as our story?"

"What?"

"That one of your grandparents was an Indian. Some of the folks in this town knew my great grandparents. They'll never accept that any of my ancestors were Indians. They don't know yours."

"I suppose that is as good as anything. I just can't remember if they were supposed to be Creek or Navajo. And Henry, that just may be family gossip. It might not even be true."

"At this point it doesn't have to be. The Navajos are primarily out West. There are still Creeks in this part of the country. Let's just say that one of your grandparents was a Creek Indian."

"If you think that will work."

"We're about to find out." Henry glanced out the living room window to see Mary Alice Smythe and Martha Dexter coming up the front walk. They were each carrying a small gift. Henry rose to greet them at the door. "Ladies, how kind of you to call."

"Oh, we're just so anxious to see the new baby. Is this a good time?"

"Dee is awake. We are sitting in the living room. I think the baby is sleeping."

"Oh, pooh." Mary Alice dropped her lower lip. "We so wanted to see the little one."

"I think we'll be able to tiptoe into the nursery. He's a very sound sleeper. Follow me. Let's visit with Dee first."

Dee rose to greet them. "Ladies, it's so nice of you to visit."

Martha Dexter extended her gift. "I bought you this present. It's a silver rattle from Morris Jewelry. You know, they're the most expensive jewelry store in town. They only have the best stuff."

Mary Alice gave Dee and Henry an apologetic look. "Yes, Martha, Morris Jewelry is excellent."

Dee took the package from her. "Thank you for being so thoughtful."

Mary Alice handed Dee her offering. "There's a gift receipt inside. You can return it should you receive another."

"Thank you. You're so sweet to remember us this way." Shady entered the room with a silver tray. It had some small cakes on it and a tea service. "Please ladies, be seated. Let's enjoy a cup of tea. Shady baked these cakes for our guests that come to call on the baby."

Martha Dexter did not wait for Shady to put the tray on the table. She immediately grabbed two of the cakes and popped one in her mouth while reaching for a third. Mary Alice gave her a disapproving look. "Let's sit down, Martha, I'm sure their *Help* would prefer to serve us."

"What have you named the baby?" Mary Alice asked, balancing the cup and saucer on her lap.

"We're naming him after his daddy." Dee smiled.

"And his granddaddy and his granddaddy before him," Henry boasted.

"So, he'll be the Fourth." Mary Alice cooed. "That's so sweet."

Cries came from the nursery. "Sounds like our son is awake." Dee started to stand.

"Honey, you stay seated. I'll get Shady to bring him in."

A few minutes later, Shady walked into the room carrying the baby. Martha saw him first. Her cake-filled mouth hung open. She splattered cake crumbs on herself as she asked, "Henry, is that your baby?"

Henry stood and took his son from Shady. "Ladies, I'd like for you to meet Henry Mudd the Fourth."

Both women stood so they could get a better look at the baby. "Well, he has your hair, Henry, only he has more curls."

Henry tried to lighten the moment. "He almost has more hair. Mine's beginning to thin."

"He has your eyes." Martha chimed in.

"He's a Mudd, that's for sure." Henry announced reassuringly. "He did luck out on one thing. He didn't get my pasty white skin. He inherited his mother's beautiful coloring. He'll be able to go out in the sun and not worry about turning bright red."

Both women turned to look at Dee. "Yes, I see." They nodded.

Dee smiled. "One of my grandmothers was a Creek Indian, so I inherited her coloring. Fortunately, our baby got those genes."

"No sunburn, blisters, and peeling for him." Henry agreed.

"Well, Martha, I think we should be going. I'll bet Dee needs to feed this young man."

"That I do. Thanks so much for calling, and thank you both for the gifts."

Mary Alice turned to leave and then turned back to indicate it was time for Martha to follow. Martha was busily collecting the remaining cakes. "I hope you won't mind, but I'd like for my Howard to taste these. They're so good."

"Please, help yourself." Dee said.

Once Martha and Mary Alice were in the car, Mary Alice asked, "Did that baby look like a Creek Indian to you?"

Martha started laughing. "Not in the least. They're going to have to do better than that."

"You can say that again. There's more to that story than meets the eye. And I plan to get to the bottom of it."

"Are you going to tell anyone?"

Mary Alice pulled the car away from the curve. She glanced back at the Mudd house. "I plan to tell everyone I know."

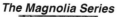
The Magnolia Series

Dennis R. Maynard

Chapter 19

"What in God's name are you watching?" Canon Jim Vernon asked.

"Watch this for a minute." Bishop Sean Evans responded to his longtime lover and partner. "This is incredible. There must be over five thousand people in that congregation."

"Don't forget all the people watching him on television." Jim responded. "Why would you watch that circus?"

"I just don't understand." Bishop Evans muted the volume on the television. "Yesterday I conducted my visitation over at All Saints. It was a beautiful Mass. The rector there is doing a great job. And he's a much better preacher than this television clown. But Jim, there were only about one hundred fifty people in attendance. Most all of them were seasoned citizens. When they brought the Sunday school children in at *The Peace,* there were only four of them."

"That's a pretty typical congregation in this diocese."

"I know that. I've been listening to this guy here. It's all *feel good* stuff. He doesn't talk about sin, or sacrifice, or self-discipline. There's no message of discipleship. He's standing there telling his listeners that God wants them to be rich, successful, happy, and they're eating it up."

"Sean, it's the *Gospel of Prosperity.* It's not unlike the snake oil salesmen in the past. Take this elixir and it will cure whatever ails you. Only the elixir for these folks is their form of religion. Honestly, if you listen to them, they sound just like a medicine man in a gypsy circus. *Swallow a little Jesus every day and all your problems will go away.*"

"It's not just that. Jim, there's no liturgy. There's nothing that requires the members of the congregation to think. They do a pledge of allegiance to the Bible, but the scriptures aren't being explained. Even the music they sing is mindless. They project it on these big screens. A bouncing ball points them to the words they're supposed to sing. They don't even have to know how to read music. Some of them get so caught up in it, they actually sway while they sing the jingles."

"Honey, you're answering your own question."

"How's that?"

"Sean, our Mass is the polar opposite of what's being offered in that arena. The bottom line is that our liturgy and music require you to think. It does speak of sin and sacrifice. Given a choice, people are going to choose the message that promises them happiness over one that challenges them."

"I suppose you're right." Bishop Evans turned off the television. "Did you bring me the files on Saint Michael's?"

"I've looked through them. The pattern is obvious. It's been going on for at least thirty years. I talked to Bishop Petersen. He said that there is a core group in that parish that's just plain mean. His words. He'd observed that they were not only mean to their clergy, but they're mean to each other. They call a rector and give the appearance of being all excited about them. The rector begins to grow the parish and bring in new leadership. Usually around year three, the new rector starts reporting that a group in the parish is bullying them."

"That's happened with all of them?"

"According to Bishop Petersen, that's the first shoe to drop."

"And then?"

"As in this case, two or three of them show up down here complaining about the rector." Jim wrinkled his brow. "I'm curious. Were any of their complaints valid?"

"Hell, Jim. There's no perfect priest. Some of them are valid, but none of them would be enough to get him written up in any other business or organization."

"So just ignore them." Jim shrugged.

"Those aren't the ones that concern me. The ones that really tell the story are the ones they manufacture, or at least exaggerate."

"So if that doesn't work, then what do they do?"

"In that place, they have a habit of starting a *fifty-two club*."

"A what?"

"That's the name Bishop Peterson gave it. A group of them reduce their pledges to one dollar a week."

"That's sick. They're just hurting their own parish."

"You and I know it, but the worst part is they continue to have little secret meetings to plot ways to intimidate their rector. Usually between years five and seven, each of the rectors have tossed in the towel. A couple of the priests have moved on to other positions, and a couple of them have retired. The congregation goes into decline, only to repeat the pattern. That's been their history over the last four rectors. Saint Michael's is where clergy ministries go to die. Or more accurately, it's where clergy ministries get assassinated."

"Did he give you some names?"

"He did."

"Is that who you met with?"

"It was a representative sampling. It was a most unpleasant meeting. I confronted them with their history. I gave them examples of the ways they have bullied and abused their last four rectors."

"How'd they respond to that?"

"They basically told me to go back over to the diocesan office and mind my own business. They were in charge of Saint Michael's."

"They said what?"

Sean nodded. "You heard me."

"Well, then I don't blame the past four rectors for giving them the finger and walking out."

"The problem is that they're not only hurting some good clergy, but they're alienating a lot of faithful lay people.

I called a few of their former lay leaders on the phone. They want nothing else to do with any parish after their experience at Saint Michael's."

"What are you going to do?"

"First, I wanted to make sure that their history confirmed what I'd been hearing. I am not going to give them another rector to persecute. That little game has got to come to an end."

"It's a toxic parish for sure, but that hasn't kept them from finding another rector."

"No, it hasn't." Sean agreed. "You and I both know that there are plenty of clergy that want to believe they're the exception. They think they're different from the last priest, better or smarter."

"Oh, I think it's more than that. I think clergy really want to believe that when there's been a divorce between a rector and a parish, it was the former rector that was at fault."

"I think it's probably a combination of both."

"I agree. They would probably have a long list of priests anxious to prove that they're better than the last rector." Jim wrinkled his brow. "Are you certain you don't want to give them another rector?"

"I don't know any other way to try to stop this pattern."

"The place is really sick."

"It is. And it's never going to be any more than it is as long as that group is allowed to repeat their pattern with each new rector. That core group is not going to go anywhere. They really don't want to grow. I'm not so sure but that they get jealous of their own rector's success. They definitely resent any new leadership he brings into the congregation."

"So how are you going to handle the place?"

"I'm going to start by sending them this letter." Sean handed Jim a manila folder with the letter in it. Jim read the letter.

"Wow! This is strong."

"I don't see I have a choice. I'm going to send it to every member of that parish. I am going to lay their history out. As you can see, I don't name names, but I do state that there's a group in the parish that has not been happy with any of the past four rectors. I've pointed out their pattern of behavior, including their *fifty-two club*."

"I honestly think this needs to be done. No sickness can be cured until it's acknowledged. But Sean, are you sure about not letting them call another rector?"

"I am. I'm just going to send them a series of Sunday supply clergy for the next five years. We won't leave any one priest in place long enough to become a target."

"You're not going to give them an interim?"

"No. They've even turned on a couple of their interims. Let's just see how they respond to a different priest every few weeks."

"Well, that's an idea."

"They'll either figure out how to get along with each other, or chase each other off in the process. Either way, the parish wins. There's one thing I'm certain about, especially after my meeting with them and reviewing their history. I'm not going to let them keep repeating their pattern. That's the definition of insanity. This is the only thing I can think that might get their attention."

"What would you really like to have happen?"

"In all honesty, just between you and me, I'm hoping that the few healthy members of that congregation that are left will make it so uncomfortable for the antagonists that they'll go elsewhere."

Jim shrugged. "It just might work."

"I'm not hopeful at all, but I refuse to let them destroy another faithful priest." Sean stared deeply into his lover's eyes. "Now Jim, I want to talk about us."

"I know you're trying."

"I've lost ten pounds."

"I can tell."

"Are you ready to move back into our bedroom?"

"No, it's too soon. Ten pounds is a start but you have at least another thirty to go."

"But I miss you."

"And I miss the man I used to make love to."

Sean nodded. "Do you still love me?"

Jim walked over and kissed him on the cheek. "It's precisely because I love you that I'm doing this. I'm not ready to lose you. I want you to stay on your program. I'm just afraid if I move back in, you'll stop."

"I promise I won't."

"And I promise I will when you get back in shape."

The Magnolia Series

Dennis R. Maynard

Chapter 20

"Hey, Parson. "It was Chief Sparks calling. Steele was working on his sermon in his study at home.

"What's up, Chief?"

"One of the guests in my fine hotel down here at the law enforcement center has requested that you visit her."

His statement raised Steele's curiosity. "So why are you calling to tell me that? I usually get those calls from one of your dispatchers."

"This is a unique situation."

"Go on."

"You know we're holding the wife of the pastor from the Presbyterian Church?"

"I only know what I read in the newspapers."

"Well, she wants to see you. She didn't say what she wants. She just asked if you'd come visit."

"Has she had any other visitors?"

"None."

"Who's her lawyer?"

"The judge assigned her a public defender."

"A good one?"

"I think he will be, once he graduates from middle school."

"That doesn't give her much of a chance."

"We caught her dead to rights. She's guilty of growing and using marijuana. That's a slam dunk."

"You think she was selling?"

"I do, but the Feds haven't found any evidence, so that appears to be a dead end investigation. Of course, someone could always come forward and point a finger at her, but that's pretty unlikely."

"I wonder why she wants to see me?"

"Preacher, I'm just the messenger. I thought I'd call you myself. Since this is a pretty high profile case, you may not want to get involved."

"Is that your advice?"

"As I said, I'm just the messenger. The media is all over this case. We've even had some network coverage."

"I know. I saw it on the nightly news."

"This is a pretty high profile case. If you do visit, it won't go unnoticed. We have at least one reporter watching the jail day and night."

"Let me think about it. Thanks for calling."

"Who was that?" Randi brought Steele a fresh mug of coffee and sat it on his desk.

" That was Chief Sparks." Steele then recounted his conversation with the Chief for his wife.

"Steele, you've got to go see her."

"I just don't know if I want to get involved."

"Honey, she's a mother. Her children have been taken from her. She's alone. Even the Chief told you that she's not had a single visitor."

"I understand all that, but..."

Randi's eyes grew wide. It was a look that Steele both loved about her, and on occasion, had come to dread. "Steele Austin, this is not like you. I've never known you not to honor anyone's request for a visit. As a favor to me, and to mothers everywhere, I want you to go over to that jail and at least say a prayer with that woman."

"Okay. Okay. As a favor to you." He stood and kissed her on the forehead. "But I'm not going by myself. I'm taking my lawyer with me."

"Steele, why do you need to take a lawyer with you?"

"Randi, I think I'm skating on thin ice here. I'm about to make a pastoral call on a fellow clergyman's spouse that is in jail. I just don't know what kind of trouble I could be making for myself. I want to at least have my bases covered." He picked up the telephone and dialed the direct line into Stone Clemons' office.

At the law enforcement center, Stone and Steele entered through the back entrance and walked directly into the Chief's office. He told them he'd have Rose brought to them. "I'll excuse myself. Y'all can use my office. I'll station an officer outside the door, but I don't think she'll cause you any trouble. She's been pretty passive."

A female officer brought Rose into the Chief's office. She started to handcuff her to the chair. "Is that really necessary?" Steele asked.

The officer took a long hard look at Steele. "You're Father Austin, right?"

"Yes, I am. I'm sorry, I don't remember meeting you."

"Oh, we've never met, but I know all about you. My partner talks about you all the time. It's Father Austin did this, and Father Austin said that. He just goes on and on."

Steele smiled. "That's nice to hear, but let me guess. Is your partner's name Simon, or is it Joseph?"

A big smile lit up and softened her face. "Quite honestly, there are days I don't know which one of the two I'm riding with. You know they're identical. They even sound just alike. But I'm supposed to be riding with Simon."

"Stone, that's one of Willie and Grace's grandsons. Remember, Willie was a sexton at First Church. When he died, I buried him in the churchyard. He was the first person of color buried in the First Church cemetery."

Stone nodded. "Yep, I remember all that. I thought they were going to tar and feather you over that one."

Steele smiled. "Well, Willie's grandsons are twins. They're now officers for the Chief."

Stone nodded. "I remember those guys. They played some great football in high school."

"The last time I saw them was at their grandmother's funeral; they each had one child. Both of their children had been born on the same day."

The officer chuckled. "Well, now they each have three."

"I think I'd better have a talk with the two of them. Sounds like they could use a short course in reproduction." They all enjoyed a brief chuckle. Rose sat stoically staring at the floor. She did not share in the laughter. "Tell your partner and his twin that we're long overdue for a visit. I expect them to drop by my office when they're free. I'll buy them a cup of coffee. I might even spring for lunch."

"I'll pass along the message." The officer glanced at her handcuffs and then at Rose. "I'll tell you what. Since it's you, Father Austin, I don't think we'll need these. Now Rose, don't you cause any trouble in here. This here is a real good man, and he just stuck his neck out for you. You need to be grateful. I'll be outside the door should you need me."

The officer shut the door as Rose MacClaren broke down in tears. Great sobs shook her body. Stone handed her a handkerchief. Once she regained her composure, she sat glancing back and forth at the two of them. "Who are you?" She directed her question to Stone.

"I'm Stone Clemons. I'm Father Austin's legal advisor."

She nodded. "Thank you for coming to see me, Father Austin."

"I have to admit, I was surprised to get the message you wanted me to visit you. Why me?"

"I've not been in Falls City long, but I've heard a great deal about you. Most of the people in this town hold you in high regard."

Steele smiled. "Don't be fooled. I have a list of names that would beg to disagree with that evaluation."

Rose shook her head. "I've met some of them. They don't matter."

"What can I do for you?"

"Melvin, that's my husband, won't let me see my children."

"Mrs. MacClaren..."

"Please, call me Rose."

"Okay. Rose, I'm not sure I can do anything about that."

More tears spilled out of her eyes and ran down her cheeks. She toyed with the handkerchief she was holding between her hands. Then her body began to shake with more sobs. Once those had passed, she looked at Steele and then Stone. "What I tell you is confidential?"

"If you want."

"I'm fearful for my children."

"In what way?"

"My husband is abusive."

"Verbally?"

She nodded.

"Physically?"

Once again she nodded. "He beats them with his belt."

Steele glanced at Stone. Stone raised his eyebrows. "By beat, you mean spank?"

"No. He beats them hard."

"Does he leave marks?"

"Bruises and welts."

"Why have you never reported this to the authorities?"

She cried, "I'm afraid of him."

"Has he ever hit you?"

She nodded.

"If I bring Chief Sparks back in here, are you willing to tell him what you just told us?"

"Isn't there some other way? Father Austin, can't you go talk to him, pastor to pastor?"

"Rose, if your husband is abusive, as you say, he will not respond well to another pastor interfering in his family life. I think he will most likely deny it, and we will have accomplished nothing. In fact, there's a chance that it will make the situation worse for your children."

Stone agreed. "Do you think your children are in danger?"

"Melvin has an awfully bad temper. I fear he may be taking what I've done out on them."

"Why have you never taken your children and left him?"

"Mister Clemons, I'm a pastor's wife. He's a man of God. Who would have believed me?"

Steele reached over and put his hand on top of hers. "I believe you."

She forced a slight smile.

"Who's your attorney?"

"He's a young man from the public defender's office. I don't recall his name. I've only seen him once for about five minutes. He just told me to say nothing to the police unless he was present."

Stone sat back in his chair and folded his arms across his chest. "Were you growing marijuana?"

A fearful look washed over Rose's face. She looked like she wanted to run out of the room. Once again, Steele patted her hand. "You're in a safe place. What you say in here stays here."

Rose looked down at her hands resting in her lap. "I didn't start out that way. You've got to understand what it was like to live with Melvin. I think he loves me... or... I think he did love me in his own way. He's a very hard man. His temper kept me fearful and upset continually. I met this woman at a laundromat one night. She taught me how to smoke. It relaxed me. It made me feel good. It made me laugh. I could never laugh around Melvin. He thought laughter was the devil's folly."

"And he never knew?"

"I hid it from him."

"So you grew your own?"

"I had to. I didn't know where to buy it. That woman gave me some seeds so I could grow my own. That's how I got started."

Stone leaned forward. "Now, I am going to ask you a very specific question. I want you to listen carefully to my question, and then answer it truthfully. Do you understand?"

Rose nodded.

"Rose MacClaren, did you personally sell any marijuana to any person living in or residing in Falls City, Georgia, or the great state of Georgia?"

Rose thought for just a moment and then shook her head.

"Rose MacClaren, did you personally drive marijuana to any other state for the purpose of selling the drug?"

Again, she shook her head.

Stone chewed on his lower lip for a moment. "Do you have any family or friends helping you?"

"I have no one."

Steele asked, "If we were to arrange for you to get out of here, where would you go?"

"I don't know. I don't have any money. Melvin controls all the money." Rose started sobbing again. "I don't have anyone. I don't have a home. I've lost everything."

Stone studied her for a few more minutes. "Let me discuss all this with Father Austin, but Rose, I think I'd like to represent you."

"Mister Clemons, I don't have any money to pay you. I probably won't ever have money to pay you."

"Don't concern yourself about that. There will be no charge. I can assure you that you'll get a lot better representation from my firm than you will from the public defender's office."

"Thank you."

"Don't thank me yet. Like I said, I want to discuss all of this with Father Austin. Now, we're going to leave and I'm going to send the Chief back in here. I want you to tell him just what you told us about your husband and your children. Can you do that?"

"Melvin will never speak to me again."

"It doesn't sound like he plans on doing that whether you report his abuse or not." Steele reassured her. "Right now, you need to think about your children."

"I'll tell him."

Steele and Stone stood. Steele asked, "Rose, would you like for me to give you a blessing before we leave?"

"Please. Please pray for me."

Steele nodded and blessed her. He made the sign of the cross on her forehead.

In the car driving back over to Stone's office, Stone began, "That is one abused woman."

"It sounds like the entire family is living in fear of that man."

"If my intuition is correct, the police are going to find more than bruises on those children."

"I think you're right." Steele then expressed an idea he'd been mulling over. "Stone, I'd like to bail her out of that place."

"Do you have that much in your discretionary fund?"

"No, but I think I know someone that will help me with her bail."

Stone smiled. "You're really good at finding folks to fund special needs."

Steele shrugged. "Oh, I don't know about that. It's just a matter of knowing who is interested in which ministry, and then asking them for help."

"Nevertheless, you're good at it. If you do raise her bail, where would she go? She may be better off where she is."

"I have an idea, but I need to discuss it with Randi."

The Magnolia Series

Dennis R. Maynard

Chapter 21

Virginia Mudd was struggling to breathe. She grabbed each end of the nightstick being held at her throat and tried to push it away. Javiar's breath was hot against her face. It was rancid. His eyes were filled with anger. Virginia's lungs ached for air. He continued to push her head against the concrete wall in the yard. Virginia's eyes darted from side to side looking for someone to help her. No one could see what he was doing to her. The other pot-smoking inmates had formed a visual barricade around them. Virginia whined. She felt the darkness overcoming her. Then, in an instant, he removed the club. She bent over, gasping for breath. When she stood back up, he slapped her hard across the face, over and over again. She began to cry. "Shut up, bitch!" He threatened her. "You don't come down here and smoke my stuff without paying for it."

"I will. I will." Virginia wailed.

"You're damn right, you will."

"What do you want from me?"

Javiar gave her a toothy grin. He firmly patted her on the cheek. His pats stung her tender face. "I hear say you got a rich lawyer boyfriend that visits you."

"I have a boyfriend, but he's not rich."

Javiar hit her in the face again. This time he did so with his fist. Virginia yelped. "Don't lie to me, you *Puta*. How stupid do you think I am? I know all about your *stud*. He shows up here in his Mercedes, wearing suits that are worth more than us guards get paid in a month."

Virginia was rubbing her cheek. Tears were streaming down her face. "What do you want from me?"

"That's better."

Once again, Javiar patted her, but this time he used his club and he patted her on the head just enough to hurt. "You've been smoking my good stuff. It's not cheap."

"I didn't know I was going to have to pay for it."

"Did you think I was running a charity for potheads? Damn girl, are you an *idiota*?"

"I didn't know."

"I figure you've smoked four of my joints over the past week. You now owe me one thousand dollars."

"What?" Virginia whimpered. "I could buy a couple of joints on the street for ten bucks or less."

Javiar let out a big laugh. "You're not on the street."

Virginia pointed to the other women. "Do they pay that much?"

Javiar pulled his hand back as though he was going to hit her again. She covered her face. He stopped himself. "You do have a smart mouth on you. None of these *muchachas* have Mercedes-driving boyfriends. Everyone pays what they can. You, my *chica*, can afford the most."

"How am I supposed to get a thousand dollars to you? I can't just have him bring it to me in a paper bag."

Again, Javiar chuckled. "Do you think I'm *tonto*? I'll be dropping by your cage before your man whore visits again. I'll give you my bank account number. He can deposit it there." He slapped her hard one more time and poked his finger at her eyes. "You will get me my *dinero* or else... cash, no checks!"

Virginia nodded.

"Now, would you like another smoke?"

Virginia shook her head. "No. Can I go?"

"Now, that's no way to be." Javiar pulled a joint out of his shirt pocket. He lit it and blew the smoke in Virginia's face. She breathed it in. "Here, take it. This one's on the house. Let's just call it a customer appreciation gift." Virginia took the joint and pulled the smoke deep into her chest. Each draw was followed by multiple coughs from her hurting lungs.

"What ·the hell happened to your face?" Adrianna touched Virginia's face.

"Javiar." Virginia whispered. "Where was my protection?"

"I tried to tell you not to get mixed up with him. Virginia, none of these guards are going to cross Javiar."

"Why not?"

"I told you everyone thinks he's connected. Some say his connections run deep into one of the most violent drug cartels in Mexico. He's a mobster. Most of these guards have families. They're not going to risk having one of them hurt, or worse. If nothing else, they'll keep their mouths shut to protect their own skin."

"How'd he get a job as a prison guard?"

"Well, Virginia, I don't think he put *mobster* on his job application."

"He wants me to pay him a thousand dollars for the joints I've smoked."

"So he's figured out that you have a rich boyfriend."

"He said so. I just don't know if Thackston is going to pay it."

"Oh, he'd better pay it. Virginia, there's been more than one sister in here that got on the wrong side of Javiar. It didn't turn out very well for them."

"What happened to them?"

"Let's just say they mysteriously died in their sleep."

Virginia collapsed on her cot. She ran her hand over her cheeks. "My face hurts. Should I go to the clinic?"

"Only if you don't want to come out."

"What do you mean?"

"They'll ask you lots of questions. If Javiar finds out you're there, he'll have to silence you for good."

"Won't the other inmates or guards question me?"

"Everyone will mind their own business. No one will say a word."

"Not even the guards?"

"You're not the first masterpiece Javiar has painted. They'll recognize his work."

"So what should I do?"

"You don't have a choice. You have to pay him."

"Well, I will, but then that's it. I won't go near him again."

"It's not going to be that easy. You don't start with Javiar and just stop. He won't let you. He knows a pot of gold when he sees it."

"Well, I'll just stay away from him. I'm not going near his smoking circle."

"You should have listened to me and not gone near him the first time."

"I know."

"Do you, Virginia? I think you live with an awesome burden."

"What burden?"

"The burden of being smarter than everyone else."

"I don't understand."

"I've been listening to your life's story and all the trouble you've gotten yourself into over the years."

"So?"

"Here's the bottom line. You have refused to listen to anyone. You thought you were smarter than anyone you knew. You didn't listen to your old man, your lovers, or your friends. Being the smartest woman in the world must be a terrible burden to bear."

"Now you're just being mean."

"No, girl, you need to look at this latest mess you've gotten yourself into. I told you to avoid Javiar, but you didn't listen. It's just possible that your own stubbornness is the primary reason you're in this fine establishment."

"So when did you get your degree in psychiatry?"

Adrianna lit a cigarette. She stared at Virginia for a long moment. Then she broke the silence. "I've seen a lot of them come and go during my time, but you, Virginia, are a real piece of work. I'm beginning to wonder if you're so smart you just might never get out of here."

"What does that mean?"

Adrianna shook her head. "You had it all. Down there in Falls City you were one of the fine ladies moving around in society circles. If I believe your life's story, you had a husband and children that really loved you. Now you're in a cage, but you're too damn smart to realize it's all your own doing."

"Oh, I'm going to get out of here. Javiar, you, or no one else is going to stop me."

"That's not the question, Virginia."

"Well, then just what is the question?"

"You're so much smarter than me and the rest of the world. You figure it out."

The Magnolia Series

Dennis R. Maynard

Chapter 22

One of Steele's favorite meetings each week was when he gathered with the staff clergy. The meeting always began with the parish deacon, Lois Smith. Her report included those in the parish that were ill. Deacon Smith carried the lion's share of the pastoral care in the congregation. Her ministry included weekly visits to the nursing and assisted living facilities. She also routinely checked on the elderly that were still living in their own homes. She'd advise Steele and the other clergy on any members they should visit in the coming week. Mother Graystone's report followed. She was in charge of the visitor and new member ministry in the parish. She updated the other clergy on those that had joined the parish. She included her plan for getting them networked with other members and ministries in the congregation.

Doctor Drummond, as the senior associate, oversaw the staff responsible for the education and outreach. This morning he had a particular request. "Did any of you read the article in Sunday's paper about that Auburn professor's new book?"

Steele nodded. "Are you talking about his research on the rise of fundamentalism as it relates to the rise and fall of television preachers?"

"That's the one."

"I've read a couple of his other books. He's got some interesting insights into current religious trends."

"What's his name?" Mother Graystone asked.

"Doctor Richard Walling." Horace answered. "I think he's got a couple of PhDs and a host of other degrees. Anyway, he's going to be here in Falls City in a couple of weeks. He's speaking at the community college."

Steele nodded. "I'd love to hear what he has to say."

"How would you feel about having him speak here at First Church? He could teach one of the adult forums."

"He'd be willing to do that?"

"I spoke to him on the phone. The problem is his fee. The Director of Christian Education just doesn't have enough in his budget to pay him."

"If he'll come, I'll take his fee out of the Rector's Discretionary Fund. It would be wonderful to have him here. That could be a real treat for the congregation. It could also be a first rate teaching opportunity."

Horace and the other clergy agreed. Horace said that he'd take care of the details. Then he raised a question. "Have any of you been keeping up with the events over at Saint Andrew's Presbyterian?"

"It's just awful." Mother Graystone clicked her tongue against her teeth. "My heart just goes out to that poor pastor. How embarrassing for him. It must be tearing his heart out to have his wife's mug shot smeared all over the news. How did she keep him from finding out that she was a drug dealer?"

Steele leaned toward her. He put his hand on her arm. "Things aren't always as they're reported in the news. I fear there's a lot more to the story."

Horace raised his eyebrows. He looked Steele in the eyes. "It sounds like you have some information that can enlighten us."

A slight smile crossed Steele's face. "Okay. Everyone mentally put your purple stoles around your necks. For now, the following is under the seal. Agreed?"

All at the table nodded.

"The first thing you need to know is that there is absolutely no evidence that Rose MacClaren was selling drugs. The only facts in evidence are that she was in an abusive marriage. She was growing some marijuana and using it medicinally to cope with the stress she was living with. That's where the facts end. Nothing else has been discovered."

"Abusive?" Deacon Smith asked.

"I'm afraid so. It seems the good pastor has a violent temper and has been known to strike his wife and children."

"What about the children?"

Steele shrugged. "The only thing I can tell you for sure is that Child Services examined them. There was evidence of welts and bruising on all of them. The children are now in foster homes."

"Is their mother still in jail?"

Steele chuckled. "Well, it seems that a certain Episcopal priest raised some money for the rector's funds and then used them to bail her out. She's now living in his guest room."

A deep baritone laugh came from Horace, "And I take it that priest would be you?" Horace gave a knowing look to Mother Graystone and Deacon Smith. "Does any of this surprise either one of you?"

"It does, but I guess it shouldn't. It sounds just like something Steele would do." Mother Graystone glanced back at Steele. "What about the children? Are they in the same foster home?"

"No. As of right now, they've been separated."

"Is there something that can be done about that?" Horace asked. "Those children should be kept together."

"I agree, but I'm not sure there's anything I can do. I fear that Child Services gets to make that decision."

"What about the preacher over at Saint Andrew's?"

"The only thing I know is that he has been forbidden to have contact with his wife. His visits with his children have to be supervised. Beyond that, I don't know anything."

Deacon Smith cleared her voice. "I'd like to move on to another subject."

"Go ahead." Steele encouraged.

"I have an idea I'd like to present. A lot of our elderly members are lonely. That's especially true for those that are still living in their homes by themselves. I'd like to make a plan to periodically take each one of them to lunch after Church on Sunday. I'm not talking about an expensive restaurant. I was thinking about places like *Applebee's.*"

"That's a wonderful idea, but it will take up a great deal of your time on Sundays. Are you sure you want to make that kind of commitment? I'm afraid that once you start doing that, it will have a way of snowballing. Some of our seasoned members may be lonely, but they also talk to each other."

"I realize that, but I think it's a real need. It's something we can do to minister to them."

"If you're willing to make the sacrifice, you certainly have my blessing."

Deacon Smith hesitantly raised her hand. "There's just one problem."

Steele asked, "Oh?"

Deacon Smith smiled, "I don't have any money."

The entire table broke out in laughter. "Well, that is a problem." Steele mused. He thought for just a minute. "I'll tell you what. I received a gift to be used for another project a couple of days ago. It was actually more than I needed for that particular purpose. Let me ask the donor if we can use the remainder for this ministry. If they agree, the business office keeps the *American Express* card for the Church. I'll tell them to get a duplicate card for you to use on the weekends. Just scribble something that looks like my signature on the receipt. Since I have the worst handwriting in the world, that ought to be easy enough. Bring me the receipts each week and I'll pass them on to the business office. What's left in that gift should cover your start-up costs. In the meantime, I know a couple of our other members that have expressed an interest in our ministry with our elderly members. I'm sure they'll also want to make a contribution. Give me a list to take to lunch as well. I think Randi and I would like to take some of them out for Sunday lunch from time to time."

"Thank you, Steele. I think this is going to be a wonderful ministry."

"Are you free to talk about Texas?" Horace asked.

"I'm willing to talk about it, but there's not much to say. I've done their questionnaire and had a telephone interview."

"How do you feel about it all?"

"I'm not sure. That's an honest answer. I can't say that it's something that excites me. To the contrary, the more I hear about the job, the more anxious I become."

"You'd make a wonderful bishop." Mother Graystone interjected.

"I agree." Deacon Smith smiled. "But I'd really hate to see you leave First Church."

"Let's not get ahead of ourselves. As you all know, these elections are so unpredictable. If they present four candidates, only one will get to be the bride. All the rest will be bridesmaids."

"From what I hear from my friends that have done it, the best day they've had was the day of their consecration. After their big service of ordination, it's all downhill." A frown crossed Horace's face. "The old expression among clergy is that the only people that should get that job are the ones that really want it. Then they have no one to blame but themselves."

Steele sat back in his chair and looked around the table at each of the clergy now focused on him. "The only thing I can tell you is that I'm praying about it. I'm listening, but as of right now, I don't have an answer."

The Magnolia Series

Dennis R. Maynard

Chapter 23

Steele took Dawn in his arms. Her tiny waist felt so good. She melted into him as she yielded to his embrace. He looked into her ocean blue eyes and stroked her long black hair. He was so in love with her. He gently put the palms of his hands on each side of her face so that he could cradle it in his hands. He brought her lips to his. She opened her mouth to receive his tongue. She issued a low moan. He continued to kiss her on the mouth and then he slowly moved his kisses to her forehead, her cheeks, and the small of her neck. Her body sought his caresses. When their mouths came together again, her tongue playfully sought his. He nibbled on each of her ear lobes. He whispered huskily, "I am so crazy in love with you, Dawn, I almost can't stand it."

He picked her up and carried her to the bed. She was so light in his arms. He gently laid her down. Steele stood above her, staring down at her. He ran his eyes over her, from her black hair that was now spread over the white pillowcase, to her long legs that were wrapped in her tight blue jeans. He knelt on the bed beside her and began unbuttoning her blouse. She wasn't wearing a bra. The beautiful blue blood vessels on her breasts took his breath away. He pulled her blouse to the side and bent down to take one of her dark nipples in his mouth. She put her hands on each side of his head as he gently absorbed them into his lips. Her body quivered, and once again she moaned with pleasure.

Steele stood and removed her boots and socks and then her jeans. She lay naked before him. Quickly he removed his shirt, jeans, and shorts. He lowered himself on the bed until he was just above her. He returned his kisses to her neck, and continued to work down her body. "Oh, Dawn, I love you so," he uttered over and over again. "I worship you. I never want this to end." His tongue lingered on her smooth stomach before making his way to her thighs and legs. He turned her over so he could smother the back of her neck, shoulders, the small of her back, and her bottom with his kisses. He nibbled on the backs of her knees. He knew that was one of her sweet spots. "Oh, Steele," she moaned. "Oh... oh... oh..." she screamed as her body quivered.

She turned over so that she could look up at him. Dawn took his face in her hands. She brought him to her lips. He kissed his way down her body, loving the feel of every inch of her beneath his lips and tongue. Then he found her smoothness. The taste of her drove his passion even further. He spread her legs so he could enter her. He started moving in her, slowly and gently at first.

She wrapped her legs around him and moved with his motion. He began to move faster. "Harder. Harder." Again and again her moans rose to a scream, "Oh, Steele, my God, Steele. I love you. Steele, Steele... oh... oh..."

As he exploded inside her, he shouted her name over and over, "Dawn... Dawn... I love you. I am so crazy in love with you."

After, he lay beside her, holding her and stroking her hair. Her body melted in his arms. He wrapped himself around her. He never wanted to let her go. He took her hands in his and wrapped his fingers around hers. They were a perfect fit. He smelled her hair. The scent was so familiar. He felt as though he'd known her all of his life. Perhaps he'd known her in a previous life. They were meant for each other. "Steele, you know that I can't stay here with you, don't you?"

He was caught off guard. Panic entered his body. "No, what do you mean? I want you to stay with me forever. I've really missed you. I need you."

"Honey, you know I can't. Think. I have to go back."

"Where? Are you going back to Texas?"

"Steele, you know I'm not in Texas anymore."

Steele felt his eyes fill with tears. "Dawn, please don't leave me. Please stay with me."

"Baby, I only wish I could. It's just not possible."

"Will you come back to me?"

"One day we'll see each other."

"In Texas?"

"No, silly. I'll never forget you. I'm never far from you."

Dawn stood and started walking away from him. He reached for her hand, but her hand slipped through his. He tried to stand to follow her, but his body was paralyzed. An unseen force was holding him on the bed. He watched her naked body slowly cross the floor toward the door. Dawn turned and looked back at him. Her blue eyes were radiant. She smiled and blew him a kiss. A bright light invaded the room. Dawn faded into it.

Steele woke. Tears were running down his cheeks. His arms were outstretched as he reached for her. His body was covered with sweat. Reality hit him. He felt for his wife with his right hand. Randi was sleeping peacefully beside him. Steele quietly moved from the bed and walked into the bath. He gently closed the door and turned on the shower.

The Magnolia Series

Dennis R. Maynard

Chapter 24

"I have your ancestry DNA results, Henry." The doctor telephoned just before Henry and Dee were going to sit down to dinner. Dee had been helping the girls with their homework. Henry had been feeding his son a bottle of formula.

"Let me get Dee. She's in the other room with the girls. I'm going to put you on hold. We'll go up to my home office. I want to put you on speakerphone so that Dee can hear." When Henry and Dee were both in his home office, they shut the door and locked it. "Okay, doctor, what did the tests show?"

"Let's start with you, Henry. Yours was the easiest to review. Henry, you are as European as any *blueblood* living in Kensington Palace."

"I can't say I'm surprised. Does that surprise you, Honey?"

Dee shook her head, but she'd actually stopped listening. If Henry's bloodline was completely European, that could mean only one thing for her. "What about my ancestors?" She blurted. Dee could not control her anxiety any longer.

"Well, Dee, that's going to explain things, but let me finish with Henry. There is no DNA evidence that your ancestors ever reproduced outside the European Continent."

Henry could see the anxiety on Dee's face. He took her hand in his. "That's all well and good, but we need to move on to Dee's ancestors."

"Your ancestral DNA is a bit more colorful, Dee."

Dee turned white. Henry feared she was going to become ill. "Are you all right, Honey?" She nodded. She whispered to Henry. "Tell him to get on with it."

"You have our attention. What do you mean by a little more colorful?"

"Exactly that. Dee, you have some Native American in your DNA. The best I can tell from these results, it's not very far back. Maybe only a generation or two."

Dee sighed a breath of relief. "I've always heard that my great grandmother was either a full blood or part Indian. I just never knew which tribe."

"This particular test isn't designed to answer that question. There is a more detailed analysis that can be done, if you really want to know." The doctor cleared his throat. "But there's more."

The anxious look returned to Dee's face. "What do you mean, more?"

"Dee, I don't know how you and Henry are going to feel about the next thing your analysis revealed. I suppose we should have discussed it before doing this test."

Henry was growing impatient. "What is it you discovered? The suspense is not helping either one of us."

"Okay." The tone in the doctor's voice became more soothing. Henry figured it was the voice he used when he was giving a patient bad news. "Dee, your DNA shows that one of your ancestors has origins on the Dark Continent."

"Africa?" Dee gasped.

"Yes, Africa."

"That's just not possible."

"I'm afraid it is. I asked the lab to review their conclusions twice. There's no mistake."

Henry put his arm around Dee and squeezed. "How far back?" She asked.

"Dee, that's the question I really was hoping you wouldn't ask."

"Why?" Dee's voice was quivering. Henry took both of her shaking hands in his.

"Dee, the strength of the DNA indicates that this part of your ancestral heritage is no more than one or two generations back."

"You've got to be kidding. There must be some mistake. I never met my grandparents, but I've seen photos.

They were not black. My daddy's as white as Henry. My mother isn't black. It's just not possible."

"Dee, I understand your reluctance to accept this, but I'd stake my reputation on the fact that there's no mistake. The results of these tests explain the features that your son has inherited."

Henry concluded the conversation and disconnected the call. Dee broke down in tears. Henry wrapped his arms around her and held her while she cried. "Would you like a drink?"

She nodded.

He called Shady on the intercom. "Shady, please bring Mrs. Mudd a white wine up to the study, and a scotch for me."

The two of them sat in silence until after Shady had presented their drinks. Dee then asked Henry the fear-filled question that was haunting her. "Henry, does this change the way you feel about me? Do you still love me?"

Henry put down his drink and took hers and sat it on the table. He took both of her hands in his. "Delilah Mudd, I love you, and nothing in this world is ever going to change that." He then put his arms around her and kissed her.

"Oh, Henry, I'm so lucky. You are the best husband in the world."

"And you are the woman I've always wanted to love. I thank God every day of my life that I found you."

"Henry, I don't know how to explain this. I'm at a complete loss."

"Are your parents still coming this weekend?"

"Yes, they're so excited to see the baby."

Henry patted her hand. "Let's just put all this behind us for now. When they get here and the time is right, let's ask them about these results. I think that your parents are the only people that can give us the answer we need."

"I can only hope so, but Henry, don't you think that my mother or dad would have said something about a black relative in our family tree?"

"Not necessarily. I'm not sure that's something too many white families want to admit. Granted, times are changing, but if your parents are anything like mine, they'd never admit to it voluntarily." Just then, their son began to cry. "There's one thing for sure," Henry smiled.

"What's that?"

"His ancestors have given him a good set of lungs." He picked up his drink and handed Dee hers. He then clicked his glass against hers in a toast. He followed the toast with a gentle kiss. "Now, let's go play with our son."

The Magnolia Series

Dennis R. Maynard

Chapter 25

Steele's secretary, Crystal, buzzed him on the intercom. "Father Austin, Bishop Powers is returning your telephone call. He's on line four."

"Thanks, Crystal. See that I'm not disturbed while I'm on the line with him."

"Yes, Father."

"Hello, Bishop. Thanks for returning my call. How are you?"

"Oh, we'll get to me in a few minutes. The first people I want to know about are the really important ones. How's Randi?"

"She's just great. Things couldn't be better."

"So the two of you came through everything just fine."

"Bishop, we're stronger for it. We're keeping our promise not to have any secrets. We try to remember to tell each other the most insignificant detail if there's the possibility that one of us could misinterpret it. I never dreamed our love could be more than it was on the day I married her."

"It's not rocket science. Communication is the key. People grow intimate verbally before they can merge their spirits. Open and free flowing communication brings a couple together. Now, tell me about my great-godchildren."

Steele smiled. "Randi will be pleased to hear that you think of our babies as your great-godchildren. They're growing like weeds. Of course, you realize that they both possess above average intelligence. Travis is the most handsome little guy you could ever hope to see. And Amanda is a beauty."

"And she has her daddy wrapped around her tiny little finger."

"I fear so."

"Well, give Randi a hug for me and kiss those beautiful children."

"That's easy work."

"That's not work. That's a godly admonition from your former bishop."

"Understood. Yes, your Lordship."

"Now you've gone and done it. Let's move on before I have to get my purple wading boots out. Where are you with San Antonio?"

Steele caught him up on the search process. "I think I'm on track. I'm just not sure I want to be. Bishop, I've talked to a couple of other guys that have gone down that road, and they're not happy. Are you happy?"

"I choose to be happy. If you're asking me if this job is what I thought it was going to be, then the answer is a resounding no."

"Would you do it again?" The bishop didn't respond. Steele's question was met with silence. Steele thought the bishop must be lighting a cigarette. He waited. "Bishop, are you there?"

"I'm here."

"Did you hear my question?"

"I heard. It's actually a question that no one has ever asked me. You've caught me unprepared."

"I'm sorry."

"Don't apologize. It's a good question. Steele, if you're asking me if I miss the parish, the answer is yes. I loved being a parish priest. You're a part of a community. You become a part of people's lives and they yours. You can make things happen in the parish. You get to see the results."

"You don't feel like you see any results in the diocese?"

"The results happen in the individual congregations. They actually have little to do with anything I've done. In this job, it's different. Every Sunday it's a different congregation. You are not a part of any of their communities. Most of the people there don't even know who you are. A lot of the regulars actually stay away from church on the Sundays you visit. They know there will be baptisms and confirmations.

They realize it will be a long service. If it weren't for the family and friends of the candidates, the attendance would be even more sparse. And Steele, even though your photo is plastered on the narthex walls of every congregation in the diocese, the average person in attendance still doesn't recognize you."

"Oh, I'll bet the people in Oklahoma know who you are."

"I'd like to think so, but I've tested it. I didn't wear my clerics when I visited a couple of my congregations. When I approached the visitor's table, those attending it asked if I was a visitor. They proceeded to make me a nametag. They failed to recognize me as the bishop, even after I told them my name."

"Ouch. So you miss the parish?"

"Yes. I am even envious of some of my rectors. I don't mind confessing that to you. I've got a couple of rectors that have more resources in their congregational budget than I have here in the diocese. Hell, they even make a whole lot more money than I do. They can make things happen in the parish that I can only dream about on the diocesan level." Again, there was a long pause. "Steele, let's be honest. Do you really want your bishop hanging around First Church?"

"Now you've put me on the spot."

"Come on. We've always been honest with each other."

"Okay. In all honesty, I'd just prefer that he show up, do a quick service of confirmation, and leave."

"Now that's an honest answer. I agree. If rectors weren't needing the bishop for confirmation, most would be just as content not to ever see them."

"What bothers me is that during the telephone interview, it seemed like every constituency was asking me what I was going to do for them."

"Oh, that's when they do want the bishop. If they think you can open that great vault filled with diocesan gold, and pour money over their pet project, then you are welcomed with palm branches and hosannas."

"Excuse me, Bishop, but that really does sound pessimistic."

"Steele, do you want me to blow smoke your direction, or be truthful?"

"You know the answer to that. I trust you."

"I appreciate that. What else do you want to know?"

"Let's just say that I think I pretty well understand the downside of the job. What's the upside?"

"Well, you get to wear a pointed hat, carry a stick, and of course, there's those purple shirts."

"But you don't wear a purple shirt."

"I am only one of about a half dozen bishops that don't. I think they're pretentious. Why would I want to wear the color attributed to an abusive Roman Emperor?"

"What else?"

"There's something about looking in the *Directory of Episcopal Clergy* and seeing your name listed as one of the successors to the original twelve apostles."

"Okay."

"So I take it that doesn't impress you."

"I'm afraid not. I doubt if many lay people have even seen the *Red Book*. I think very few clergy buy one. I doubt those that do even look at that chart."

"I guess the biggest upside is that I get to administer the Sacrament of Confirmation. I preside at ordinations and I get to ordain other bishops."

"But, bishop, I get to prepare those confirmands, and take those priests through the discernment process. And I get to help elect the bishops."

"You're not going to make this easy, are you?"

"I'm sorry."

"Quit being sorry. You're asking the right questions, and making the correct observations. Let's try this. How would you like to have tea with the Queen at Buckingham Palace? Or how would you like to be in a photo with all the

Anglican Bishops in the entire world? That photo is only taken every ten years at the Archbishop of Canterbury's Palace in Lambeth. Now think about it."

"I don't know what I'd say to the Queen, but I think being in that photo might be pretty neat."

"Neat? Neat? Crap, this is frustrating."

"Am I making you angry?"

"No, you're forcing me to ask questions of myself I'd just rather not ask."

"I'm so...."

"Don't you dare apologize!"

"Okay."

Bishop Powers was silent for several minutes. Steele listened patiently, waiting for him to speak. "Steele, how many bishop's homes have you been in?"

"I suppose a half dozen or so."

"And how many of those bishops have erected shrines to themselves in their houses?"

"I don't know what you mean."

"They've dedicated an entire wall to themselves. It's covered with their ordination certificates. There's the inevitable linear chart depicting their apostolic succession. And of course, there will be a wall covered with photos of themselves with the other Anglican Bishops at the worldwide Lambeth Conference. Finally, the *pièce de résistance* is to have their photograph standing next to Bishop Tutu or one of the Archbishops. Now, how many of those have you seen?"

"A couple of them. I just never thought of one of those displays as a shrine to themselves."

"What else would you call it?"

"I don't know."

"Of course it's a shrine. They might as well be burning incense and have lit candles in front of it. That shrine is there to impress anyone that sees it, but more so, it's there to reassure themselves that what they've done with their lives and ministries is important."

"Now that really is cynical."

This time Steele could hear the bishop light a cigarette and inhale the smoke into his lungs. He waited. "Steele, the job of a bishop is not like anything you think it will be. Absolutely the best day of your life is the day of your ordination. I'm sure I'm not the first bishop to tell you that. You've heard it before. After that, the glory fades."

He paused before continuing. "As I said earlier, most of the laity don't know who you are, and an even greater number don't care. Your clergy tolerate you, but would prefer you just stay the hell away and leave them alone. You are in charge of a diocese that has very little money to run programs. But then, the clergy and lay people don't need you to duplicate their programs. They can run them just as well, or better, in their own parishes. You're going to be on the road every weekend. If the diocese is spread over a wide geographical area, you'll become familiar with every fleabag motel in it. Now, my friend, that's the job of a bishop."

"Is that it?"

"Oh, let's not forget all those studies and reports you get to discuss at General Convention and at the House of Bishops' meetings. All of us present deceive ourselves into believing that we're doing something that really matters. We further deceive ourselves into believing that when we issue our report, it will be front page on the *New York Times.* The fact is that the world couldn't care less what the House of Bishops thinks about anything."

"Wow! I don't know if it's that bad."

"Please be a realist."

"I really don't know how to respond."

"You don't have to. Now, is there anything else you want to know?"

"I'm curious. What are the dynamics in the House of Bishops?"

"Just like they are in any feeding frenzy where the large fish and small fish gather in the same pond. The bishops of the larger, wealthier dioceses have the power.

The bishops of the smaller dioceses have to be content with the scraps."

"Wow!"

"Frankly, I'm amazed you're surprised by that. It's just like any gathering of clergy. It often turns into a pissing contest. Too often, it's nothing more than a tussle for bragging rights."

"That's disillusioning."

"It shouldn't be. You asked; I answered. Face it, Steele. You actually have more people in your congregation there in Falls City than some of our bishops have in their entire dioceses. The biggest parishes in several dioceses only have a couple hundred members in attendance."

"Do you trust the other bishops?"

"Some of them, but not all of them. Steele, I like some of my colleagues. I don't have any affection for others. Some I include in my friendship circle. There are others I wouldn't trust as far as I could throw them."

"How does that play out?"

"Primarily when it comes to clergy references. You never know for sure their reason for giving a good or bad reference. It could all be contingent on whether or not they want to keep a priest or get rid of them. Of course, I have some pretty big theological and political differences with several of them. That alone makes trust difficult."

"Have you ever known a bishop that torpedoed a priest?"

"What do you mean?"

"Have you ever known a bishop to destroy a priest's opportunity to get another parish? Or... have you ever known a bishop that actually so slandered a priest's character that their ministry was destroyed?"

"What made you ask that question?"

"I received a telephone call from a priest friend that had received a call to a very desirable parish. His bishop called the chair of the search committee and talked him into withdrawing the call. The chair of the search committee called my friend and repeated the disparaging remarks that the bishop made about him. My friend denied the accusations and insisted they were not true, but the damage had been done. The chair of the search committee told my buddy that he believed his bishop was jealous of him, but his hands were tied."

" Regrettably, that does happen."

"Do you think that the search committee chair is correct? Can a bishop get so envious of a rector's success and popularity that they would try to destroy their ministry?"

"Steele, becoming a bishop doesn't make you a saint. In some ways, I think this job makes you even more vulnerable to temptation. I've known bishops that never got over not being called rector of a particular parish. They then take their anger out on the poor sap that did get the call. You'd think that being the bishop would be enough for them. Obviously, it's not." Bishop Powers took a deep breath. After a period of silence, he continued. "Steele, I'm beginning to find all of this a bit disconcerting. Your questions are taking me to a place I'd rather not go. Unless there's something else you absolutely need to ask me, I need to hang up."

"Bishop, I know you don't want me to apologize, but I feel like I need to do so. I'm sorry this has been a disturbing conversation for you, but you've really helped me. I now have the clarity that I need. Before I let you go, I need to tell you about a dream I had a few nights ago. I don't know if it has anything to do with all of this, but something tells me I need to share it with you. I haven't told anyone about it, including Randi."

"Go on."

"When I was at the University of Texas, I fell in love with a girl by the name of Dawn. I loved her like I'd never loved anyone in my life. We had plans to get married. In fact, she's the reason I'm an Episcopalian."

"Continue."

"Bishop, she had juvenile diabetes and died before we could get married. I grieved over her for years. It wasn't until I met Randi that I could allow myself to fall in love again."

"And your dream?"

"She came to me in a dream."

"That's not unusual. We often dream of people from our past."

"No, Bishop, you don't understand. It wasn't just a dream. We made love in the dream. I actually relived making love to her. It was as real as if we were actually having sexual intercourse. It was as real as it could be. As far as my body is concerned, we made passionate love."

"So it was an erotic dream?"

"Completely."

"You say you knew this girl in Texas?"

"Yes, at the university."

Steele could hear Bishop Powers light another cigarette. He waited to hear him exhale the smoke. "Steele, I'm not a psychiatrist, but for what it's worth, I think you can put two and two together."

"How?"

"You're wresting with a potential move back to Texas, right?"

"Yes."

"And you met your first love in Texas, right?"

"Yes."

"I don't think it's hard to analyze. Steele, just make sure that your draw back to Texas doesn't have more to do with past memories than it does with present day realities."

"You really think it's that simple?"

"Like I said, I'm not a shrink, but past happiness in a particular locale is no promise of history repeating itself."

"I guess that makes sense. Should I tell Randi about the dream? Remember, we said *no secrets*."

"Hmm, should you tell your wife about an erotic dream you had of an old girlfriend, albeit a dead one?" Bishop Powers chuckled. "Boy, give me a break."

Steele relaxed. "I guess that was a stupid question."

"You said it. I didn't."

"If you had one final piece of advice to give me about running for bishop, what would it be?"

Once again, Steele could hear the Bishop inhale the smoke from his cigarette. The Bishop exhaled. "Forget about theologizing it. Don't let yourself get caught up in all the talk around God's will. Just remember, there will be three or four other priests that believe it's God's will that they be the next bishop. Either God doesn't care, or the Almighty is playing with some of your heads. If it's all about God's will, then only one of you is receiving the correct message. That means the other candidates have all deceived themselves into believing that God was talking to them. Mind you, I'm not suggesting that you don't pray about it. By all means, pray over your decision, long and often."

"Then what are you suggesting?"

"Steele, you're like a son to me. In fact, I love you just like you are one of my sons. I don't want you to make a mistake."

"Thanks, Bishop. I love you too. How do I keep from making the wrong decision?"

"Steele..." Bishop Powers paused before continuing. "Listen to your guts. If you have fire in your belly for the job, then by all means pursue it. But son, if there's no fire in your belly for it, run like hell in the opposite direction." The line went dead as the bishop put his phone back on the receiver. Steele was left sitting in stunned silence.

The Magnolia Series

Dennis R. Maynard

Chapter 26

"Steele, I have some wonderful news." Randi telephoned Steele at his office on his private line.

"Okay, dish. I have some news as well."

"Me first. Rob and Melanie's baby was born this morning. Melanie just called." Rob and Melanie were Steele and Randi's best friends. At one time, Rob had been a priest. He met Melanie at a church conference. Even though Rob was married at the time, they fell in love and had an affair. If it hadn't been for Steele and Stone Clemons, Rob would be in prison today for the murder of his first wife. He arrived home from one of his weekends with Melanie to discover his wife's dead body in their home. All the evidence pointed to him as the murderer. Stone and Steele discovered that Rob's wife had also been having a lengthy affair with her boss. The boss, overwhelmed with guilt and the evidence against him, confessed to the murder. Rob was then free to marry Melanie and begin a new life in California.

"Is the baby a boy or a girl?"

"A boy."

"That's wonderful news. I'll give Rob a call in a few minutes."

"Do you have any regrets?"

"About what?"

"Not being their donor."

"Gosh, no. We made that decision; it's behind us. I hate that Rob is sterile, but I believe the donor father they picked is the right one."

"You know what's interesting?"

"What?"

"Melanie says the baby looks just like Rob. She says he's a perfect combination of the two of them. They were looking at their own baby photos and can see the resemblance in both of them."

"That's just great. Rob is such a jock; it will be wonderful for him to have a son."

"Are you saying girls can't be athletes?"

"Oh my, how did I get myself into this one?"

"Yeah, big boy, you'd better retract that statement. You have a daughter, and if you ask me, she just may be on her way to the Olympics."

"Well, that would be lots of fun. Should I make our plane reservations now?"

"Funny man. Listen, Rob and Melanie want us to come out to California the week after Christmas so you can baptize the baby. Can we do that?"

"I don't see why not. I always take the week after Christmas off. They just need to get their rector to invite me, but they know that."

"Melanie has already taken care of it. The letter is on its way."

"How's Rose doing?"

"I catch her crying from time to time, but she's a very courteous houseguest. In fact, I enjoy her company. She's a really nice lady. I just don't understand how her life could take such a turn."

"There's a lot you don't know."

"I've figured some of it out on my own. When you are not around, she's more outgoing and talkative. As soon as you walk in the room, she pulls into her protective shell. Steele, I think she's afraid of you."

"I don't think it's just me. I think she's afraid of men in general."

"Why?"

"I think when all the facts come out, you'll understand. Just continue being her friend. Stone is working on her case. Hopefully, we can get her life back."

"Steele, did you know she's an incredible seamstress?"

"No, I don't think I did."

"Remember, a couple of weeks ago we went over to her house and retrieved some of her things? Her husband had to stay away long enough for her to get what she wanted. One of the things we loaded up was her sewing machine, and all the stuff she had in her sewing room. We set it up in the guest room."

"I remember. It seems like she has been sewing on something every free minute since then, or at least when I'm home that seems to be what she's doing."

"No, you're right. I think it might be therapy for her. She has been sewing pretty continually from sun up to sun down. Well, you aren't going to believe the cute little outfits that she made for Travis and Amanda. I can't wait for you to see them. They're absolutely professional. On the front panel of each, she did these beautiful designs. She had to do that part by hand. She called it *smocking*. Have you ever seen it?"

"I can't say I have."

"You won't believe these outfits. She put a fire truck on the front of Travis' outfit, and the cutest little kittens on Amanda's."

"Wow, they sound cute."

"There's something you need to know."

"Oh?"

"Almeda came by. Not only was she impressed with Rose's handiwork, but she wants to do something about getting the children back with their mother."

"I don't know how she plans on doing that. Not even the Chief has authority over child services. They're calling the shots on that one."

"Well, just prepare yourself. She left here with a full head of steam. Let's just say if I were those children's case worker, I wouldn't want to see Almeda coming at me."

Steele laughed. "You've got that one right. I do remember the days when she was anything but my friend. Almeda is not someone you want in the opposing camp."

"Just keep in mind that you've been warned, and you heard it here first."

"Ten-four."

"Almeda said that she wants Rose to move in with her when she gets the children back."

"Well, she does have a lot more room than we do. We could make it work, but it would be crowded."

"Rose went over to Almeda's. She doesn't want to hurt our feelings, but she agreed that they would have more room over there."

"It works for me if it works for Rose. We need to do what's best for her and her children."

"I told her that. Now, what news did you have for me?"

"I talked to Bishop Powers about San Antonio."

"And?"

"Randi, he didn't say anything to persuade me to pursue a purple shirt. In fact, most of what he said has me leaning in the opposite direction."

"I'm relieved," she blurted out.

"What?"

"I was afraid he was going to try to talk you into it."

"No, to the contrary. He was really fair. He described the things he likes about the job, and the things he doesn't."

"Steele, we've been so focused on the job that I'm afraid we haven't given much thought to what that job would do to us and to our children."

"I thought I had."

"Maybe you have, but I want to give you some additional things to think about."

"Okay."

"If this is what you really believe God is calling you to do, I'll not stand in your way."

"I know that."

"It's just, as your wife, I don't relish the thought of your being gone every weekend."

"I was thinking you could go with me."

"Steele, we have two small children. Soon their Saturdays are going to be filled with activities and friends. They won't want to be out visiting churches."

"We could get a sitter."

"Sorry, Charlie, I'm not leaving my children every weekend for the next fifteen years."

"Maybe I hadn't thought that part through."

"Steele, you're still a young man. If you got elected, you'd have to do that job for the next twenty-five or thirty years. You used to say that no one should become a bishop before their sixtieth birthday."

"I know."

"Do you? Do you really? I know intellectually you do, and I understand how flattering it is to think that a diocese might want you as their bishop, but gosh... I just don't know."

"So what are you really saying?"

"Honey, unless God strikes you with a bolt of lightning, I'm getting down on my knees and begging you not to do this. I'm afraid of what being a bishop will do to us and to our family."

"Gosh, I had no idea you felt so strongly."

"I should have spoken up sooner. It's just that when it comes to these things, the conversation gets so spiritual, and the practical gets lost. How do you interject what appears to be selfish into a conversation around God's Will and the leading of the Holy Spirit?"

"I'm glad you did. Can we talk more about this when I get home?"

"Let's."

The Magnolia Series

Dennis R. Maynard

Chapter 27

"What happened to your face, Virginia?"

"Oh, Thackston, I got into a fight in the yard."

"A what?"

"Yes, this mean girl attacked me. I had to fight back."

"Why did she attack you?" It was visitor's day, and Thackston had come to see Virginia. They were seated in the room set aside for visitation. The room was filled with metal picnic tables that were bolted to the floor. Thackston sat on one side of the table and Virginia on the other.

"She wanted me to get her something from the commissary, and I refused."

"Why did she think you'd get her something?"

"Prison gossip. She learned that I have a nice balance on my account."

"How'd she find that out?"

"Oh, Thackston, there are no secrets in here. Everyone talks."

"Did you report the girl that attacked you to the warden's office?"

Virginia put her hand over her breast. "Oh Thackston, that would be the worst thing I could do. It would only make things worse. If her tribe were to find out that I'd gotten one of them in trouble, they'd all be after me."

"Tribe? What tribe?"

"It's all about tribes in here. They keep telling me it's not a racial thing, but the tribes are divided according to race. We white inmates have the smallest tribe. Thackston, I'm terrified."

"Did you do something to provoke her?"

"No, Thackston, I didn't. I was just minding my own business when, out of the blue, she came up to me. She pushed me into a corner of the yard where the guards couldn't see us. She wanted me to buy her a carton of cigarettes. I told her I wouldn't, and she just started beating on me. Some of her tribe stood guard. They were blocking us so that the guards couldn't see us. I fought back the best I could, but she was just too big and strong."

"Gosh, Honey, I feel so helpless. I want to do something to help. What if I were to talk to the warden?"

"No, please don't. I promise that your visit won't be a secret. It will get out, and then her entire tribe will be after me. Next time they might actually let her kill me."

"Isn't there something that I can do?"

It was then that Virginia noticed that the two people sitting at the table next to them weren't conversing. They were listening to her conversation with Thackston. She recognized the woman. She'd shared a joint with her in Javiar's circle. She'd never seen the Hispanic man sitting with her. Clearly, they were there to make sure that she did not say anything that would get Javiar in trouble. At the same time, she knew that if Thackston found out that she had been smoking pot, it could be worse for her. He might actually break up with her and walk away. Then she would have no one on the outside to help her. His final words before each visit ended were that she should be a model prisoner and stay out of trouble. "Thackston, I'm so scared. I can't eat. I can't sleep. Every time I leave my cell, I'm afraid I might be attacked."

"There's got to be something, Virginia. Maybe if I bribed one of the guards to keep an eye on you?"

"You're so sweet, but no guard can watch me continually."

"I've got to do something."

Virginia leaned forward and whispered, "There is one thing that I've learned about that seems to work."

Thackston leaned in and whispered, "What?"

Virginia looked around the room before continuing. "My cellmate pays insurance to one of the guards in here. Her family deposits money in his back account. He then distributes a share to the heads of all the tribes. He does so through their commissary accounts. The heads of the tribes then put the word out to protect her. Since she signed up for the insurance, she's never had one bit of trouble with anyone in here."

"That sounds crooked to me. I'm sure it's not legal."

"Thackston, I only know what my cellmate has told me. I'm afraid we're way beyond the law in here. The guards only think they're in control. The thugs are running this place."

"Still, it sounds like blackmail to me. That's a scheme that needs to be busted."

Virginia forced some tears. "And then what? Let's say you're successful in breaking up this scheme. Who is going to protect me then? What if they find out my fiancé is behind it all? Then I'll have the head of every tribe in here out to get me. I'll end up dead for sure."

"Okay, maybe getting you this insurance is our best option for right now. How much is the insurance?"

"It's rather expensive."

"How much?"

"I only know the amount to get started."

"How much?"

Virginia forced even more tears followed by a sob. She wiped at her face with her hand. She whispered, "One thousand dollars."

Thackston shrugged. "It doesn't sound like we have any other option right now."

"Thank you, Honey. I love you. It will be nice not to live with this fear in the pit of my stomach."

"How do I pay the... well, let's just call it *the premium*?"

Virginia reached into the sleeve of her prison blouse and brought out a small scrap of paper. She slipped it into Thackston's hand. "Here is the bank account information you'll need. The deposit has to be made with cash. I can't thank you enough." The couple at the next table saw Virginia pass the account information to Thackston. They waited just a minute to insure that he kept it. When they saw him put it in his pocket, they left.

"Will there be another payment due?"

"I think so. I just don't know when. I just know that my cellmate says that the insurance works."

"Well, it doesn't matter, because I think I've worked out a way to appeal your case. We may even be able to get the entire thing thrown out."

Virginia's eyes widened. "How?"

"Remember, you told me that you had been set up. You told me, the prosecutor, and the judge that you thought you were auditioning for a movie."

"Yes, that's correct. I wanted to surprise you if I got the part. This guy told me that the director of the movie would be at that bar. He said that if I was going to get the part, I had to make it all sound real. That's why I used your ex-wife's name in my audition. I thought that I could make that sound more realistic. Honestly Thackston, I just thought I was auditioning for a movie."

"I believe you, Honey. We just have to convince the judge. I think we can. I've discovered some evidence that just may prove your story."

"What?" Virginia gasped.

"You told me that it was a fellow by the name of Mark that introduced you to a man pretending to be Lobo Solatario."

"That's right. I met him through my friend Alicia Thompson. I can't remember his last name."

"His last name doesn't matter since that wasn't his real name anyway. And as for Alicia, she may not be of much help with this. Her testimony will be questionable since she's in prison for interstate drug trafficking."

"I'm afraid I don't understand."

"It's simple, Virginia. I've learned that the fellow who introduced himself to you as Mark was really an undercover DEA agent."

"Oh." Virginia clutched her breast.

"As for the fellow that pretended to be the movie director auditioning you for the part, *Lobo Solatario*, well, that's not his real name either. He was an undercover FBI Agent."

"I still don't understand."

"Virginia, I found out the two of them knew each other. They're actually best friends. I'm going to make the case that they set you up. It's a clear case of entrapment. If I can convince the judge, I'll have you out of here and home by Christmas."

Virginia squealed, "Oh Thackston, Darling, that would be wonderful."

"Don't get too excited. I still have a lot of work to do, but I think this just might be the break we need."

The guard announced that visiting time had ended. Prison rules allowed Thackston and Virginia a farewell embrace. "I'll take care of the deposit," he whispered in her ear. "I want to keep you safe. I should have some news on your appeal next time I visit."

Virginia felt like a load had been lifted off her shoulders. She was a happy woman. She wanted to celebrate. She knew that Javiar had received a report on the deposit by now. Surely he'd want to give her a smoke to celebrate.

The Magnolia Series

Dennis R. Maynard

Chapter 28

Franklin and Caroline Cummings were wedded to all forty feet of their Class A recreational vehicle. Since Franklin had retired, they'd driven it from coast to coast, and from the Canadian to the Mexican border. They'd used it to chase the good weather. They wintered in Florida and summered in the mountains of North Carolina. They retained their family home and did check in from time to time, but the majority of their time each year had been spent in their beloved RV.

"They called." Dee was so excited. "They'll be here in about thirty minutes."

"I'll be right home." Henry hung up the telephone. Finally, he thought, we'll get some answers.

"Daddy, no." Henry walked in to hear Dee arguing with her father. He extended his hand to shake Franklin's. He gave Dee's mother an embrace. "Henry, please tell my dad that he's not sleeping in his RV."

Henry chuckled. "Dee has been counting on you all staying in our guest room. She's bought new sheets, towels, and ordered fresh flowers for you. I think she even had Shady put a fruit basket and a bottle of wine in your room. We'd really like you to stay here in the house with us."

"That's mighty kind of you, Henry, but we just don't want to be a bother. It's just as easy for us to sleep out there. All I need is access to some electricity."

"Daddy, please. Mom, can't you talk to him?"

"Franklin, it does sound like they've gone to a lot of trouble for us."

"Well, all right, I'll go out and pack us some things to spend the night."

"Nonsense, Franklin, I already packed us a bag. I knew Dee wanted us to stay in their guest room. We can go get it later. Right now, I just want to see my grandson."

Dee's eyes widened as she looked at Henry. He nodded. "The baby's sleeping, so let's not wake him just yet.

Do you think we could sit down, have a drink, and a little conversation?"

"Well, if you're pouring, I'm drinking." Franklin smiled. "I'd be happy with a cold beer."

"Mom, what would you like?" Dee asked.

"Do you have white wine?"

"And for you, Honey?"

"I'll have white wine as well."

When Henry returned with the drinks, he proposed a toast to celebrate the birth of Henry Mudd the Fourth. "Franklin... Caroline, if you don't mind, I'd like to get the conversation started. I believe Dee has some questions she'd like to ask you about her family ancestry."

Caroline looked at Dee and then at her husband. "Like what?"

Dee put her glass of wine on the table and sat forward on the couch. "Mom, do we have any Indian blood?"

Caroline took a sip of her wine. "Why, yes we do. My grandmother was either full or part Creek Indian. She died when I was just a little girl, but I do have some memory of her. She had dark skin and long, long black hair. She didn't have a grey hair on her head. I'll never forget. When she took her hair down, it would hang almost to the back of her knees. I don't think she ever cut it. I also remember her conversing with one of her brothers in Creek. I wish I could tell you more, but my memory of her is really sketchy. I think I have a photo back home. If you want, I'll try to find it and send it to you."

"I'd like to have that photo." Dee picked up her wine glass and took another sip. "Do we have any other kind of Indian in our bloodline?"

"Not that I know of. Why do you ask?"

Henry took Dee's hand in his and squeezed it. "Franklin, maybe it would be better if I direct this question to you first. We found the need to have our son's DNA tested."

"Now why on earth would you do that?" Franklin sounded exasperated.

"I understand your confusion. When you meet young Henry, you'll understand. He has features and a skin tone that led us to run the test."

"Like what?" Caroline blurted.

"You'll see for yourself. His hair is curly and cropped close to his scalp. As I said, his skin is dark and his facial features just don't resemble either one of us."

Caroline put her glass down on the table. All the blood rushed from her face. She looked like she was about to faint. Franklin's face turned bright red with anger.

"Mom... Daddy... are you okay?" Dee's voice was shaking. Tears were flooding her eyes.

"Where's this conversation going, Henry?" Franklin sounded angry. He hurled the question at Henry.

"We didn't mean to upset you folks. This is supposed to be a happy visit, but I'm afraid we need some answers. I regret that you are the only ones that can provide them." Henry struggled to keep his voice calm, but he knew that they'd hit a nerve.

"What about your ancestors?" Franklin shot the words at Henry.

"That's a fair question. We had my DNA checked as well. First, I am definitely young Henry's father. Second, my ancestral heritage came back purely European."

"So that's why you're asking about Indian blood?" Franklin was becoming more and more agitated.

Henry studied the two people sitting before him. He'd examined enough clients in his law practice to know when they were sitting on a secret. These were Dee's parents. He needed to move cautiously. "I really hate that we are having this conversation, but for my wife's peace of mind... for your daughter's peace of mind, we've got to have some answers."

Franklin sat stoically staring at his wife. He turned his beer up and swallowed the contents. "I don't think I need to be here for the balance of this conversation," he mumbled. He stood. "I'll just go on out to the RV for awhile."

"Daddy, what's going on?" Dee asked desperately.

Franklin walked over to Dee and put his arms around her neck and hugged her. "Little girl, you need to know that I love you with all my heart. You are the light of my life and nothing will ever change that."

"What are you saying?" Dee could see the tears welling up in her daddy's eyes.

"I love you. You are my precious daughter. I would never change one second of our life together." He kissed her on the cheek. "I'll leave now so your mother can explain." He then reached over and hugged his wife. His voice broke as he kissed her and uttered, "I love you, Caroline. I love our life together and I love our daughter."

Dee watched her mother cover her face with her hands and break into sobs as her daddy left the house. Henry put his arm around Dee and held her close to him. They sat quietly waiting for her mother to compose herself.

"Can I get you another glass of wine?" Henry asked.

"Do you have something stronger?"

"I have whatever you want."

"I don't care. Scotch, bourbon, vodka, tequila, whatever... just make sure it has lots of alcohol in it."

"Mom?" Dee begged. "Tell me what's going on."

Caroline wiped at the tears on her face. "Honey, your daddy and I have been praying that this day would never come. I guess we were counting on it. We were foolish and naive. There is something I should have told you long ago."

"Mom, you're scaring me."

"Dee, Honey, you know your daddy loves you."

"Mom, please tell me. Get to the point. Yes, I know my daddy loves me. He's a wonderful father."

Caroline nodded. "Dee, your daddy is your daddy and he will always be your daddy. He's not..." Caroline's voice failed her. Her body shook as she gave into deep sobs. Through her cries she pounded her legs with her fists, "I was such a fool. I was so stupid. I was young and stupid. You have to believe me. I was just so damn dumb."

Dee had never heard her mother say the words *stupid* or *damn*. She moved next to her and put her arms around her. Henry stayed close with his hands on Dee's back. He patted her gently. "Mom, just get it out. This is torture. Let's just get it out."

Caroline composed herself first by swallowing the glass of bourbon that Henry had brought her. She held her empty glass up for him to bring her another. "Okay, here it goes. Your father and I had dated for almost three years. We were living together. I know that I never told you that. You young folks don't realize that our generation actually did that sort of thing. You all didn't invent it."

"Okay."

"Anyway, I got so angry with him. I thought he was going to give me an engagement ring for Christmas. I knew he'd been to the jewelry store. One of my friends had seen him there. I just knew he was picking out my engagement ring, and he was going to ask me to marry him. Did I mention that we'd been living together for three years?"

"Yes, Mom. So what happened?"

"He gave me a goddamn charm bracelet for Christmas!" She blurted out the words.

Henry and Dee started laughing.

"It wasn't funny. He hurt my feelings. I was really disappointed. I got so mad at him that I broke up with him and moved back to my parents' house."

"Momma, over a charm bracelet?"

"It wasn't just that. I'd given that man or... oh... back then he was such a boy. I gave that boy three plus years of my life, and he didn't have the gumption to marry me. I figured he was never going to marry me. I threw that damn charm bracelet at him and went home."

"Mom, I've never heard you cuss before."

"Well, that's just how mad it still makes me to think about it."

"Okay, we understand all that." Henry tried to soothe her with his voice. He handed her another glass of bourbon.

It was twice as full as the first one he'd given her. "But Caroline, the DNA tests show that Dee and our son have some African blood in them."

Caroline's eyes brightened. "African? No, Dee's biological father wasn't from Africa, he was from Jamaica."

"Mom!" Dee shouted. "What are you saying?"

"Dee, I'm sorry. Your daddy, or rather Franklin and I, were separated for almost six weeks before he came to his senses. After Christmas, I went to Jamaica with a couple of my girlfriends. I had a fling. You've got to understand. I was so angry. I was hurting. I needed someone to tell me just how pretty I was. There was this cabana boy that did all that. He had a big, beautiful smile. He spoke with the cutest accent. He was built. His muscles had muscles. Hell, he was hot! We had a passionate week. It was sweaty and wonderful."

"Mom, stop! I don't want to hear that."

"Dee, I'm just trying to help you understand. That boy is your biological father."

"But what about Daddy?"

"He came to me on the Valentine's Day after that Christmas I broke up with him. He got down on his knees and asked me to marry him. He gave me this engagement ring." Caroline held out the ring for them to see.

"I've always thought that was a beautiful ring."

"Were you pregnant at the time?" Henry asked.

Caroline nodded. "Yes."

"Did daddy know?"

"I told him everything. He said he didn't care. He wanted to marry me anyway. He would raise you as his own. He believed that blood didn't make a man a daddy. Only love could make a man a daddy. He never treated you in any other way. From day one, you were his daughter. And you still are."

"Dee is a little darker than you are, Caroline, but other than that, she doesn't have any qualities that would suggest that her father was anything but a white man."

"I know. I guess that's one of the reasons we figured we'd never have to tell her. You do remember that you had a nose job when you were a teen?"

"Oh, Henry, I had a deviated septum. My nose was..." Dee stopped herself.

"Mom, did I really have a deviated septum?"

"Honey, your daddy and I did what we had to do. We believed we were doing the best thing for you."

"Do you know where he is?"

"You mean, the Jamaican?"

"Yes."

"I never saw him again or heard from him. As far as both of us were concerned, it was just a fling... nothing more. Do you want to try to find him?"

Dee sat quietly staring at the floor. She then looked at her mother and smiled, "No. I have a daddy. I don't need another." Dee then whispered in Henry's ear. He whispered something back. She smiled. He nodded and returned her smile. He hugged her, and kissed her on the cheek.

"Caroline, I'm going to go out to the RV to get Franklin. It's time for him to come back."

Caroline nodded. "I'd appreciate that."

Henry and a shaken Franklin walked through the front door to find Dee and Caroline waiting for them at the entrance to the living room. Dee was holding her baby. "Grandpa, I want you to meet your grandson." Dee handled the baby to Franklin.

He held him in his arms and studied him for a minute. "Well, he's got a really good tan." The tension in the room evaporated as the four of them laughed.

"Daddy, I have something to ask you."

"Okay."

"Daddy, we've named him Henry Mudd the Fourth. My Henry's grandfathers and father didn't have a middle name."

"Well, that sounds like a nice name. Are you going to call him Hal or Henry?"

"Neither." Henry smiled.

"Daddy, we'd like to give him a middle name. We'd like to name him Henry Franklin Mudd the Fourth."

Tears filled Franklin's eyes. "Really?"

"Yes, Daddy. Henry and I have discussed it. I want to name my son after the best Daddy in the world. I want to name him after you."

Franklin's mouth began to quiver as he spoke. "Gosh, Dee, I love you."

"And I love you, Daddy. Is it okay if we call him Frank?"

The Magnolia Series

Dennis R. Maynard

Chapter 29

"We all know how she can be." Mary Alice Smythe had invited Howard and Martha Dexter, Colonel Mitchell, and Tom Barnhardt to join her at the Falls City Country Club for lunch. "She's already hired an architect. She's moving forward with remodeling the sanctuary on her own authority."

"She won't be able to undo one screw without the consent of the vestry." Howard countered.

"When is the last time the vestry of First Church stood up to Almeda and her money?" Martha Dexter buttered another one of the dinner rolls on the table. She lifted the silver bowl for the waiter to bring more.

"Hell, I've got just as much money as she does. I might even have more." Tom Barnhardt pushed his chair away from the table.

"This is not about money. This is about Almeda. She is a force to be reckoned with, and you all know it." Mary Alice was determined to put an end to Almeda's plans to remodel the church sanctuary.

"She'll destroy the beauty of our historic church if we don't stop her. Imagine moving our beautiful altar rail to the nave floor. That rail has been in its current location for over two hundred years. Just who does she think she is?" Martha queried.

"Quite frankly, I don't care." Tom Barnhardt signaled for the waiter to bring him another martini. "I don't have any investment in that church. My only interest is in the school. And you all know my feelings on that subject. If it weren't for the church, the school could become a real community asset."

"Let's stay on subject," Colonel Mitchell offered. "I believe Mary Alice and Martha are correct. Once Almeda has unleashed her demolition crew in the sanctuary, there's no end to what she might do. Lord, we won't be able to recognize the place when she's finished."

"Once again. I don't care. I don't know what I'm doing here. Why did you invite me?" Tom Barnhardt could not hide his lack of interest.

"I invited you because you've done battle with Almeda and the rector before. I thought maybe you could give us some insight as to the best way to handle them." Mary Alice was afraid he was about to leave.

"Mary Alice is correct, Tom. You've been here before. You can help us strategize," Howard Dexter patronized.

"You aren't hearing me. I don't care. Steele Austin has a Teflon coating. No matter what you try, it just slides off him. He's as greasy as they come."

"I don't see how this concerns the rector. I happen to like him," Mary Alice pleaded.

Tom smirked. "And do you really think that Almeda could remodel the church without the rector's support and blessing?"

"I hadn't thought about that." Mary Alice shrugged.

"Well, think about it. It was probably his original idea. He just talked her into heading up the project. If you want to stop Almeda, you're going to have to take down the rector."

"I've grown weary of that song." Howard Dexter shrugged. "We've already tried doing that too many times. He has the support of the bishop and most of the leadership. Hell, he's as popular as any rector we've ever had. The vast majority of this congregation is crazy about the man."

"He's not a god," Tom exhorted through gritted teeth. "We just need to find his soft spot."

"I don't know," Mary Alice stated reluctantly. "I don't want to hurt the rector. I just want to stop Almeda."

"Well then, grow up. You're not going to be able to do the one without the other." Tom pointed his finger at Mary Alice for emphasis.

"I'd like to find another way," Mary Alice muttered.

"I don't even know what she wants to do. What's this all about?" Tom asked.

"She wants to move the altar out and put the choir behind it. You know, like some Baptist Church. Then she wants to put the altar rail down on the nave floor. My biggest objection is that she wants to turn the priest's sacristy into a bathroom, and move the clergy vesting room to the north entrance." Colonel Mitchell could not disguise his disgust.

"And that has you all exercised?" Tom mused.

"As I said earlier, she'll destroy the historical significance of our church. We might even lose our place on the historic registry."

"I'm willing to help you, but let's make it clear that my only investment in all of this is getting rid of Steele Austin. Once he's gone, we'll be able to gain the school's independence from the parish. As for all this remodeling nonsense, I could not care less."

"You keep bringing up the school's independence." Howard Dexter interjected. "Colonel Mitchell and I have already told you that we're in favor of that, but I don't see it happening anytime soon. I think it's wrong for the school to be taking money out of the offering plate. Our money is being used to underwrite the educations of those in this town that are already financially privileged."

"I agree with Howard," Colonel Mitchell stated. "The overwhelming majority of the students are not even members of First Church. Why should my pledge dollars be used to underwrite the private school education for the Presbyterians, Methodists and Jews?"

"If the school is independent, it will have to pay its own way. Why can't you guys understand that?"

"Then, why can't they do that now?"

"Because people, like me, that have little interest in First Church, are not going to give our money until we also have control over how it's spent. If we're paying the bill, we want to decide who runs the school. Right now, the rector makes that decision. I'll give my money when I can have a say in hiring and firing the faculty and the headmaster."

"Just as you don't have any investment in the parish, I don't have any investment in that school. However, I would like to get it off the parish financial statement." Howard Dexter directed his comment to Tom.

"Howard, you do remember that I guaranteed that the school accounts would be kept in your bank if it became independent?"

"I remember."

"Well, let me increase your interest a little further."

"How?"

"I've looked into the land adjacent to the school campus. It seems that you and Colonel Mitchell own that acreage."

"Yes, we do. Howard here talked me into buying it several years ago. It has been nothing but a tax drain. We'd hoped to develop it, but the town hasn't grown that direction. We're just stuck with it."

Tom Barnhardt leaned in closer and indicated for those at the table to do the same. "What if I could get the property appraised for ten times what you paid for it?"

"Who would do that?"

"Leave that to me. Here's the part where you boys win and the school wins as well." Tom glanced around the room to make sure no one was listening. "You admit you can't sell it or develop it, right?"

"That's right." Howard nodded. "It's just sat there since the day we bought it."

"But if it were appraised for ten times what you paid for it and you donated it to the school, both of you would get a handsome tax deduction."

"Is that legal?" Mary Alice Smythe gasped.

"It's not illegal." Tom sat back in his chair. "I guarantee you that if the school is independent, I can make that happen. If the IRS ever challenges it, I'll have my firm defend you pro bono."

Howard and Colonel Mitchell exchanged glances. Colonel Mitchell studied Tom Barnhardt's face for a minute. He then asked, "How would you suggest we proceed?"

"Aren't you the Junior Warden?"

Colonel Mitchell nodded. "I am."

"So you can get access to the rector's financial records."

"Oh, stop right there. We've tried that before." Howard Dexter shook his head. "We've audited his discretionary funds. He was able to refute our every objection. They're audited every year by the church auditors, and they've never found anything to be amiss."

"Yeah, I watched you all botch that. However, you were able to plant a few seeds in the minds of some of the congregation that we need to keep watering." Tom chuckled.

"What do you mean *botch*?" Howard asked defensively. "And just what is it we need to keep watering?"

"It's not about proving anything. It's about planting questions that raise suspicions in people's minds. Listen to me. Clergy are the most vulnerable in three areas. Sex is first, but we all know that Austin is head over heels for his wife, so that's a dead end street. The second is heresy. That won't work without the bishop's cooperation, and I don't think we can get it. So that only leaves money. We don't have to prove anything, and we sure as hell don't give him the opportunity to do a rebuttal. We only need to start planting seeds of doubt in the minds of the congregation. By doing that, we keep the pressure on Austin. It's like a slow form of torture."

"I don't understand." Mary Alice murmured.

"Of course you don't." Tom tried to comfort her. "You're a nice lady. You need to leave everything to us."

Mary Alice nodded. "I'm still confused. How are you connecting the rector's expenditures with Almeda's plan to remodel the sanctuary?"

"Nothing and everything." Tom smiled. "Mary Alice, it's just a means to an end. In order to stop Almeda, we have to destroy the rector's credibility. As I said, we begin by planting doubts in the minds of the congregation about the rector's financial affairs. Thanks to the work that Ned, Howard, and Colonel Mitchell have done in the past, the clouds of suspicion are still out there. We just bring it all up again, and then we stand back and let the town gossips do their work. It won't take long for Austin to throw in the towel. He'll simply quit. Once he's gone, Almeda will find herself up a creek without the proverbial paddle."

"I still don't understand." Mary Alice shook her head.

"Listen, the beauty of the plan is in the safety net. If we start getting blowback from the congregation after he leaves, the justification for getting rid of him is already in the wind. We only have to formalize our suspicions in writing. And here's the real beauty in it all." Tom Barnhardt could hardly contain his excitement. "The rector won't be here to defend himself. Hopefully, he'll be a thousand miles away. We can go before the vestry, the bishop, and the congregation with our suspicions, and they'll stick. It will be like putting on a trial with no defense attorney or defendant present. The town gossips will insure that we win and Austin loses."

"I don't know. It just seems like we've tried all that before," Howard Dexter stated reluctantly.

"Just leave it to me." Tom Barnhardt started to unveil his plan. "Colonel, get copies of the expenditures the rector has authorized. I'll take them over to my office and have my paralegal prepare a spreadsheet on them. We're going to give them the same attention as if we were preparing a case for a jury."

"I don't think you'll find anything illegal." Howard objected.

Tom smirked. "I don't have to. The only thing we have to do is plant more seeds of doubt in the minds of the vestry and members of the parish. Trust me. We don't need facts. This is not about proving anything. We only need to ask the right questions about some of his expenditures.

Once we do that, the gossips on the rumor mill will do our work for us. Austin will become discouraged and leave."

Mary Alice grimaced. "Well, you'd better hurry. Almeda has already started moving the furniture around in the church. When folks arrive next Sunday, she will have set up a temporary altar and altar rail. She thinks that if people can see what it will look like, they'll support her proposal."

"She's doing what?" Colonel Mitchell exploded.

"Just what I said." Mary Alice responded, through tight lips.

"Then she and that rector have to be stopped. And they have to be stopped permanently." Colonel Mitchell slapped his hand down on the table. "Count me in. I'm at the end of my rope with The Reverend Mister Father Steele Austin and his army of liberals." All at the table nodded their heads in agreement.

The Magnolia Series

Dennis R. Maynard

Chapter 30

The various officials in charge of administering the laws, ordinances, and regulations in Falls City, Georgia, routinely try to do so without bias. However, they're only human. The handful of caseworkers at child services spends most days overwhelmed by their workload. There are more children than foster homes. But then, monitoring the children in those homes is exhausting in itself. If a caseworker is fortunate, they're able to get to each of those homes every other month. Even then, their visit has to be limited to just a few minutes. The required paperwork following each visit takes longer than the drive to the home, the visit, and the return trip to their office.

Meesha Jones had graduated from Falls City Community College. Her studies had focused on sociology and psychology. The supervisor in charge of child services offered her a position as a caseworker when she graduated. For over ten years, Meesha had struggled to keep up with her caseload. The last thing she needed on her calendar was a visit from a rich white woman.

Almeda walked down the hallway past the other caseworker's office directly into Meesha's office. She did not knock on the door. She didn't wait to be invited to enter. She didn't hesitate before sitting in one of the two metal folding chairs opposite Meesha's desk. Meesha was typing on her desktop computer when Almeda entered. She looked up. "May I help you?"

"I am Mrs. Horace Drummond. I believe we have an appointment."

Meesha looked at her calendar. "Yes, we do, but not for another thirty minutes."

"I believe in being prompt." Almeda countered. "Do you know who I am?"

"Yes, you just introduced yourself. You're Mrs. Drummond." Meesha did not follow the society pages. She'd never even driven down River Street. She certainly didn't have any idea as to just how important Almeda considered herself to be.

"My husband is one of the priests at First Church."

Meesha still wasn't impressed. She'd heard of First Church and the controversial rector they had, but she knew little else. "Okay."

Almeda thought this woman must really be uninformed. "You know he's an African-American."

"No, I didn't know that."

Almeda felt herself growing exasperated with the girl's ignorance. "Well, he is. How do you feel about that?"

"About what?"

"That my husband is an African-American."

Meesha studied Almeda's diamond bracelet and earrings. She then noticed the ones on her wedding band. "Did he marry you because you're rich?"

"I beg your pardon. He married me because he loves me."

"If you say so."

"Do I detect disapproval?"

"Look, lady, I'm really busy. You don't want to know what I think about our black men marrying rich white women. Now, what can I do for you?"

Almeda decided she needed to follow another tactic. "I understand that your aunt works for one of my best friends."

"Which auntie?"

"I believe her name is Shady."

"Yes, Shady is my auntie. She works for the Mudd family. Mister Mudd has been very good to her. He even gave her a house."

"Oh, I wasn't aware of that."

"Mister Mudd was just helping my auntie. He wasn't looking to have his photograph on the society pages handing her the keys. That's just the kind of man he is."

"Well, I think I can help you."

"Oh, how?"

"I understand you've been assigned the MacClaren children."

"Yes, I'm managing their case."

"They're in three different foster homes."

"I'm not free to discuss my cases with you."

Almeda was not about to be deterred. "Well, I think those children have been through enough. They need to be together."

"Look, lady. Like I said, I'm not free to discuss this with you."

Almeda ignored her comment. "I'd like to move those three children to my home. My husband and I will be more than happy to care for them. I moved their mother to my home last week. Those children need to be with their mother."

"Wouldn't that be a bit crowded?"

Almeda chuckled. "I have the largest home on River Street. I have rooms in my house that I've not even been inside of for weeks. We have plenty of room."

Meesha took the pencil from behind her ear and started tapping it on her desktop. She continued to study Almeda. "You do realize that there's a long investigative procedure that must be followed before we can license a foster home?"

"Oh, I'm sure we can find a way around all that paperwork."

"You are?"

"I am."

Meesha reached for the three case files on the children. She needed to refresh her memory. The youngest was in a temporary situation that was due to end at the close of the week. She'd have to reassign him anyway. That is, if she could find a vacancy. The same was true with the oldest. This could be an answer to her dilemma. She had two more children she needed to place by the end of the day. Meesha's eye caught a glimpse of Almeda's walking cane. Her cane alone was worth more than she earned in a week. "Why do you want to do this?"

"As I said, my husband and I have more than enough room. Their mother is currently residing in our home. I've gotten to know her. She's a wonderful woman that has gone through a terrible ordeal. She misses her children. I want to help her. You realize her husband is a minister, but he abused her and those precious children."

"As I said, I shouldn't even have discussed this case with you as long as I have."

"Well, for the life of me, I don't understand why you would object to placing these children in an expansive home with their mother. I did tell you that my husband is a priest?"

"And the man that abused his wife and children was a priest as well." Meesha countered.

"Young woman, Presbyterians don't have priests. They have preachers. As for my husband, he's a loving man. He's never abused anyone in his life. We are simply trying to help."

"And then what?"

"What are you asking?"

"So you keep them for a few weeks. What happens when you tire of them? Are you going to send them back to me?"

"Absolutely not!" Almeda pounded her cane on the floor. "I am going to help Rose MacClaren put her life back together. I'm going to help her have a home of her own."

Meesha was at a loss to argue with that. She had already concluded that this snooty white woman had more than her share of money. She'd also concluded that Almeda just might have a heart of gold to go with her fortune. "I'll tell you what I'm going to do. I want to come out later today to inspect your home. I'm going to want to talk again with you, and I need to interview your husband. Is that agreeable?"

Almeda tried to conceal her look of satisfaction. She'd won. "I believe you'll find my home more than adequate. As for my husband, you'll be just as pleased with him."

"I'm also going to call Mister Mudd to get a reference on you." Meesha slid a yellow legal pad across the desk toward Almeda. She handed her a pen. "I need additional references. Please give me the names and telephone numbers for three more people. Of course, I will also need your address. I'll be at your house sometime after four."

Almeda tried to suppress her humiliation at having to give references. She really wanted to blast the girl for not knowing that she was one of the most important people in Falls City. She wanted to tell her about all the people that mattered in this state that were in her acquaintance. She considered them to be close personal friends. Then Almeda smiled. The girl said she wanted references. I'll give her some references she won't forget. Almeda opened her address book. She wrote on Meesha's legal pad the names and private telephone numbers for the Governor of Georgia and the two United States Senators. When she'd finished writing, she slid the pad back across the desk. Meesha took the pad and glanced at the names. Her eyes widened. "Are you kidding me?"

Almeda leaned on her cane and pushed herself up from the chair. She turned and walked to the door. She looked back and gave Meesha her most haunting smile. "Call them." She then turned and walked down the hall, making sure that the sound of her cane echoed on the tile floor.

The Magnolia Series

Dennis R. Maynard

Chapter 31

The Reverend Melvin MacClaren had taken refuge in the manse of Saint Andrew's Church for the past couple of weeks. He'd pulled the blinds and had taken the telephone off the hook. He unplugged the television and radio. He canceled the newspaper. A few people had rung his doorbell, but he'd refused to answer. The investigators from the police department had grilled him twice. They advised him that his wife was accusing him of abusing his children. Child Services had examined the children and found evidence of bruises and welts on their legs, backs and buttocks. They also found evidence that young John Calvin had suffered a bone fracture in his right femur. Pastor MacClaren hired an attorney. The attorney advised him not to talk to them again without him being present. As long as he was under investigation, he could only have supervised visits of one hour a week with his children.

As far as he knew, his wife, Rose, was still in jail. Her scandalous behavior had been the lead story in the local newspaper and on the television news for days. He'd received a call from the denominational Presbytery Board. They advised him that they also would be investigating the allegations against him. Until all the issues had been resolved, his license to preach the gospel had been suspended. So day after day, Melvin sat in his dimly lit study, working on sermons he would preach once his name had been cleared. He prayed continually that the Lord would deliver him from the hands of his enemies. His doorbell rang. He ignored it. The ringing was combined with knocks on the door. He continued to ignore the visitor. Before long, the knocking and ringing ceased. He reasoned the visitor had given up. He returned to his sermon preparations. Then there was a knock on his study window. The knocking continued. He pulled back the curtain. Judith Idle was smiling up at him. She motioned for him to open the door.

"Judith, it's so nice of you to come, but I just don't feel like receiving visitors."

"Nonsense, Pastor MacClaren. I'm not a visitor. I'm your friend. I've been worried about you. Have you eaten?" Judith picked up the straw basket at her feet and rushed past him into the house. "I've prepared some food for you. Which way is the kitchen?"

Melvin closed the door behind her and led her through the darkened living and dining room into the kitchen. "I don't think I can eat anything."

Judith turned on the kitchen lights and lifted the blinds over the kitchen counter. "I can tell you've not been eating. You look like you've lost weight. It looks good on you, but you need to eat. Sit down at the table; I'll fix you a plate."

Melvin sensed that he was not going to be able to get rid of her until he'd eaten. She prepared him a plate and one for herself. She brought both to the table and sat down opposite him. "Eat," she instructed.

Out of habit, Melvin took her hand and closed his eyes. "Heavenly Father, I thank you for this food we are about to receive. I ask you to bless the hands that have prepared it. I ask..." Melvin's voice broke. He began to sob.

Judith squeezed his hand. "Let me finish. Dear Lord, I thank you for this good man. He is your faithful and loving servant. He is being mistreated and abused for your sake. Holy Jesus, I beg you to have mercy on him and come to his aid. Deliver him, Father, from the troubles that have been brought down upon him. He is innocent of all wrong. With the mighty power of your Spirit, defeat those that have falsely accused him and return him to the pulpit at Saint Andrew's. You know that he preaches your pure and unblemished word. Deliver him; deliver him for your sake. Thank you, Jesus. Thank you, Jesus. Ohhh... Jesus... Ohhh... Jesus... Jesus..." She hummed.

Melvin patted her hand and wiped the tears from his face. "You are a good Christian woman, Judith. Elmer is so blessed to have you as his wife."

Judith smiled. "Thank you. Now let's eat."

"This is wonderful. You're an excellent cook."

Judith took his plate and filled it again. She returned it to the table. "It's so gratifying to watch a man enjoy his food."

"You know everything that's happened to me, don't you?" Melvin asked her, after he'd finished his third piece of apple pie.

"I read in the newspaper about your wife being a drug dealer. That's got to be so embarrassing for you."

"Believe me, Judith, I had no idea."

"I do believe you. Have you had any contact with her?"

"I don't want any. As far as I know, she's in jail, and that's where she belongs."

"So you don't know."

"What?"

"She's out on bail."

"Who paid her bail?"

Judith shook her head. "It really pains me to have to tell you. I have it on good authority that the rector of First Church got her out on bail."

"What?"

"I'm sorry, but it's true."

"Why would he do something like that?"

"Because he's pure evil. That man should not be a priest. He has no business going near a pulpit. I could spend the rest of the afternoon rehearsing all of his evil deeds for you."

"I've heard about some of them. I guess I'd just written him off as one of those liberals."

"He's so much more than that. Elmer thinks that he's a communist."

"I just don't know what's wrong with The Episcopal Church. They keep ordaining men like him. They're even making some of them bishops."

"All of that is why Elmer and I left them and joined Saint Andrew's. We realized we didn't belong over there."

"Do you know that Rose is accusing me of abusing her and the children?"

"I just know the gossip. She's filing for a divorce against you. Who's her attorney?"

"The papers came from the law offices of Stone Clemons. Do you know him?"

Judith's eyes grew wide. "Know him! He's one of Steele Austin's primary defenders. That man is every bit as evil as that so-called priest. I can't stand him."

"Do you know where Rose might be living? They've put a restraining order on me. I can't have any contact with her or the children without supervision. That pagan holiday, Halloween, was last week. This is the first time I wasn't able to protect my children from the works of Satan. I never allowed them to dress up in hedonistic costumes and go out begging for sweets. Do you keep that awful day?"

Judith shook her head. "No, we don't. When the children come to our door, we give them index cards with Bible verses printed on them. We also give them a copy of a pamphlet explaining how they can accept Jesus and be saved."

"That's a wonderful idea. I wish I'd done that. We just turned out our lights and refused to open the door." A large tear dropped from Pastor MacClaren's eye and rolled down his cheek. "I don't know what I'm going to do about Thanksgiving this year. Rose always prepared such a feast for me. And then Christmas..." His voice broke. "I just don't know how I'm going to get through Christmas. Did you tell me if you knew where Rose is living?"

Judith reached across the table and took his hand. "Oh, Pastor MacClaren, I hate to be the bearer of all these sad tidings. Rose was living in Steele Austin's home. Now she and the children are living with this rich white woman and her black husband."

On hearing that his wife and children were living in the home of a Negro man, the blood rushed to Melvin MacClaren's face. Judith was afraid he was going to have a stroke. She ran to the kitchen sink and poured water over a towel. She brought it back to him and put it on his forehead. "Thank you." She gently patted his face with the damp cloth.

"Did you have any idea about your wife? I mean, were you happy with her?"

Melvin took the cloth from her and laid it on the table. "I thought we were happy. I thought we had the perfect marriage. In my mind, we were a model family. We were living a Biblical marriage. Yes, I had to discipline my children. The Bible is quite clear on that subject."

Judith resumed her seat at the table opposite him. She took his hand and squeezed it. "Yes, *spare the rod and spoil the child.*"

"My children were well behaved. They were learning the scriptures as well as their school lessons. I just can't believe my life has come to this. Tell me, Judith, what have I done wrong? I've simply tried to be God's obedient servant. I've wanted nothing else but to obey His sacred word and teach my wife and children to do the same."

Judith put her other hand on top of Melvin's hand. She was now clasping his hand between both of hers. She watched the tears stream down his face. "Did you think that Rose loved you?"

"I had no reason to believe otherwise. May I show you what I'd been working on? I got the idea from you and Elmer."

"From us?"

"Yes, remember you told me you always recited the Stations of the Cross before you entered your marriage bed?"

"We don't do the one about Mary, but we do the others."

"Well, they all just smell too much of the Bishop of Rome to suit me. I was working on something similar that Rose and I could do."

"I'd like to see it."

Melvin led her up the stairs to the hallway. At the top of the steps, he pointed to a framed Bible verse on the wall. It was labeled *Step One*. "This is where I'd wanted us to begin. We'd hold hands and I'd read her this verse. *A woman shall leave her father and mother and cling to her husband. The two shall become one flesh.* See, I thought that it would be fitting to begin by reminding ourselves that marriage is a part of God's plan."

"I think that's just wonderful. It's from the *Book of Genesis*. Then what?"

"Let me show you." He led her through the open door into the bedroom and pointed her to a second framed Bible quote. He read it to her. "*Wives be subject to your husbands as the Church is subject to Christ. Husbands love your wives as you love your own body as no man despises his own body.* Don't you think that makes a good second reminder about the essence of marriage?"

"Oh, I do. I do. That one is from *Ephesians*. I recognize it. I've always loved that passage." Judith murmured sweetly. She put her hand on his back and rubbed his shoulder. "You poor man. You've put so much thought into this. My heart just bleeds for you."

He smiled at her and took her hand. Let me show you the third step. They moved further into the bedroom. He continued to hold her hand as he read, "*Let him kiss me with the kisses of his mouth! For your love is better than wine.*"

"Oh, pastor, that's beautiful. Where is it from?"

"All the rest of these are from the *Song of Solomon*."

Still holding hands, he led her to the next. He read the text to her. "*You are beautiful my love; you are beautiful; your eyes are doves. Ah, you are beautiful, my beloved, truly lovely.*"

Judith once again rubbed his back and shoulders with her free hand. "Pastor MacClaren, I've never read these passages. I didn't know they were in the Bible."

He led her to the next. Again, he recited the framed passage for her. "*Your eyes are doves. Your hair is like a flock of goats. Your teeth are like a flock of shorn ewes. Your lips are like a crimson thread and your mouth is lovely.*"

Judith loved the sound of his voice. "You read those passages with such feeling. I could listen to you all day. Your voice stirs something deep inside of me."

He pulled her to the last frame. He began, "*Your breasts are like two fawns...*"

Judith stopped him. She put two fingers on his lips. She moved closer to him so that he could feel her breasts pushing against his chest. His eyes dropped to her cleavage. She lifted his face with her hand so that she could look deep into his eyes. Her eyes were begging him to take her. He started to pull away when she ripped open her blouse to reveal her naked breasts. His eyes widened. Once again, he started to back away. Judith wrapped her arms around his waist. They stood, coupled together, staring into each other's eyes in silence. Again, Pastor MacClaren's eyes dropped to stare at Judith's naked breasts. He took them in his hands. He looked into her pleading eyes and surrendered. He grabbed her with both of his arms and pulled her even closer. Their lips found each other as her tongue sought his. Together, they fell onto the bed. He smothered her breasts with kisses before taking one of them in his mouth. Judith gushed, "Ohhh... Jesus... Ohhh... Jesus... Jesus..."

The Magnolia Series

Dennis R. Maynard

Chapter 32

Doctor Richard Walling stood before a packed parish hall. Steele and Horace were actually surprised by the number of people in attendance. "What's going on?" Steele asked.

"Look over there on the right," Horace offered in a hushed voice. "Take note of that group seated on the front row. There's Colonel Mitchell sitting with Howard and Martha Dexter. They've brought their entire fundamentalist army with them."

"Do you think they're here to learn, or to criticize?"

"Do they ever come here to learn anything?" Horace questioned. "They're here to load up with fresh ammunition."

"Maybe having this guy here is a mistake."

"We shouldn't deny the good folks in this congregation the opportunity to learn just because a few small minds won't like what they hear."

"I hope you're right."

"Ladies and gentlemen, I want to thank you for the opportunity to present my research findings." Doctor Walling began. "I want to make it clear that my research has been limited to the television preachers that have a mass appeal. While some of what I have discovered will apply to all television evangelists, there is a segment of that population I did not include. As you are aware, the channels are filled with a lot of low budget evangelical operations. Most of these are harmless enough. The local congregation, or a couple of benefactors, are their primary source of support. My research did not include the regional evangelists either. These are the ones that have a larger operation and seek funding from their viewers. They tend to have a more political agenda. Their appeal is to those that want to wrap the Gospel in the American Flag. I focused my research on the big budget operations that have a national appeal. These evangelists are names that would be recognized by people that have little or no religious affiliation. The production budgets for their broadcasts number in the millions of dollars each year. With that introduction, let me begin. If I could get someone to dim the lights."

Doctor Walling held a remote control in his hand. A photo of a congregation gathered in an arena appeared on the screen. "Can anyone find me an empty seat?" There was no response. He projected another congregation in a different facility and then another and a few more. "Did anyone see an empty seat?"

A couple of people smirked, "There aren't any."

"That's correct. These are slides that I took off the actual opening scenes of several popular evangelists' Sunday broadcasts. *Rule Number One* is that you never show an empty seat or a half full congregation." He projected another slide. "Now notice the date of this broadcast. I was actually in this congregation on the day this service was videotaped. It was only half full, but when it was broadcast on television, they showed a packed house. That brings us to *Rule Number Two*. Never do a live broadcast. Always prerecord your broadcast so that you can edit it to include a packed house."

He projected several more slides and then positioned them together on the screen. "What do you notice about this view of the congregation?"

A lady volunteered, "There are people in wheelchairs up front."

"Is that normal?" There was silence. "Where are most handicapped accessible spaces? For example, where are they in a theatre or casino? Not that anyone here would frequent such places."

Another man offered. "They're usually in the back."

"And why is that?"

"Closer to the exits in case there's a fire or a need to evacuate. It would be easier to get them out."

"Exactly." Doctor Walling continued. "But in the television church, you want to put them up front and you want to group them together. Any guesses as to why?"

Several people answered at the same time, "To appeal to your emotions."

"Again, correct." He projected several slides of various choirs. "Now, what did you notice about these choirs? They all have something in common." That question was met with silence. "Oh, come on, this one's easy." More silence. "Let me run through them again." Silence. "Okay, does anyone see, oh, let's call them, seasoned citizens?"

"They're all young."

"Correct. And what else?"

"They're beautiful."

"Oh, you all are good. In order to sing for one of these broadcasts, I discovered that you had to be young and attractive. Do you see any overweight people?" Silence again. "No, any one of these choir members could have just returned from running the *Boston Marathon*. Now, you also need to know that none of them are volunteers. They are paid. These are professional choirs."

Someone observed, "Now that you've pointed these things out I see them, but I'd never noticed them before."

"That's the idea. They don't want you to remember, or turn away, because one of the entertainers is overweight, or old, or unattractive. They are manipulating you into not changing the channel."

"As long as we're talking about music, let's see what else can be discovered." He projected some photos of the various congregations in his study singing. "What do you notice?"

"There are no hymnals."

"Again, you are correct. The words to the songs, and I'm using that word descriptively, are not hymns in the traditional understanding of that word. The words to the songs are projected onto a screen. That way, you don't have to flip through the pages of a book looking for the song. Now, what's missing from the words on the screen?"

Silence.

"Anyone?" More silence. "There's no music score. You don't have to concern yourself with those little black and white notes. My studies discovered that most all the songs the congregations sang utilized only five notes. But then, notes weren't needed since the bouncing ball pointed the people to the words they were supposed to sing. The congregation and choir don't have to concern themselves about singing in four-part harmony." Most of the listeners found that remark humorous.

"Now, here's the most interesting discovery about music in these productions. The words to the songs were all bright and happy. They were *feel good songs*. Hymns in the traditional Church often remind the worshipper of their responsibility, and the disciplines that God requires of them. We are reminded to love, serve, and forgive in the hymns that we sing. The *Feel Good Gospel* preached in these television productions makes no demands on those present. The primary distinction is that the hymns a mainline denomination might use require you to think. They also require you to know a little bit about reading music."

He projected a view of several of the preaching platforms. "There are no bulky pulpits to block your view. If there is one at all, it will be see-through plastic. These preachers are masters of the teleprompter, although you'll never see one in the broadcast. Their preaching platform and the entire cathedral or arena is set up for television. They have designed them for entertainment. Have you ever noticed that one of their favorite broadcast tools is to show members of the congregation?" Silence. "Okay, start noticing. They know that talking heads are boring. They show the preacher parading around the stage. They broadcast his sermon points on a screen. There is action as they focus on the various faces in the congregation that are either crying, or smiling, or nodding in agreement. There is action in these broadcasts." He projected the same slides again. "Did anyone see a cross or a crucifix?"

"No."

"These are Christian services, but the platform is decorated with trees, green plants, brightly colored flowers, and, in a couple of cases, waterfalls. These are television studios. I was at this broadcast. I want you to listen to a portion of the sermon as it was broadcast." He played the videotape. "Now, I want you to hear the same part of that sermon as I recorded it on my equipment." He played it for them. "Did you hear what he said?" The listeners nodded. "Midway into that portion of his sermon, he stopped and looked up at the director in the sound booth. He said, and I quote, 'I'm going to do that again. Let's edit out the other part.' He started over before continuing, but there is no way that you would know that it was a do-over unless you were in the congregation. Which, by the way, was only about a third full. That's the way that the television preachers are able to broadcast sermons that are flawless in their delivery."

He projected a list of words onto the screen. "I'm going to close by showing you a list of words that you will never hear one of these popular evangelists use. I read over a hundred sermons from each of the preachers I studied. The following words never appeared. They are *sin, guilt, sacrifice, discipline, repent, discipleship, Church, and service*." He projected another slide. "On the other hand, these words and phrases appeared in one form or another in every sermon. *Happy, happiness, prosperity, wealth, rich, richer, blessing, love, joy, and joyful.* I leave it to you as to which set of words are most compatible with the Gospel as Jesus proclaimed it."

He paused as he folded his lecture notes. "Now, there is one more closing observation. These evangelists live a lifestyle that Elmer Gantry could only have dreamed about. They reside in huge mansions; they stay in five star hotels, drive luxury automobiles, and fly first class or on private jets. To their credit, few of them draw a salary from the congregations they preside over. They don't need to. Each week on national television, they sell their books, videotapes, announce their schedule of paid speaking engagements around the world, and paid appearances on talk television shows. On those shows, they promote their published works to yet other national audiences. They don't need to draw a salary. In fact, drawing a salary from their congregations would only create problems for them with Internal Revenue. Now, are there any questions?"

Colonel Mitchell was the first to rise to his feet. "Sir, I've sat here and patiently listened to you defame these faithful servants of God. I want you to know that I find your presentation to be most uncharitable."

"That was certainly not my intention. My research is intended to shed light on what I consider to be one of the most interesting sociological phenomenon in this century."

"Some of us have no use for sociology or psychology." Howard Dexter had risen to his feet to stand next to Colonel Mitchell. "I listen to a couple of these fine preachers that you've demeaned. I also have read their books and bought their tapes. I like hearing what they have to say. Some of us here at First Church need to hear the Bible preached the way they do."

"But that's my point. They don't preach the Bible. They use the Bible to sell a product. They proclaim a popular gospel that requires nothing of its followers, and promises them comfort, wealth, health, and happiness."

"Well, I disagree."

Steele walked up to stand next to Doctor Walling. "Folks, I regret that we are out of time. We need to bring this to a conclusion, but I'm sure all of you will join me in thanking Doctor Walling for his presentation." The vast majority of the people in the room stood to applaud.

Colonel Mitchell and Howard Dexter approached Steele. "We want to know where you got the money to pay this man to come here."

"I paid him out of my discretionary fund." Steele answered. Howard and Colonel Mitchell grinned. Steele could not help but wonder what their satisfied looks meant. The two men walked away from him, only to gather in the corner of the parish hall with a couple of others. The four stood huddled, engaged in hushed conversation. Steele really didn't know much about the other two men. He only knew that they had not kept their dislike for him a secret. He'd often heard their critiques of his ministry through the grapevine. He never came out favorably. One of the men actually brought a book with him to church. He would read it during Steele's sermons. A sick feeling stirred in Steele's stomach. He needed to calm himself. He still had two more services to preach this morning.

The Magnolia Series

Dennis R. Maynard

Chapter 33

Steele left his house early on Monday morning. Last evening after the five o'clock Mass he'd discovered a homeless girl hiding in the shelter of the porte cochere near the parish hall entrance. She was a sixteen-year old runaway from Maggie Valley, North Carolina. She and her boyfriend had left home, looking for a new life in Florida. When they got to Falls City, her boyfriend dumped her for another girl they'd met at the First Church Soup Kitchen. She was now broke, hungry, cold, and frightened. She just wanted to go back home. Steele took her to his office and had her call her parents. He promised them that he'd make sure she was safe for the night, and he'd have her on the first bus home in the morning. Steele used the parish credit card to rent her a room at the hotel near First Church. He fed her dinner and agreed to meet her in the lobby at seven the next morning for breakfast in the hotel restaurant. Once she was on the bus, he drove to his office. He had a full day waiting on him.

His first appointment was with Henry and Dee Mudd. They wanted to plan their son's baptism. Henry was carrying the baby when they entered the office. "This is our son, Frank. You'll notice he has a tan."

"I've heard." Steele reached for the baby. "Now let me hold this guy. He needs to get to know his priest."

"What have you heard?" Dee asked.

"Dee, eventually all gossip reaches this office. I choose to ignore it."

"Do you want us to explain it to you?" Henry asked.

"Only if you want."

"I do." Henry then proceeded to tell Steele about Dee's biological father. "Do you think that we need to tell our friends here at First Church?"

"Henry, Dee, I don't think you owe anyone an explanation about anything. Your true friends don't require an explanation. Your enemies won't believe anything you have to say. This baby is your son. The details are no one's business. If I could offer any advice at all, it would be that you stop calling attention to his skin coloring. Just introduce him as your son. Besides, he's simply a photo of the future of America."

"How's that?"

"We're a bit protected here in Falls City. Once you get out of here and observe the growing population in America, you'll realize that America is changing. More and more, children are born today with a skin color that looks more like coffee with cream. Love is breaking down the racial barriers, and the children are a product." Steele chuckled. "Heck, Henry, the day may be coming when you're going to have to explain just why you're so white."

Henry looked shocked while his wife laughed. "So what are you saying?"

Steele handed the baby back to Henry. "Stop calling attention to your son's skin pigmentation. He's your son. That is all anyone is entitled to know. Now, let's plan a baptism."

Steele's next appointment was with a woman he feared was on the verge of a panic attack. Her daughter was up for homecoming queen in the local high school. "You don't understand. She has to win, Father Austin. My grandmother was homecoming queen, my mother was queen, and I was homecoming queen. My daughter just has to win. If she doesn't win, she'll be absolutely traumatized. It will simply be awful if she doesn't win. I don't know how we'd be able to live through it all if she loses. We won't be able to show our face anywhere in Falls City ever again. I simply cannot allow that to happen. I need you to pray, and to pray really hard, that she wins."

Steele attempted to explain that he didn't think the Almighty was in the business of picking winners and losers. He suggested that if her daughter won, that meant other girls would be brokenhearted because they lost. "The Lord does not want to break any teenage girl's heart." When his explanations failed to satisfy the woman, he assured her that he would keep her daughter in his prayers.

"That's not enough. You have to pray that she wins." Steele walked her to the door.

He looked forward to his next appointment. His old friends, The Reverend Josiah Williams and his wife, Rubidoux, wanted to meet with him. Josiah and Steele became friends after Josiah invited Steele to help him do the funeral for one of the sextons at First Church. Willie and Grace were the first people of color to be buried in the First Church cemetery. Since then, they'd done several other services and outreach projects together. Rubidoux was known for her colorful dress. This morning, she did not disappoint. She led her husband into Steele's office. She had to bend a bit to get the feathers on top of her hat through the door. She was dressed in bright blue from head to toe. That was also her signature; Rubidoux never mixed colors. Her outfits were always of one uniform bright color, with emphasis on the word *bright*.

"Father Steele, come here and give Rubidoux some sugar." Steele knew he had no choice but to yield to her embrace, and be marked with her lipstick on his cheek. "How are your beautiful wife and those precious children?"

Steele shook Josiah's hand and invited them to be seated. After catching up on each other's news, Josiah stated the purpose for his visit. "Rubidoux has taken on a new project that I'm hoping you can help her with."

"Oh?"

"That's right, Father Steele, now let me explain it to you. Black mommas just can't handle having queer sons."

"Rubidoux!" Josiah interrupted. "I've told you to quit using that word. They want to be called *gay*."

She waved her hand dismissively at her husband. "Josiah, these mothers don't care what you call them. They believe their sons are sinning. The Bible forbids men to lay with men as though one of them was a woman. As far as black women are concerned, that makes them *queers*.

202

Father Steele, in black society homosexuality is *taboo*. These young men know that, but they aren't willing to live on the *down low* like so many of the older men have done."

Josiah shrugged. "Rubidoux has been trying to counsel these mothers and educate them, but in some cases, the damage has already been done."

"Damage?" Steele asked.

"They are throwing their babies out onto the street. They are disowning them."

"I hate to hear that." Steele sympathized. "But I'm not sure how I can help."

"I've started a support group for these mothers. Now, this is just for black women. Not all of them come to our church, but we are growing in numbers. I'm trying to help educate the women, and in some cases, get them to reconcile with their sons."

"That sounds like an important ministry." Steele reassured her. "I still don't know what I can do."

"Here's the problem, Father Steele. Before we can intervene, some of these boys disappear. They take off for Atlanta, New York, or out to San Francisco. Then we can't find them."

"Well, those cities would be more friendly to them than Falls City. They would have a welcoming community."

"We want to try to keep them here at least long enough to get their mommas and daddies to come around."

"Have you thought about trying to get them into Noah's House? We started that home for such teens."

Josiah shook his head. "That won't work. They seldom have a vacancy. And Steele, all the residents over there are white."

"I have to confess; I wasn't aware of that."

"We think it would be better if we could have a house that could be a temporary home for our black children."

"I understand. And that's what you need from me."

"My church has some money to put into such a project, but we don't have enough. Rubidoux and I were hoping that we could do this project with you folks here at First Church."

"How many teens would you need to house at a time?" Steele asked.

"I don't think more than eight or ten."

"Have you done some cost projections on such a project?"

"I've sketched out a few things."

Steele sat quietly for a few minutes. "I think we need to put together a joint committee of number crunchers and attorneys to explore the regulations, and give us some dollar amounts. Would that be agreeable?"

"It sounds like a start, but time is of the essence."

"I understand that, but we need to have the facts before proceeding."

"Agreed." Josiah stood. "We'll leave you be for now, but you and Randi have to come for dinner soon."

"We'd like that."

Steele left his office to drive to a restaurant at the edge of town. He'd received a call from a young man needing to meet with him. Steele had presided at his wedding just a few weeks ago. He worked in one of the carpet plants and only had an hour for lunch. He needed Steele to meet him at the restaurant near his work. "How's it going?" Steele began.

The young man blushed. "Thanks for meeting me here. I have to be back at work in one hour or my boss will get very angry with me. But first, I need to apologize. Father Austin, I can't afford to pay for lunch."

Steele smiled. "That's all right. First Church will buy lunch. Now, what can I do for you?"

"Father, my wife has a spending problem."

"What makes you think so?"

"I didn't know this before we got married. She has maxed out all her credit cards. They're charging us enormous rates of interest. I just found out she's applied for another in my name."

"That does sound serious. She didn't tell you about any of this before you married?"

"No. I don't know what I'm going to do."

"I think we need to get both of you to a credit counseling service. They may be able to get some of your debt canceled or reduced. If not, I have a banker friend that might consolidate your debt at a reasonable interest rate. I think the greater issue is to discover whether or not your new wife is an addict."

"An addict?"

"There are different forms of addiction. Spending can be an addiction. She may have just been immature and foolish. I'm not going to try to diagnose her. Obviously, she has a problem, and by virtue of your marriage, her problem is now yours. How does going for credit counseling sound to you?"

"At this point, we have to do something."

"Great. Now let's relax and enjoy our lunch."

Steele always reserved Monday afternoons to begin his research for the following Sunday's sermon. As he opened the Bible on his desk, he paused. He sat back in his chair and turned to look out at the churchyard. The sun glistened off the First Church bell tower. The autumn leaves were loosening their hold on the trees and falling gently to the ground. The fading green grass provided a perfect background for the colorful carpet the leaves were painting. He turned again to look at the open Bible on his desk. Once again, he relaxed into his chair and leaned back. This time his eyes fell on the crucifix sitting on his desk. He picked it up and gently ran his fingers over the image of Jesus. He heard a little voice whisper. "You like being a parish priest."

The Magnolia Series

Dennis R. Maynard

Chapter 34

Steele had asked his secretary, Crystal, not to disturb him while he was doing the research for his next sermon. Of course, she had a short list of people that were exceptions to that rule. "Father Austin, Bishop Evans is on line two."

"Thanks." The bishop's letter complaining about Steele's salary flashed through his mind. He had never responded to it. Stone Clemons told him not to respond and that he would take care of it. Steele picked up the receiver and pushed the blinking button. "Bishop Evans, how are you?"

"Please, Steele, when it's just the two of us, call me Sean."

"Okay, Sean, how are you?"

"I'm actually doing quite well. I've lost over twenty-five pounds. I'm getting myself back in shape with exercise and diet."

"Congratulations. Finding time to exercise in these jobs is a challenge in itself. We all work such weird hours."

"Agreed." The bishop cleared his throat. "Steele, I want to begin by apologizing to you."

"For what?"

"I should have done my homework before sending you that letter about your compensation."

"Oh?"

Sean chuckled. "Yes, Stone Clemons showed me the research that the finance committee had done on the compensation packages for similar rectors. I guess I just had no idea what rectors of larger congregations were being paid."

"I want you to know I had nothing to do with any of that. I didn't ask them for a thing."

"I know that. Stone shared that with me. Actually, you probably should ask them for more."

"Why?"

"Have you seen the work they did?"

"No."

"Well, you're actually being underpaid. Compared to what other rectors of congregations with schools earn, you're in the bottom half."

"I don't have any complaints. Randi and I have all that we need."

"Have you made a decision about running in San Antonio?"

"Sean, I think I have. Randi and I have discussed it at length. I just don't think I have a passion for the job. That might change sometime in the future, but I have too many years left to make such a dramatic change right now. I also have to think about what the job would do to my life with my children."

"You're a young man."

"So are you. Sean, you're not much older than me. Are you happy being a bishop?"

"It's really not a matter of being happy. The only thing I can tell you is that I don't think it's anything like being a rector. I was already working at the diocesan level, so in some ways, it wasn't much of a change for me. On the other hand, there is no way I can really explain this job. It's not what I thought it was going to be."

"That seems to be a story I hear over and over from other bishops."

"Steele, I understood from Bishop Petersen that you are the sole administrator of an endowment designated for outreach ministry."

"That's correct."

"It's rather sizeable, I was told."

"I can only use a percentage of the income. I can't touch the principle. A percentage of the income is returned to the principle to hedge against inflation."

"Bishop Petersen said that you used some of the income in partnership with the diocese on a project."

"That's true. We started a shelter for homeless gay teens."

"I have a project in mind, but no money to fund it. I think if it's successful, it could also save some of our dying congregations. In addition, it would be a wonderful outreach to our growing Hispanic population in Georgia."

"You have my attention and interest."

"Good. Do you know anything about the mission in Mount Stater?"

"Maybe I should know more, but I do know that it's one of the oldest congregations in the diocese. I know that at one time they were a thriving parish, but as the town has declined, so has the church."

"That's pretty accurate. How do you even know that much?"

"The priest you have there approached me at clergy conference. He told me the congregation's story. He also wanted to see if I had the need for another associate."

"Yeah, he'd really like to get out of there. I may need to move him anyway if I can get funding for an idea I have."

"Okay."

"As I said, there's a growing Hispanic community down there. These are not the migrants. These are folks that have settled there and are making Mount Stater their home. The Roman Catholic Bishop shut down his church. I think if I could put a Spanish-speaking vicar in there, we could start a Hispanic service and build up that congregation."

"And you'd like me to help you fund it?"

"That's the reason for my call."

"I think you're right. It could be a wonderful opportunity. The only hitch is that it doesn't actually meet the guidelines for the fund that the donor gave me."

"That's disappointing."

"Could First Church use some of the funds in their outreach budget?"

"I can always present it to that committee, but Sean, like the diocese, they have more need than money. The funds also tend to go to the organizations that the committee members have a history of supporting."

"Well, I thought I'd at least ask."

"Sean, don't give up. Let me see if I can't find a way to make an exception, or maybe even expand the guidelines of the trust."

"You'd do that?"

"I will. I'll call you back in a couple of days and let you know if I've figured out a way to fund it."

"I really appreciate that."

"I'm not making any promises, and I don't want to give you any false hope, but I'll do my best.

"God bless you, Steele. Next time I'm in Falls City, let's have lunch."

"A healthy one," Steele chuckled.

"Agreed."

The Magnolia Series

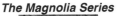

Dennis R. Maynard

Chapter 35

Steele had made only a couple of sermon preparation notes when Crystal buzzed him again on the intercom. "Father Austin, I have Mrs. Gordon Smythe standing by in the waiting room. She insists on seeing you. Father Austin, she's crying."

Steele walked down the hall to the waiting room. Mrs. Smythe's face was wet from the tears she'd been shedding. "Mary Alice, what on earth is wrong? Please, come into my office."

"No, Misturh Austin, I don't want to go to your office. I am so mad and upset I could just bite nails."

"I'm sorry. What can I do to help?"

"I want you to walk with me over to the Church to see what that woman has done to our beautiful sanctuary."

"What woman?"

"Almeda!" She spit the name from her lips. She then stood and started walking toward the waiting room door. "Are you coming?"

Steele nodded. "Yes, I'm anxious to see what has you so upset."

Once they were in the nave, it was evident that Almeda had proceeded with the temporary setup they'd discussed. "Did you know anything about this?" Mrs. Smythe barked at Steele.

"I've discussed Almeda's suggestions with the executive committee and the church staff, but I had no idea that she was going to put the temporary arrangement up so soon."

"So you didn't okay this?"

"Yes and no. I agreed that it would be a good idea to do a trial run with the congregation. But quite honestly, I thought we were going to wait until after the historical architect had done some drawings. We could distribute the drawings to the congregation to consider before actually rearranging the church."

"That's just like her!" Mary Alice was furious. "She doesn't think she has to get anyone's permission or agreement for anything. If she wants to do something, she just goes ahead and does it. The rest of us don't matter."

"Okay, let's sit down here on the first pew and have a look at the situation."

"I don't want to sit down. I want you to call the sextons and have them put everything back where it belongs."

"Mary Alice, please. Let's take a few minutes to survey the situation."

"As a courtesy to you, Misturh Austin, I'll sit for a few minutes, but I can tell you right now, I don't like it. I can also assure you that the majority of this congregation won't like it."

"Let's just try to consider what she's thinking." Mary Alice sat down next to him. "Okay, let's look at it from her viewpoint and the viewpoint of other disabled, elderly, and wheelchair bound members. Climbing those three stairs and crossing past the choir to the altar rail is quite a challenge for them. In addition, they have to come back down the three stairs on either side. Those in wheelchairs can't even receive at the altar. They have to have communion brought to them in the back of the nave."

"I've not heard anyone else complain about our current arrangement. It's been this way for over two hundred years."

"I understand that. And just because someone hasn't complained doesn't justify not changing. I'd be curious to know how many disabled and elderly have simply quit coming to church because of those stairs."

"Like I said, no one that I know has issued a complaint."

"Let me ask you, what harm has been done by setting up a communion rail here on the nave floor? The church is just as pretty as ever. No walls have been moved."

"Father Austin, I am not the person that should be giving you a lesson in church architecture, but if I must, I will. This is a cruciform church. The altar rail belongs on the other side of the choir near the altar itself."

"Mary Alice, I understand that. Would it surprise you to know that many of the great cathedrals in Europe and here in America have done exactly what Almeda is proposing?"

"Well, we're not a cathedral."

"No, we're not. But I can name several parish churches every bit as old as this one that have done this very same thing. They didn't do it to destroy their architectural integrity. They did it to accommodate their disabled and elderly members. They considered it the charitable thing to do."

"Now you are sounding just like her. I don't know why you can't just leave things the way they've been all these years."

"Believe me, Mary Alice, I'm as opposed as the next person to change for the sake of change. I don't like experimentation just to rile folks up. But in this case, I have to agree with Almeda. I believe this is the loving thing to do in order to better serve all who want to worship here."

"Well, you'd better think again. This idea has already been tried on some of the more important members of our church, and they don't like it. Misturh Austin, for your own sake, you'd better have the church put back together by next Sunday."

"I'll consider your counsel, but since Almeda has already set things in motion, I think I'll let it stand for a few weeks. There's nothing like a visual to help people better comprehend the idea."

"You're playing with fire. I believe you're already on thin ice after you brought that liberal professor here to speak last Sunday. He really upset a lot of people that matter in this parish."

"Did you hear his talk?"

"I did."

"What part of it was liberal? I don't remember him even mentioning politics or anything about a social issue."

"He defamed some of the most inspirational preachers we have today. I watch a couple of them on television. I like listening to them. I like what they have to say. One of them in particular has really helped me. I also buy his books."

"I'm not opposed to folks finding spiritual nourishment in other places. I believe what Doctor Walling had to say was factual and really non-threatening. It was a sociological analysis and nothing more. I thought it was quite insightful."

"There was nothing insightful about it!" Mary Alice rebuked Steele. "It was an attack on some of the finest preachers this nation has ever produced. Those men of God did not deserve to be slandered."

"Mary Alice, please, I don't believe that was Doctor Walling's intent. He was simply revealing the methodology they utilize. It's part of what makes them and their churches so successful. Honestly, I don't believe any harm was done. Personally, I found his presentation very informative."

"Well, I was at a little gathering Sunday night. I can tell you that he really upset some folks in this congregation. I think you need to know they're not the ones you want to upset."

"Thanks for the warning."

"So you're not going to move the furniture back?"

"No. Let's just leave it up at least through Christmas. That will be a good trial run. We always have to rearrange things and set up folding chairs for the Christmas services anyway. With the rail down here it might actually expedite the length of time it takes to distribute communion. That's always an issue with so many folks attending Mass."

Mary Alice stood and looked down at Steele over the top of her glasses. She wagged her finger at him. "You're going to ruin Christmas for a lot of us. I don't know how we're even going to decorate the church with it set up this way. Christmas is just not going to be very merry or jolly. I don't envy you the response you're going to get when our important members see what you've done to their church." Mary Alice started to leave and then she turned around and shouted. "If I were you, I'd be praying that this disaster is not the last thing you ever get to try here at First Church." She left through the sacristy door, slamming it loudly behind her.

The Magnolia Series

Dennis R. Maynard

Chapter 36

"This is the Lafitte residence." Steele recognized the oriental accent.

"Shing, this is Father Austin."

"Oh, Father Austin, long time since Shing hear your voice. So nice to hear you call. You want speak Mistuh Lafitte or Mistuh Schneider?"

"Mister Lafitte, please."

"One minute. I take him the receiver."

"Steele, this is a pleasant surprise."

"Well, I promised I'd stay in touch."

"I'm glad you are. Are you calling from a secure phone?"

"I'm calling from a pay phone."

"Good. Tell me, how's Almeda?"

"She's bounced back. She has to walk with a cane, but other than that, you'd never know she'd had a stroke. In fact, some of her detractors believe she doesn't even need the cane. They think she's only using it as an attention getter."

"Either way, that's good news."

"How's Eric?"

"Eric is Eric. His primary task is to keep looking good for me. Needless to say, I am well pleased. What is the latest news in Falls City?"

"Oh gosh, Earle, I don't know where to begin. The scandals have dominated the front pages the last few weeks."

"Anyone I would know?"

"Well, did you hear that Virginia Mudd is in prison for trying to hire a hit man to kill her lover's wife?"

"She was always such a prissy little thing. Quite a looker, if I remember."

"Yeah, she really broke her husband's heart. Her daughters want nothing to do with her. Henry has remarried. His wife is a real fine lady. They have a new baby."

"Wasn't he quite a pain in the butt when you first arrived?"

"Yes, he was. But now, he's actually one of my best friends and supporters."

"Well, I'm thankful he finally came around. I'm also glad things have worked out for him."

"Ned Boone was killed in a fiery car crash. Did you hear about that?"

"I remember reading that in the state newspaper. I never liked that man. He was one of the most homophobic people at First Church. No, homophobic is not the right word. He was a hater."

"I think you've got that right. He was leading the attacks on me. Things were getting pretty tough for me here. He finally left and went over to Saint Andrew's Presbyterian before he was killed. But then *Karma* caught up with him."

"How's that?"

"It seems they'd made him into some kind of saint over there. He helped them call what has turned out to be a pastor that is even more homophobic than Ned was. Anyway, after he died, they named the chapel in his honor. Then it came out that he was responsible for having child pornography planted on the previous pastor's computer in order to get rid of him. They've had to reverse their decision to name the chapel in his honor."

Earle chuckled, "I'm just happy to hear that his true colors were discovered."

"Here's the funniest part of his legacy. He left instructions to have a statue of himself erected in the little park over by his house. Stone Clemons and Chief Sparks take turns going by and sprinkling birdseed at the foot of the statue to insure a constant flow of bird poop on it."

Earle erupted in laughter. "Wait. Isn't that a city park? How could he get a statue erected in a city park?"

"Stone told me that it's a real screwy deal. Evidently he gave it to the city on permanent loan. One of the conditions was that it be named in his honor and the statue be erected in it. The crazy part is that the city has to maintain it."

"What the devil is permanent loan?"

"I have no idea. Stone has his law firm looking into it."

"Anything else?"

"Oh, the usual. The new Presbyterian pastor that Ned is responsible for calling is in trouble. His wife was arrested for growing marijuana. He has been forbidden to go near her or his children. They're accusing him of abusing them. Oh, and the part you'd find most interesting. Almeda has taken them all in."

"Are you serious?"

"As a heart attack."

"Will wonders never cease?" Earle chuckled. "Now, what's happening with you?"

"I think I've settled in for the long run. The Diocese of San Antonio contacted me about pursuing their purple shirt, but I'm not going to do it. I just don't have the heart for it."

"Steele, it's your decision. You're a good parish priest. Personally, I think we've lost too many good priests to the cope and mitre society. They would have been better off if they'd remained in the parish."

"I think I might be one of them. Hey, before I forget, I've got to tell you about two of your old adversaries."

"Who?"

"Tom Barnhardt and Gary Hendricks."

"I hated those guys. You could insert a piece of coal up either one of their butts and get a diamond back in minutes. They tried to screw up every business deal I put together."

"Well, it seems they got in partnership with Ned Boone. They went after me in an effort to separate the school from the parish. Their tactic was to discredit me. They thought that was the best way to gain the school's independence."

"Why don't you just dump the school?"

"It's not my decision. It will probably happen, but not until we've had a few more funerals here at First Church."

"I know exactly who you mean. Well, what happened to Lex Luther and the Joker?"

"Who? Oh, Tom and Gary. Well, Tom was disbarred, but that hasn't slowed his wheeling and dealing. He's still making money hand over fist."

"He's not making anything. He's stealing it from any unsuspecting victim he can discover. What about Gary?"

"That's the most interesting. Did I mention both of them were implicated in Ned's scheme to plant child porn on the bishop's computer?"

"No. You didn't tell me about the bishop."

"It doesn't matter because Gary has disappeared."

"What do you mean disappeared?"

"Exactly that. He sold his house, his cars, and his business. He sold everything. He closed out all his financial accounts and has disappeared from the face of the earth."

"Wow! I never thought Gary Hendricks would ever do anything like that. I remember him as one of the most uptight men in Falls City. He was such a perfectionist. I used to ask him where he bought his suits. Man, that guy was always in control. I figured his immaculate dress mirrored an equally perfect life." Earle paused to clear his throat. "Steele, you have more drama going on in Falls City than we do here in San Francisco."

"I can truthfully say there's never been a dull moment."

"You know, Steele, I've been feeling guilty about something."

"Oh, what?"

"I just wonder if things would have gone smoother for you there if I hadn't set up that trust fund for you to administer. It seems like everything you've done with it has been controversial. You're the one the uptight in that town went after."

"Everything we've done has met a real need and healed a real hurt for some portion of this community."

"I know, but maybe if you took a step back, things would go easier for you. If you would just go along with them, hell, they might even name a parish hall in your honor after you leave."

"Earle, you know that's not in my DNA. I would have found a way to set up every ministry we've undertaken, even if there were no trust fund. I don't regret a single one of them, and we're not finished yet. There are other hurting people in this town we can help."

"I figured you'd say something like that, but you know, that will mean there will be no parish hall. You won't even get a brass plaque in your honor when you leave."

"I'll survive. Will Rogers said that *a lot of good can be done by the man that doesn't care who gets the credit.* I guess I'll just be satisfied with the good that is being done."

"Tell me about Randi and your children. You still have just the two?"

"Yes. Randi, Travis, and Amanda are all in great shape. They are the center of my life."

"Steele, you're going to have to excuse me. I have an appointment. It's over at the cathedral."

"Before I let you go, I need to ask you about a project."

"Okay."

"The bishop called. He'd like for me to use some of the trust money income to fund an experimental Hispanic Ministry in one of the mission congregations. He thinks that if we're successful in that congregation, they could be a model for others."

"That's not exactly what I had in mind when I set up that trust."

"I know. That's why I'm asking."

"Do you want to do it?"

"I'd like to give it a try."

"I hear rumors that your bishop is gay."

Steele chuckled. "It's the strangest thing I've ever seen in my life. Here we are in one of the most conservative dioceses in the nation. Every person in it whispers about the bishop being gay, but no one will acknowledge it publicly. Basically, I think every one likes the guy. It's all so surreal."

"There's no explaining, is there?"

"I can't."

"Steele, I trust you. If you think this is something you'd like to try, I'll have my lawyer in Atlanta amend the trust guidelines to provide for it. But let's re-evaluate after three years. Okay?"

"Sounds good to me."

"Now, my friend, I'm late and I really have to go. Come see me again."

"You can count on it. God bless."

The Magnolia Series

Dennis R. Maynard

Chapter 37

Almeda couldn't contain her excitement. She led Rose MacClaren into a small vacant building just off Main Street. It was empty except for a steel desk and a couple of metal folding chairs. "Well, this is it."

"This is what?" Rose was confused.

"This is where I want you to start your business."

"Almeda, I don't understand."

"Rose, you are an excellent seamstress. I want to help you go into business for yourself. You can sell the clothes that you make. I think there's a real market for your children's clothes with various smocked designs on them. Smocking is almost a lost art. You can also do alterations and repairs."

"Do you think that I can earn enough to support my children?"

"Not in the first few weeks. Maybe you won't earn enough in the first year, but I just know you'll be a success."

"How much is the rent on this space?"

"Until you get going, there will be no rent. I own this building. Once your business is a success, we'll discuss rent."

"This is just too much. I don't know if I'll ever be able to repay you."

"Nonsense. I don't expect you to repay me anything."

"But what about my trial?"

"I have wonderful news. I talked to Stone Clemons earlier this morning. He's talked to the prosecutor. They'll agree to a parole as long as you have a source of income and a place to live."

Rose began to cry. "That's such a relief."

"In the greater scheme of things, you are a small fry in their war on drugs. Stone argued that with all that has come out about your husband's abuse, it would be best if you're not separated from your children."

"I'm so relieved."

"We just have to demonstrate that you are gainfully employed and that you have a place to live."

"My children and I can't continue to impose on your hospitality for another year."

"That's the next thing I want to show you. Horace and I want you and your children to live in one of our rentals."

"You are being too kind."

"No, Rose, I believe in you. We've become very fond of you and your children."

"Horace has been a tremendous help with the boys. He has really turned things around for John Calvin. You know that he has stopped wetting his bed?"

Almeda nodded. "That's what my housekeeper told me."

"I owe all that to Horace."

"Horace says that he believes both of them have some real athletic potential. They have really taken to the batting cage at the park. He also enjoys coaching their soccer games."

"And you've done so much to help my daughter learn proper etiquette."

"Well, I never had a daughter of my own. It has been a joy to have the opportunity to teach her all the virtues of being a *Southern Lady*. Now, let me drive you over to the house. Mind you, it might be a bit crowded. The boys will have to share a bedroom."

"They've done that before. The main thing is that we're together."

"If it's acceptable, we'd like for you to stay with us through the Christmas holidays. It's been so long since I've had any children in the house for Christmas. Horace has already gone shopping for the boys. I promise you that your children will have a wonderful Christmas."

"That sounds really nice."

"After we see your house, I want us to go shopping for your daughter. Horace freely admitted it had been so long since he'd shopped for his own daughter, he needs us to do that."

"You both are being so considerate. I don't know if I'll have any money to shop for my kids or for the two of you. Melvin only allowed one present per child. He gave me a very small budget. He and I never exchanged gifts."

"We're going to give your children the best Christmas ever. As for us, Rose, you and your children are our gifts."

"God bless you, Almeda. I am just overwhelmed by your generosity. I've never known anything like it." Rose walked around inspecting what would be her new shop. "I know I'm probably not supposed to ask, but did Mister Clemons have any news about Melvin?"

"You don't need to worry about him. The restraining order is still in effect. Stone didn't know for sure, but he'd talked to one of the elders at the Church. He said they are going to allow Melvin to resign."

"Oh, that will be hard for him."

"Well, it seems there's a little more to it than that."

"Like what?"

Almeda drew in a deep breath. "I guess you're going to hear about it sooner or later. It seems that one of our former members has issued a complaint with the session at Saint Andrew's against your husband. He says that Melvin is breaking up his marriage. He contends that his wife and Melvin are having an affair."

Rose collapsed into one of the folding chairs sitting in front of the desk. "He's what?"

Almeda sat down in the chair next to her and took her hand. "I wouldn't repeat any of this had I not heard it directly from Stone Clemons' mouth."

Rose nodded. "It's just such a shock. We haven't even been separated two months yet. What do you know about the woman?"

"She was one of those *holier than thou* types. It's a bit surprising because she used to boast about the Christian marriage that she and her husband had. She was so pious.

223

I never trusted her. She was just vicious in her criticism of Father Austin. I couldn't stand her. It sure didn't take her long to toss her Christian husband aside in order to seduce yours."

"I guess you never really know a person."

"Did Mister Clemons tell you if Melvin's still living in the manse?"

Almeda squeezed her hand. "Oh, *sugah*, I really wish you hadn't asked that."

Rose turned to look into Almeda's eyes. "Tell me everything."

"It seems that Melvin and the man's wife have left town. No one knows for sure just where they've gone."

Rose shrugged. "I feel sorry for the husband, but I think it's better that Melvin doesn't stay in Falls City."

"I agree. Are you going to tell your children?"

"I've got to, but I think I'll wait until after Christmas. You know, they don't ask about him. They resisted seeing him even though there was an officer present at his visitations. I'll tell them eventually, but not right now."

"Are you all right, Rose?"

Rose smiled. "Yes, yes I am. Maybe for the first time in a long time, I can see a happy future for me and my children."

Almeda patted her hand. "Then let's go see your new house."

The Magnolia Series

Dennis R. Maynard

Chapter 38

"What put such a big smile on your face?" Canon Jim Vernon walked into Bishop Sean Evans' office. He shut the door behind him.

Sean was in the process of hanging up the telephone receiver on his desk. "That was the rector of First Church down in Falls City."

"Have you settled things with him?"

"Huh?"

"Has he agreed to cut his salary and add the difference to support the diocesan program?"

"Oh, that. We were both wrong on that note. Stone Clemons brought me the research they'd done on the salaries other rectors are being paid. Their finance committee discovered that in comparison to similar positions, Austin was actually being underpaid. They adjusted his compensation, but he's still in the bottom half."

"Gee, I think I'd better become a rector."

"Would you really want to put up with all the crap he's been through? I can't think of any rector I'd change jobs with. I know that neither one of us has ever been a rector, but I've seen enough to know better. I think I'll keep my current position."

"You may be right. At least we get to move around on Sundays. We just hear the complaints about the rectors. We're never in one place long enough for them to start complaining about us."

"That's one of the fringe benefits of this job. I'm sure that some of the clergy, if not all of them, bitch about me from time to time, but they really aren't in a position to do any more than just that."

"As we've already seen multiple times, they don't have the same job security. Whenever three or more antagonists unite, their jobs and ministries are in jeopardy."

"You still haven't told me what made you smile."

"You're going to like this. Steele Austin is going to use some of the income from that trust he administers to fund a pilot program for me."

"Oh?"

"I asked him if he could help me do something down in Mount Stater."

"I thought you were thinking about closing that place."

"I was. I don't see how much longer we can prop it up. But Jim, even if we closed it and put the property up for sale, there wouldn't be any buyers. That town is dying. Who's going to buy a church in a town that's on its last leg? The Bishop closed down the Roman Catholic parish. I drove by it while I was down there, and it's all boarded up with a rusty *For Sale* sign sitting out front."

"So, what's the project?"

"Well, if it works, it just may save that church. I'm not so sure but that we're onto something that just may help save that town."

"What is it?"

"On my last visitation, I learned from the vicar that there is quite an influx of Latinos moving in. As you know, Hispanics tend to be Roman Catholics. There's no Roman Catholic parish. They'll feel right at home in The Episcopal Church. In fact, they may like us better."

"What's the project?"

"I want to put a Spanish speaking vicar in that congregation."

"Sounds good. Do you know one?"

"That's where you come in. I want you to find a new assignment for the current vicar. At the same time, I want you to do a nationwide search for a Spanish speaking priest that would be willing to accept that ministry."

"That's a really good idea. You know, it may take some time. I don't think we have any clergy in this diocese that speak Spanish."

"I've checked. We don't."

"If I can find the right priest for you, we may just be onto something that could help some of our other struggling congregations."

"I agree. I think this could end up being a model to follow in other places."

"Sean, why have you not told me about this until now?"

Bishop Evans shook his head. He then stood. "Let's sit over here. We need to talk." Sean led Jim to the two wingback chairs he'd placed next to the large window in his office. They were in the same place that Bishop Peterson had placed similar chairs. The window had a view of the cathedral gardens. When they were seated, he said softly, "Jim, the lines of communication between us have really broken down. Even here in the office, you've resorted to leaving me *Post-it Notes*. We don't eat our meals together at home. We don't sleep together. We haven't made love in months. I fear it has taken a toll on my feelings for you."

"But Sean, Honey, I was just trying to help you. I wanted you to get back in shape. And it's working. Baby, you look great. I'm ready to move back into the bedroom. I want us to make love again. In fact, the door is locked. I'd like to make love to you right here and now. You really look good."

"Jim, that's the problem. I no longer have those feelings for you."

"I don't understand."

"Put yourself in my shoes, Jim. How would you feel about me if I'd given you the silent treatment for the past several months? How would you feel if I'd refused to sleep with you because I thought you were too fat? How would you feel if I'd avoided your very presence except when I wanted something from you?"

"Honey, I know that I did those things, but I just wanted you to take better care of yourself."

"I've thought about that. I understand that was your motive, but did you not consider what it would do to my feelings for you? While God's love is infinite, the love between two people can be killed."

"That wasn't what I wanted."

"It may not have been, but that's what's happened."

"Are you telling me you don't love me anymore?"

"I'm telling you that I no longer feel the same way about you."

"But I love you."

"Do you, Jim? Or do you only love me when I look the way you want me to look? Do you only love me when I act the way you want me to act? Jim, that's not love. I understand that I got fat. I was more disgusted with myself than you could ever be. But what if I'd lost a leg or an arm? Would you have loved me if I had lost my eyesight, or what if I'd gotten an ugly facial scar in an accident? No, Jim, you put conditions on your love for me. You ceased communicating with me when I needed you the most."

"I was only..."

Sean held up his hand. "There's no need to explain again. I understand that's what you thought you were doing. I'm just telling you that what you did hurt me. Your actions have caused me to question your love for me."

"But we're married, or at least we married each other in God's eyes."

Sean sat quietly looking out the window. He silently watched the gardener trim the shrubs in the cathedral garden. "Jim, I think it would be best if you found a new place to live."

"Honey, please. No! We can work this out. I want to be with you. I want to be married to you." Tears welled up in Jim's eyes and ran down his cheeks as he pleaded. "Christmas is coming. We've spent Christmas together every year for as long as I've known you. Even when we lived in separate states, we were able to be together on Christmas. Please, Sean, I don't want to celebrate Christmas without you."

"Jim, don't you get it? You hurt me. Yes, I got lonely for you, but then something else happened. I quit missing you. I'm not lonely anymore. I've learned how to sleep quite well by myself. I've allowed myself to be attracted to other men. I like the way they look at me. Frankly, Jim, I don't miss you anymore. I think I'd prefer to live by myself over having you sleep down the hall."

"I did this. It's my fault. Can you forgive me?"

"I already have. I just don't want to live with you."

"Could we go to counseling? I'm sure we could find a therapist up in Atlanta."

"I'll think about it, but for now, let's take a break from each other."

"What about my job?"

"Your job is still your job. As long as you do it, you don't have anything to worry about. I'm leaving tomorrow for a national church board meeting in Philadelphia. I'll be gone the rest of the week. I'd like to have you out of my house when I return." Sean stood to return to his desk.

"Sean, Honey, may I kiss you?"

Sean turned on his heels. He put his hands on his hips. "No! Jim, try to understand this. I don't feel the same way about you that I did. I'm going to try to explain it to you one more time in the simplest way. I don't want to kiss you. I don't want to be affectionate with you. I don't want to be married to someone that tries to manipulate me into looking a certain way by giving me the silent treatment and withholding affection. Now, you need to excuse me. I need to go home and pack. I'm going to spend the night at the airport hotel."

The Magnolia Series

Dennis R. Maynard

Chapter 39

Steele had heard through the grapevine that Howard Dexter and Colonel Mitchell were boasting to their friends about some new evidence that would discredit him. They were going to bring it to the December vestry meeting. Steele told Chief Sparks and Stone Clemons what he'd heard. None of them were surprised to see Tom Barnhardt at the meeting. The business administrator had told him that Colonel Mitchell had also requested copies of Steele's discretionary fund and the parish credit card expenditures. After Steele asked Doctor Drummond to open the meeting with a prayer, Colonel Mitchell made the motion that the items on the agenda be dispensed with. "I have a matter of critical importance I need to bring to the vestry."

Stone grinned. "Oh, we've been sitting here with bated breath."

Steele nodded. "Proceed."

Colonel Mitchell then distributed the spreadsheet that Tom Barnhardt's paralegal had prepared. True to his promise, it was laid out like a piece of evidence for a jury trial. "I have here an analysis of the expenditures the rector has made with the Church's money. I want to draw your attention to the multiple times he has used the church credit card to buy himself lunch. Gentlemen, he's romancing his wife over lunch on Sundays and various other days, and then letting us pay the bill. I find this unacceptable."

"Not this again!" One of the young vestry members started shaking his head. He could not hide his exasperation with what had become an all too familiar line of attack on the rector. Several others nodded their heads in agreement. He continued, "This is verging on the ridiculous."

"Have you asked Father Austin about these charges?" Chief Sparks asked.

"I don't need to. I can draw my own conclusions," Colonel Mitchell answered caustically.

"Very well then, I'll ask him."

Steele smiled. "Colonel, these charges are all justified expenses. Very often I meet with a member of the parish for a luncheon meeting. Sometimes I have to meet them near their place of work or business. There are times when they want to meet with me and the reason is so delicate, they don't want to come to my office."

"Why are their names not recorded on the receipt?"

"For that very reason. The meetings are confidential."

"So we have to take your word for that. I choose not to."

"That's your choice. As for most of the Sunday charges, Deacon Smith and I started a new ministry. We each take one of our lonely elderly out for lunch and conversation after church on Sunday. They really appreciate it. We think it's a good thing to do. I received some donations from parish members to specifically fund those lunches. If you'd only asked me, rather than trying to ambush me at this meeting, I could have explained it."

"No one has taken my mother out to lunch!" Howard Dexter shot the words at Steele.

Stone grinned. "Howard, doesn't your mother have a live-in cook and driver? If memory serves me correctly, she meets you and your children for the buffet at the country club most every Sunday."

"Well, if the Church is going to start picking up the meal tab for the senior citizens, my mother should be included."

Steele nodded. "I'll make a note of that, but our focus has been on the elderly that have no one to visit them."

Colonel Mitchell shook his head at Howard. "What about this charge for a hotel bill a few weeks ago?"

"Again, had you asked, I could've explained. I found a runaway girl hiding in the porte cochere after the Wednesday night program. She was cold, hungry, and scared. I took her to my office and had her call her parents. I put her up in the hotel down the street, and bought her dinner and breakfast. I then put her on a bus home. How would you have had me handle that situation?"

"Well, I wouldn't have used the church's money. I'd have taken her to the rescue mission and had her parents come get her."

"I suppose that would have been one option. I just didn't think the rescue mission was a good place to put a teenage girl for the night. I chose to get her home another way."

"That's the problem, Misturh Austin. You always have to do it your way. You used the church's money to bring that communist to teach our adult forum."

"What communist?"

"That professor from Auburn that slandered so many of our wonderful television preachers. You could learn a thing or two from those men."

"I took his fee out of my discretionary fund because there wasn't enough in the Christian Education Budget to cover it. He was in Falls City to speak to another group. I wanted to take advantage of his presence. I don't believe he's a communist."

"I just want this vestry to look at the kind of people the rector is giving our money to." Howard Dexter was red in the face. "He's using church funds to increase his popularity by taking members out to lunches. Then he's putting runaways up in hotels. Most likely she was a prostitute hooked on drugs. She probably got off the bus at the first stop. I'd stake my life that she cashed in her ticket to buy heroin. And now he freely admits to paying a liberal communist to come here and attack some wonderful preachers. Those preachers have a larger following than you'll ever have, Misturh Austin. It was petty jealousy that caused you to do that. That's all it is. It's petty jealousy, plain and simple."

"And how do we know that you didn't rent that hotel room for you and that prostitute to have sex?" Tom Barnhardt shouted.

Steele started to respond when he felt Stone's foot nudge him under the table. "Colonel, Howard..." He looked over at Tom Barnhardt. "And you too, Tom, unless you boys have something better than a spread sheet filled with innuendo and false accusations, I make a motion that this meeting be adjourned."

"Second." Chief Sparks answered.

"You're going to accept his explanation for these expenditures?" Colonel Mitchell was exasperated.

Stone's voice was firm. "I am. We could sit here the rest of the evening. I have every confidence that the rector can justify each one of these expenditures in your exhibit. But then if we did that, it would defeat your purpose, wouldn't it?"

"What I don't understand about you boys is this..." Chief Sparks was struggling to contain his anger. "What part of the word *discretion* don't you understand? This nonsense has gotten to be an annual affair with you guys. I, for one, have gotten sick and tired of your innuendos and accusations around the funds the rector administers. This crap is going to stop, and it's going to stop tonight. The entire reason for a discretionary fund is so that members of the clergy can exercise ministries that are not a part of the budget, without running to the vestry for approval. The word discretion means it's the clergy's decision and theirs alone. As far as I'm concerned, they can take it out here in the churchyard and set fire to it. It is totally up to the clergy to do with as they see fit. The three of you are going to stop trying to discredit this man's character and ministry, and you're going to stop now. Have I made myself clear?"

Tom Barnhardt shouted. "The people that matter in this parish believe his time has come. He needs to resign."

Stone's jaw muscles flexed as he attempted to control his anger. "And let me tell you something. I believe that the overwhelming majority of this congregation supports this man and his ministry as our rector. Those are the people that matter. I just complimented the rector not long ago on his ability to raise funds for the specialized ministries in this parish. That's something we should all celebrate, not complain about." Stone then turned his gaze to Howard Dexter. "As for you, Howard, I think it's pretty damn hypocritical of you to think it's okay to use church funds to take your well-heeled mother out to lunch, but then complain about the rector and the deacon doing the same for folks that don't have the means." Stone stood. "Father Rector, I've made a motion."

Steele called the question. It passed with only Howard and Colonel Mitchell voting against it. Tom Barnhardt was the first person to leave the conference room. Chief Sparks and Stone Clemons walked Steele back to his office. Stone offered, "Boys, let's go over to the club and have a nightcap. I'll buy."

"That sounds good." Steele agreed.

Chief Sparks grinned. "First, I need to relieve myself. I think the perfect place to do it is out there in the cemetery on Dexter's and Mitchell's future resting places."

Stone agreed. "Chief, you take Dexter's; I'll take Mitchell's. Let's both go over and water down Barnhardt's."

Chief Sparks nodded. "Steele, we'll meet you at the club."

The Magnolia Series

Dennis R. Maynard

Chapter 40

Steele met the Chief and Stone Clemons at The Magnolia Club bar. The two of them were well into their first drink. Matthew Mercator slid into the vacant chair at their table. "I hear you boys had another contentious meeting over at the church tonight."

"How the hell did you hear that so fast?" Stone asked. "We just adjourned less than an hour ago."

"I just finished a hamburger over at Sam's when two of Steele's biggest cheerleaders sat down in the booth behind me. I don't think they took any notice of me. They immediately began to rehearse the vestry meeting."

"Let me guess." Chief Sparks interjected. "It was Colonel Mitchell and Howard Dexter."

Matthew nodded.

"Did Tom Barnhardt show up?" Stone asked.

"If he did, it was after I left. I sat there long enough to know I didn't want to hear any more."

"What did you hear?" Stone inquired.

"That they're out to get rid of my rector. I might as well tell you that you fellows didn't come out very well either."

"I think we were able to intercept all their attacks tonight." Stone acknowledged. "But I'm sure we've not heard the last from them."

"Well, I'm on my way home. I just came in for a quick drink. But I want to make something very clear before I go," Matthew stated emphatically.

"What's that?" Stone asked.

"If those two sorry excuses for Christians think they're going to run roughshod over my rector, they're going to have to go through me first." Matthew stood to leave. "And that goes for all the troops they can muster as well."

"I appreciate your support, Matthew." Steele extended his hand to shake. "You're a good friend."

"I mean it, Father Austin. If you ever need any help setting that gang of thugs straight, you call on me."

"I understand."

After Matthew had walked away, Chief Sparks asked, "What do you know about that guy?"

"He's one of our most faithful members. He's also one of my best layreaders. He practices the scriptures in the church when he's assigned to read. In fact, he's one of the few that I can depend on not to butcher the Hebrew and Greek words. He actually takes the time to look up the correct pronunciations."

"It's nice to have that kind of support." Stone acknowledged. "But Steele, you know what really worries me?"

"No, what?"

"Chief Sparks and I are getting up in years. We may not always be here to take those boys on for you. We've already seen that they don't play by the rules. Their manipulations can go far beyond mean. They can be downright vicious."

"I know that. For now, I have the two of you. As long as you guys are alive and well, I feel safe."

"I wouldn't get carried away with some false illusion of security," the Chief cautioned. "I've seen those boys in action. They don't just restrict their antics to First Church. Remember, Stone, how they went after the museum director."

"I do." Stone nodded. "And the manager at the country club. He was one of the best we'd ever had there, but they absolutely destroyed him with innuendo and outright lies. No club in the country will ever employ him after they finished with him."

Steele cautioned, "I try to understand people like them. I think they are really compensating for their feelings of insecurity and inferiority. We all know that Colonel Mitchell is in and out of a recovery program for his alcoholism. He's not kept that a secret. I've tried to learn all that I can about the *dry drunk* behavior of non-recovering alcoholics. I feel like if I understood him better, then I could know best how to respond."

"Father," Stone interrupted. "You can spend the rest of your life trying to understand those boys. You might even be able to explain them. You're just forgetting one simple fact."

"What's that?"

"Padre, you're going to have to put on your suit of armor and just accept this one undeniable truth."

"You have my attention."

"Father Austin, some people are just *sons of bitches*."

Chief Sparks choked on his drink. He was caught between a coughing spasm and laughter. When he recovered, he pointed at Steele. "I've watched those fellows and others just like them all my life. A tiger can't rearrange its stripes, or in the case of those boys, a jackass can't shorten its ears. They are going to continue to come after you until they ultimately wear you down. I don't want to throw water on your parade, but I've seen them in action too many times. They'll just keep nibbling at you until you don't have any energy left to fight them. I hate it, but it's a fact. Stone and I have committed to try to stop them, but as he said, we may not always be around."

"Well then, we've just got to do whatever it takes to keep the two of you alive and well."

Stone looked over at Steele, "Father, you know that we love you. You know that I love you. I am so grateful to you for what you've done at First Church. Our membership, attendance, and finances are the best they've ever been. The outreach ministries in the community will be here long after you've left. And I also know that damn school would have closed down if it hadn't been for the sacrifices you made and the work you did for it. But that's precisely the problem. Those boys are jealous of you and what you've accomplished." Stone paused and took a sip of his drink. He stared at Steele with love and compassion. "Steele, as long as I'm alive, those boys will not get by with a thing. But you have to understand. They are like little kids throwing cow patties at the side of a barn. The game is to see who can get one to stick. That's what they are doing to you. They're just going to keep tossing until they find a warm one that will cling. But if the day ever comes that their viciousness cannot be contained by your supporters, I only have one piece of advice."

"What's that?"

"Get the hell out of here. When that time comes, don't let any grass grow under your feet. But don't leave without first exposing them to the entire congregation for the assholes that they are."

"Sounds like a good piece of advice to me." Chief Sparks agreed.

"Misturh Clemons, I'sa brought you and Chief Sparks' another. I woulda brung it sooner but it appeared to me youn's were in a deep conversation." Elijah was one of the Magnolia Club's most faithful bartenders. He was now standing at their table.

"Thanks, Elijah. Steele, what will you have?"

"Elijah, will you bring me a *Johnny Walker Black*, neat?"

"I'sa be right back."

"What was that prick, Tom Barnhardt, doing there tonight?" Stone asked.

"He's in cahoots with the two of them."

"Obviously." Stone agreed. "I know that he got disbarred, but that doesn't seem to have slowed him down. Have you all found that kid they hired to plant the porn on the bishop's computer?"

"No. I can't offer you much hope." The Chief shook his head. "The only way we're going to catch him is if he gets pulled over for some other violation. When they run his license, they'll see we have an arrest warrant out for him."

"It just looks like you would be able to find him."

"Stone, the most we have him on is breaking and entering. That's small potatoes by comparison. We all have much bigger fish to fry."

"I want him to testify against Barnhardt."

"And I do too, but we're going to have to find him first."

"Any word on Gary Hendricks?"

"It's like the man never existed. He's gone without a trace. Damndest thing I've ever seen in my life."

"So even if you were to catch that boy... what was his name?"

"Bruce Chance."

"Good looking boy with long blonde hair. Very athletic looking, if I remember right."

"Your memory is good."

Chief Sparks swallowed the rest of his drink just as the bartender delivered Steele's drink to him. He held up his glass. "One more. What's the latest on the happenings over at Saint Andrew's, Steele?"

"I think I'll refer that question to my counsel." Steele chuckled.

Stone grinned. "Well, the best news I've heard is that the chapel is no longer named in honor of Ned Boone."

Chief Sparks smiled. "It never should have been. What about the pastor and his wife?"

"You haven't heard?"

"Heard what?"

"The pastor has skipped town with Judith Idle."

This time it was Steele that was surprised just as he was taking a sip of his drink. He started coughing. "What? What did you say?"

Stone patted him on the back. "Oh, I get to be the bearer of all the good news tonight."

"Don't get too full of yourself." The Chief chided. "You're not the Angel Gabriel and Christmas is still a few days away."

Stone chuckled. "Okay, let me bring you up to date. The pastor and Judith were having an affair. They've skipped town. My firm represents the pastor's wife, so we've filed a divorce action against him on her behalf. She's requesting full custody of the children. I understand Elmer has filed for a divorce against Judith on the grounds of adultery. The best part is that the two of them have gotten a Mexican divorce and then got married in Mexico."

"Is that legal?" Steele asked.

Stone smirked. "In Mexico. Here in Georgia, it doesn't mean a thing."

The Chief asked, "Wasn't she that *holier than thou woman* that was giving you all the trouble, Steele?"

"She kept going to conferences led by fringe clergy and then bringing back some pretty screwy ideas. Some of her ideas were so far out, the trains and buses don't even run there. She thought I wasn't very spiritual, since I wouldn't let her implement them at First Church. The truth is, I was relieved when she and Elmer went over to the Presbyterians. I never thought they were Episcopalians to begin with. I have to confess, however, that I did think that whatever religion she had conjured up was real. Then again, I've always suspected that inside every fundamentalist is an agnostic crying for help. I just never dreamed she'd have an affair and leave her husband. I guess it's a case of crazy hooking up with crazy. When they meet, they understand each other, and their pent up lust takes it from there."

"You got to watch the pious ones," Stone observed. "I've always thought they were torn between the two devils on their shoulders."

"Don't you mean an angel and a devil?" Chief Sparks interrupted.

"No. I mean two devils. The one devil is telling them how wonderful and holy they are, and that they are so spiritually superior to everyone else."

"And the other devil?" Steele asked.

"Oh, that devil is reminding them that life is a party, and they're missing it." Steele and the Chief chuckled. "Now that pastor's wife over at Saint Andrew's, I think she's the real deal. I'm happy we've been able to help her."

"The prosecutor did tell me you'd worked things out for her with him." Chief Sparks interjected.

"It really was a no brainer. She's on probation for two years. She will need to be a model citizen, but the prosecutor agreed that, lacking any other evidence, it would be best to let her slide this time."

"What's she going to do? How's she going to support herself?"

"I can answer that one." Steele interjected. "Almeda has taken her under her wing. She's helping her start a business making children's clothes and doing alterations. She's also letting her live in one of her rent houses until she gets on her feet."

"Well, God bless Almeda." Stone lifted his glass. After he'd swallowed the last of its contents, he signaled for the waiter to bring him the check. "Fellows, this one's on me. Now if you'll excuse me, I've got a bag of birdseed in my car. I'm going to go by and sprinkle it around Ned Boone's statue on my way home."

"You're wasting your time," the Chief responded.

"Oh, I don't think so. Last time I was over there, that statue was covered with bird poop."

"Stone, the statue is gone."

"What?"

"Well, it seems it's my turn to be Gabriel and bring the good news of great joy." The Chief chuckled. "Some outfit out in California bought that park from Ned's wife and son."

"I thought the city had some interest in it. I had a couple of my young lawyers looking into it."

"You can call them off. The outfit out there found that the deed and title had never been transferred to the city. It was still in Ned's name and consequently, in his trust."

"And all these years the city has been maintaining his property for him. Damn."

"He just may go down as one of the best manipulators of all time," the Chief acknowledged.

"Why did his wife sell it?" Stone asked.

"It seems that of all the people celebrating Ned's death, she's the one leading the parade. We all know what an SOB he was. I guess he treated her with the same disdain in their marriage. His son that lives out in San Francisco hadn't talked to Ned in years."

"So she was happy to sell it?" Steele asked.

"That's my understanding from the city manager."

"What's going to happen to the park?"

"It's going to remain a park. The outfit that bought it gave it back to the city on that very condition, plus two more."

"What are the two more?"

"That Ned's statue be removed immediately was the first condition."

"And the second?"

"That the park be named *Rainbow Park* and that a large rainbow sculpture be placed where Ned's statue had been."

"Do you know who bought it?"

"Like I said, some corporation out in San Francisco made the purchase. I've never heard of them."

"Why would they have an interest in giving Falls City a park?"

"I've told you all that the city manager knew to share with me."

"Well, they've got my curiosity up." Stone mused. "I think I'll have one of my interns see if she can't find out who they are."

"I wish you wouldn't," Steele requested.

"What do you know about this, Padre?" Stone glanced over at him. "Do you know who bought it?"

"I might know. I could be wrong. I guess I'd like to ask, as a favor to me, that you just leave it alone. Ned's statue is gone. The park no longer bears his name. I'd really appreciate it if you let it all end right there."

Stone studied Steele's face. "If you say so, but I think you know who bought it and why. On my deathbed, will you tell me?"

"I'd just as soon some other priest be around to give you last rites."

"Well, if no one else is available, I hope you'll tell me. I need something to entertain me in my grave besides the Chief's secrets."

Chief Sparks swallowed the remainder of his drink. "You're not the only keeper of secrets, you old geezer. Remember, for every one of mine, I have two of yours."

Stone chuckled. "And you keep in mind that the only way two people can keep a secret is if one of them is dead."

The Magnolia Series

Dennis R. Maynard

Chapter 41

"Listen to me you *Pinche Puta*." Javiar drew back his hand to slap Virginia Mudd across the face.

"Stop! If you hit me, I'll never be able to get my fiancé to give me the money. And just why do all of you men want to hit women in the face?" Virginia was terrified. If she was bruised on his next visit, she knew Thackston would not buy her story about protection.

Javiar pulled his nightstick from its holster. He shoved it between Virginia's legs and pushed hard. She screamed in pain as tears flooded her eyes. "As far as I'm concerned, you're nothing but a *Skonka*. You mean nothing to me. You smoke my weed and then you don't pay me."

"Please, please, Javiar, you're hurting me."

"This is nothing compared to what I will do to you if you don't get me my *green*."

"I'll ask Thackston the next time he visits. He missed last week, but he's supposed to come next week. I'll ask him then. I promise. Two thousand dollars, right?"

Javiar released the pressure on his nightstick, but he continued to hold it in place. Virginia relaxed as the pain subsided. He grinned. "What two thousand dollars? It's now five thousand dollars. Let's just call it interest on your past due account."

"But that's not fair." Virginia protested. "My first payment was only one thousand. Then you doubled it to two."

"And you doubled the amount you smoked." He removed the nightstick and put it back in his holster. "You really like weed, don't you, *Bonita*?"

"I just don't think five thousand is fair." Javiar reached for his nightstick again. "No. No, don't! I'll get it."

Javiar slapped her firmly on the face several times, but not hard enough to leave a mark. "That's better."

"It's just so much money compared to the first time. I don't know how I'm going to explain it."

"You don't have to explain nothing. My man watched your boyfriend in the visitor's room. He tells me he was wearing a watch that was worth at least twelve grand. Then he left here in a brand new Mercedes. Five thousand is *nada* to him. Now, how about a smoke? I have some really good stuff that just came through the gates. It'll be on the house."

When Virginia returned to her cell, a very angry Adrianna confronted her. "What the hell is wrong with you? You come in here stinking up our cage. You reek of pot. You're going to get us both in trouble."

"That's the least of my problems. Javiar wants five thousand dollars."

"What?" Adrianna sat down on her bunk. "Your man has that kind of money?"

Virginia nodded. "I just don't know if I'm going to be able to get it from him."

"I told you not to get mixed up with Javiar. Are you completely without any self-control? Maybe you should be going to AA or something. I think you're an addict."

"There's no such thing as a weed addict. I can quit anytime I want. I just do it because it makes me feel so good. I don't have to think about this place."

"Sounds like an addiction to me."

"Nonsense."

"Inmate Mudd, the warden wants to see you." A guard was standing at their cell door.

"Me?"

"Yes, you. Let's go. NOW!" He shouted. "You don't want to keep the warden waiting."

Adrianna whispered. "Oh crap, Virginia, you've been had. You'd better tell the warden everything, or you're going to end up in the SHU. Believe me, you don't want to go there."

"NOW!" The guard shouted again.

One guard led Virginia down the corridor and another followed as they escorted her to the Warden's office.

Virginia was terrified. She was sick to her stomach with fear. She could not stop her hands from visibly shaking. Her mind was in such a state of panic that her thoughts were all muddled. She knew she could not tell the warden she'd been buying marijuana from Javiar. No, that wouldn't work. Just as they reached the door to the warden's office, it came to her. She'd just tell the warden the same thing that she'd told Thackston. Javiar was selling her protection. He'd beat her up and threatened her if she didn't pay. It worked on Thackston, so why wouldn't it work on the warden? Virginia felt a strange calmness come over her.

One of the guards knocked on the warden's office door. The warden opened it. "Thackston!" She shouted. Virginia couldn't believe her eyes. Her boyfriend was sitting in the warden's office. Thackston stood and took her in his arms. She kissed him. Then she stood back so she could look at him. "What are you doing here?"

"I came to take you home."

"What?"

"It seems the charges against you have been dropped... at least for now," the warden stated. "I'll leave it to your attorney here to explain it all to you, but you're free to go. I'll have my guards escort you out."

Virginia was trying to take everything in. Thackston saw her confusion. He took her hand and squeezed it. "How?"

"It's like I told you last time. I was able to convince the judge that you were the victim of an entrapment. The man that introduced you to the FBI officer pretending to be Lobo was also a DEA agent. They were friends. They weren't only friends; they were best friends. I asked the judge for a new trial, but that may not even happen."

"Why?"

"It seems that the DEA agent was killed in a drug bust a few weeks ago. Absent the testimony of one of your accusers, such a trial probably isn't going to happen. Now, let's go home."

"Wait. What about my things?" Virginia looked at the warden.

"The guards have cleaned out your cell and packed up your things. You can inventory them at the front before you leave."

"May I change clothes?"

The warden nodded. "That uniform belongs to the state of Georgia. We want it back. I just hope I never see you in here again."

Once Virginia was in Thackston's car, he asked, "Where do you want to go first?"

"To the nearest hotel. I want to ravage your body."

"Me too." He said. "I have a reservation at the Hilton. It's not far."

"I think I'll just get us started." Virginia put her face in Thackston's lap.

They spent the afternoon and early evening making love. Once, twice, three times, and a fourth that included pleasure, exertion, and soreness. "Now, what do you want to do?"

"Do you think that *Cracker Barrel* we passed on the frontage road is still open?"

"*Cracker Barrel*? Are you kidding me?"

"No, I've been living on prison slop. I want some real food. I want a chicken fried steak, fried okra, grits, and some fried apples."

"Sounds like you've thought this through."

"I've thought about it a thousand times."

After Virginia had cleaned her plate, including the accompanying cornbread and biscuits, Thackston asked, "Are you excited about going back to Falls City?"

"I'm sure people will talk, but frankly, I don't give a damn. I think I might even show up at First Church just to rub it in those hypocrites' faces. I think we should go together on Christmas Eve. Let's walk in holding hands for all of them to see."

"Are you that angry with them?"

"Oh, it's not anger. It's revenge."

As Thackston was paying the bill, Virginia walked around the gift shop attached to the restaurant. Suddenly, Virginia's heart skipped a beat. Staring at her was a familiar face. It was Javiar's man that had been spying on Thackston and her in the prison visitor's room. His eyes were filled with violence. He took two fingers and put them to his eyes and then pointed them at her. He followed that gesture by pulling them across his throat in a cutting motion. Virginia stood frozen in place as she watched him leave the gift shop.

"Honey, you look like you've seen a ghost. You're as white as a sheet. What's happened?"

Virginia shook her head. "Take me home."

As Thackston pulled his Mercedes out of the parking lot and onto the freeway, Virginia tried to relax. The haunting sensation that they were being followed filled her with anxiety. She turned her head to look behind them. A large black SUV was closing in on them at a high rate of speed. Virginia's heart raced when she recognized the driver. It was Javiar's man. He was smiling as he brought the SUV closer and closer to their rear bumper.

The Magnolia Series

Dennis R. Maynard

Chapter 42

Christmas comes to Falls City much like a South Georgia thunderstorm. The warning clouds begin to gather first. About the time the Halloween candy and decorations go on sale, the first signs of the impending rush appear. Christmas trees and outdoor lighting displays greet shoppers as they enter the *Wal Mart* and *Sam's Club* stores on the north side of town. As Thanksgiving approaches, the other stores and shops in the city add decorated trees and window displays to announce the coming event. By Thanksgiving, there are the first signs of tents being erected for the sale of all the evergreens needed to make one's celebration complete. The city employees hang lighted artificial wreaths and garland from the lampposts down on Main Street. Bell ringers take their stations outside the most frequently visited establishments. The lights are illuminated on Thanksgiving night. The day following the turkey feast, the impending storm explodes as with thunder and lightning. Shoppers camp outside the discount stores. They hope to be one of the select few to receive an even larger discount on the items on their shopping lists. Parking spaces are scarce as panicked shoppers begin to prepare for the inevitable day.

Almeda Alexander Drummond was anything but ill-prepared for the Christmas holidays. She began weeks in advance. This year, she had even more guests to include in her celebration. Almeda asked Rose MacClaren to accompany her to Atlanta for a weekend shopping trip. They almost stayed in the Ritz Carlton across from the Lenox Square Mall. Then Almeda remembered that was where her beloved Chadsworth had taken his life. It had almost slipped her mind. She made reservations at a beautiful little boutique hotel on a side street, but within walking distance.

Rose had never even dared enter any of the stores Almeda routinely shopped in. She was overwhelmed as Almeda had her try on dresses in Saks and Neiman Marcus.

"Almeda, this one dress costs more than Melvin used to give me to feed our family for three months."

"Just forget about him. We're going to find you several dresses. You're going into business. You need to look like a woman of accomplishment when you greet your customers."

"Almeda, I'll never be able to repay you."

"Nonsense." Almeda waved her hand. "It makes me happy to do this for you. When we finish here, we're going over to the children and teen departments. I want us to select some new dresses for your daughter, and a couple of suits and sports coats for your sons."

By Christmas Eve, most every house in Falls City was pulling down on the resources of the South Georgia Power and Light Company. Colored lights and inflatable displays adorned rooflines and front lawns. Almeda dismissed most all of them as tacky. The Drummond home did have a lighting display. The roofline and pine trees in the front were lit with tasteful white lights only. "I refuse to have my home look like a carnival ride. All those colored lights have no place on a house of distinction."

Almeda custom ordered two live Christmas trees from the local nursery. The first was a sixteen-foot tree that she had set up in the solarium. The second, a mere twelve feet, was for the formal living room. The tree in the solarium was not visible from the street. It could only be seen from the swimming pool and the surrounding back acreage. Almeda gave it to the MacClaren children to decorate. She actually found the process as enjoyable as the children did. They giggled, drank hot chocolate, and ate the Christmas cookies that Almeda had instructed her chef to prepare for them. The children's excitement over the coming celebration became her own.

She had asked each of the children to write a letter to Santa Claus. Their first lists were sparse and basic. Socks, a new ball cap, a shirt, and some candy were all they could bring themselves to write. Almeda knew that the frightful way their father had forced them to celebrate Christmas was hindering their lists. She asked them to make another. This time, Almeda was pleased to see their eyes light up as she and Horace made suggestions.

The Christmas tree in the living room, the mantle around the fireplace, the garland on the balcony and stairway, the greens from the chandelier in the entry hall, and the dining room table decorations were left to the professionals. Each year, Almeda sat with her florist in late August and chose the theme and the colors to be utilized. The decorators would spend the best part of two days arranging the carefully chosen lights, ornaments, ribbons, and greenery. Of course, Almeda was their constant and critical shadow.

So much beauty had never surrounded Rose and the children. Their gratitude to Almeda and Horace was unending. Almeda did not believe it was possible for the MacClaren children to be any more polite than they already were. She was wrong.

They all gathered around the dining room table on Christmas Eve for dinner. The MacClaren boys looked so nice and crisp in their new suits and bow ties. Almeda had instructed Horace to teach them how to tie their bows. "Every true *Southern Gentleman* knows how to tie their own." The MacClaren daughter's long red hair was accented by a new green dress. Rose was also wearing a green dress they had selected at Saks. While they were in Atlanta, Almeda took Rose to a hairstylist. Rose had never had her hair done professionally. After leaving the hair salon, Almeda took Rose to the make up counter at Neiman Marcus. "Melvin never let me wear make up." Rose declared. "He said only prostitutes and clowns should wear make up."

"Well, Melvin is not here." Almeda insisted.

Rose stared at her reflection in the mirror the makeup artist was holding for her. "Is that me?" She asked. "I'm actually quite pretty."

"You're actually quite beautiful." Almeda smiled. "I'm going to have to keep an eye on you. I can think of a couple of lonely old bachelors that just might want to come calling."

"No, thank you. I don't want anything to do with any man." Then Rose decided to tease her new friend. "That is, unless I could find one like Horace."

"Well, he's mine." Almeda retorted. "But there just might be one or two out there that know how to treat a lady."

After Horace and Almeda had made the sign of the cross, they joined hands with Rose and her children. Horace then offered the blessing. John Calvin asked, "Doctor Drummond, will you teach me how to do that?"

"To do what, John Calvin?"

He moved his hand around his forehead and chest. "You know, that thing you and Mrs. Drummond do when you pray."

"Oh, the sign of the cross." Horace chuckled. He looked over at Rose for permission. She nodded. "Sure I will. I'll teach you before we go to Mass tonight."

His brother and sister were quick to respond, "Us too, please."

The first course for their Christmas feast was lobster bisque. Almeda had instructed the chef to make sure that each bowl contained big chunks of Maine lobster. The salad was a green spring salad with blue cheese sprinkles, accented with Mandarin oranges. The main course was roast duck with dark bing cherry sauce. The sides included wild rice with mushrooms and asparagus, topped with parmesan cheese. Almeda smiled as she watched John Calvin try a bite of asparagus. He then tried to discreetly discard it in his napkin. Dessert was crème brulee.

The conversation at the table centered on all the presents around the Christmas tree in the solarium. The children were having a difficult time containing their excitement. Rose tried to change the subject. "Doctor Drummond, Almeda tells me you'll be preaching tonight."

"That's right. Father Austin and I alternate Christmas sermons. He will preside at the Mass and I'll preach. Next year, we'll reverse our roles."

Almeda took Horace's hand, "May we have a hint?"

"Sure." He nodded. "In a capsule, I've been thinking about the campaign that the atheists have launched against Christmas. They think that by exposing the origin of the celebration, they will somehow or another be able to discredit it."

"I don't think I know anything about that campaign." Rose said.

"Well, they're taking out ads and buying billboards stating that Christmas is not really Jesus' birthday. They contend that Christmas actually finds its origin in the ancient celebration of the Winter Solstice. That celebration included bringing evergreens into the house and some of the other customs that Christians have adapted for our celebration."

"Oh, I didn't know that." Rose acknowledged.

"Actually, they're correct. Jesus was most likely born in the spring or summer. They're also right that the Christians simply took the secular feast surrounding the Winter Solstice and redeemed it. Many of the customs and the date itself became our celebration of the Lord's birth. But you see, the larger question is not the customs, or even the accuracy of Christ's birth date, or the origin of Christmas trees."

Horace paused. He was suddenly aware that he had the undivided attention of every single person at the table. "The critical question is whether or not Jesus matters. The atheists can demythologize all the customs surrounding Christmas, but they cannot destroy the central message of Christmas itself. The questions that all Christians must continually ask themselves, and ultimately challenge even the atheists to ask, are these: Does Jesus matter? Has He made a difference in the way we live our lives? Has He made a difference in the way we treat others? Have each of us transferred the love, compassion and forgiveness that

Jesus brought into this world to the people in our own worlds? You see, such questions are not dependent on the origin of the feast day, the evergreens, colored lights, or the baubles on the tree. They are the questions that the very birth of Jesus makes it impossible for us to ignore. No campaign to secularize Christmas can destroy that."

"Wow!" Rose nodded. "I've never heard a sermon like that."

"Oh, *shugah*, that wasn't the sermon. You haven't heard anything yet. Just wait until my Horace adorns his robes and climbs up into that big pulpit at First Church. Then you'll hear some preaching." Almeda smiled proudly as she squeezed Horace's hand. She then reached across the table and took Rose's hand in hers. Her gaze fell on the beautiful redheaded MacClaren children sitting at her Christmas table. A chill washed over Almeda. She felt tears of gratitude welling up in her eyes. This just may be the best Christmas she'd ever had in her life. The words of Tiny Tim from the *Christmas Carol* came to her mind, *God bless us every one.* "No." She whispered. "God has blessed us. Every lovely person at this table is *a Christmas blessing.*" She let go of Horace's and Rose's hands and made the sign of the cross.

"Are you going to pray again?" John Calvin asked her.

Almeda fought back her tears of joy as she smiled at him. His bright blue eyes and freckled face were alive with curiosity. She answered him softly, "Honey, I just did."

The Magnolia Series

Dennis R. Maynard

Chapter 43

The Reverend Father Steele Austin gazed out at a church nave brilliant with bright reds, evergreens, and glowing candles. The smell of fresh pine filled the air. The reredos behind the high altar was covered with magnolia leaves. They formed a beautiful dark green background for the bright red poinsettias strategically placed in their midst. Two large Christmas trees stood stoically on either side of the altar. They were covered with white and gold chrismon ornaments. At the foot of the altar sat a beautiful Christmas creche sitting in yet another bed of magnolia leaves. Steele chuckled as he remembered that Almeda was in charge of the large magnolia tree in front of the church. He mused as to whether or not she'd given her permission to cut the branches for Christmas decorations. The shelf of every stained glass window was lined with evergreen and a lit hurricane lantern. Two large evergreen wreaths hung on the narthex walls facing the nave. They were adorned with huge red bows.

Steele had stationed himself in the back of the nave by the baptismal font. He wanted to listen to the congregation sing the pre-service carols. He tried to forget the two previous encounters earlier in the evening. Mary Alice Smythe had accosted him in the sacristy as soon as he walked through the door. "You've ruined my Christmas!" She had hurled the words at him.

"Mary Alice, how have I ruined your Christmas?"

"You and that woman."

"What woman?"

"Almeda!" She glared.

"Is this about the altar rail?"

"It looks just awful. The flower guild had a terrible time decorating the church this year."

"Mary Alice, I've seen the decorations. They look wonderful. You all did a fantastic job."

"Well, I guess we just have a difference in taste."

"I really don't see how making the altar rail more accessible to the elderly and disabled has ruined your Christmas."

"Well, it has. I'm sure there will be others that tell you the same."

"I'm sorry that you feel that way, but for now, let's just focus on celebrating Christ's birth."

Mary Alice looked over her glasses at Steele. "I'm trying, but you've not made it easy." Mary Alice's lips trembled, and a tear dropped down her cheek. "I just don't understand why you can't leave things be. I've been coming to Christmas at this church since I was a little girl. Each year it has looked just like it did the year before. It was comforting. Now..." She turned and walked away. Steele heard her mumble, "Maybe some of those folks are correct. You're just not suited to be the rector of First Church."

His second encounter came with the head usher, Colonel Mitchell. Thankfully, he'd already been warned. "I called the Fire Marshall about all these chairs you instructed the sextons to set up. We're breaking the fire code." Folding chairs had been set up on the side aisles at the end of each pew and one row down the center aisle. Steele had also instructed folding chairs to be set up in both narthexes. As he looked out over the congregation, not only was every pew packed with worshippers, but each folding chair was occupied as well. In addition, people were standing along the walls. One of the sextons had heard Colonel Mitchell complaining about the chairs. He'd heard him say that he was going to call the Fire Marshall. The sexton called Steele at home to warn him. Steele called Chief Sparks. "That man is a real piece of work," the Chief responded. "The old fool has forgotten that the Fire Chief is my cousin. Leave it to me. I'll handle it."

Steele could tell that Colonel Mitchell was not happy. If Colonel had his way, he would turn people away rather than allow them in the church. "So what did the Fire Marshall say?" Steele asked calmly.

Flames shot from Colonel's eyes. "You know what he said. He and his wife are sitting up there with your buddy and his family." Steele's eyes followed his pointed finger. Sure enough, the Fire Chief was sitting on the third pew with Chief Sparks. The sight of Tom Barnhardt presiding over an empty pew interrupted Steele's amusement. He was turning away anyone that approached it for a seat. Steele resolved not to let that upset him, but he didn't understand the audacity. Tom Barnhardt seldom came to church. He could not find any record that he'd ever contributed so much as one thin dime to First Church. But on this Christmas Eve, he believed he could reserve an entire pew for his wife, children and guests. Then again, this was the night when all of Falls City believed that First Church was the place to be. He shrugged it off.

"Merry Christmas, Father." One of the acolytes tugged on his alb and smiled at him. "I want to thank you again for lunch yesterday." Each year, Steele invited the former acolytes that were now in college to be the acolytes at the midnight mass on Christmas Eve. After the rehearsal, he treated them to a nice lunch. It was a way he could keep in touch with some of the college students and keep them connected to their church. He mused that if Colonel Mitchell found out about that discretionary expenditure, he'd want to accuse him of mismanagement for it as well.

"Merry Christmas." Steele responded.

The congregation began singing *Away in a Manger*. Steele's thoughts went to his home and his little family. They'd spent the afternoon decorating their Christmas tree. It was an old Anglo-Catholic practice that Steele was having a difficult time releasing. He'd purchased the tree over a week ago and had kept it in a bucket of water in the garage. He just didn't believe that the tree should be decorated until Christmas Eve. He realized that his children's friends decorated their trees earlier in December. Steele resolved, for his children, he'd leave his guilt between the pages of his Anglican Missal, and decorate the tree earlier next year.

Travis and Amanda were delighted to hang ornaments and candy canes on the tree. Of course, they were all placed on one side of the tree and bunched near the bottom. After they'd gone to bed, Randi and Steele, along with the children's sitter for the evening, rearranged most of the ornaments and finished decorating the tree. Getting Travis to bed on Christmas Eve was not a problem. His toddler sister, sensing from her big brother that something big was about to happen, went to sleep just as easily. Steele knew that, after the midnight Mass, there were two large boxes waiting for him in the attic. Both were marked *some assembly required.* He would assemble the big wheel tricycle that Travis wanted first. Then he'd tackle the little pink table and chairs for Amanda. The best part of the evening would come when all was in readiness. He will make a fire in the fireplace. His beautiful wife and he will sit on the sofa, hold hands, drink a glass of wine, and bask in the glow of the fire and the Christmas tree.

"Christmas Blessings, my brother." Two large black hands reached out for him. Steele reciprocated and hugged The Reverend Josiah Williams. "Where are you sitting?"

"Up front with Randi. Can't you see Rubidoux's hat?"

Steele chuckled as he spotted a red hat with a large red feather on top. "I do now." He stretched up to see that Randi, Rubidoux, Rose, and her children were all on the front pew.

"I just wanted to tell you again how happy I am that we're going to be able to do Rubidoux's project together."

"I am too." Steele nodded. "And thanks for the loan of your choir."

Josiah leaned in so he could whisper in Steele's ear. "I've heard your choir. Seems they are stuck on some really old Latin music that could put an insomniac to sleep. It's nice enough, but my choir will bring this place to life. These white folks are going to be clapping their hands before this night is over."

Steele patted him on the back. "Well, that will be something if it happens." Steele had convinced the choir director to allow Josiah's choir to participate in the *Midnight Mass*. Several of the choir members were not happy about it and had made their complaints known, but Steele prevailed. Josiah's choir would help them lead the hymns, sing an anthem after the Gospel reading, and sing during communion. Several members of Josiah's parish also were in attendance tonight. They'd come to support their choir. Steele loved looking over the congregation and seeing the black faces intermingled with the elite of Falls City. A chill washed over him. He realized that, without planning it, he had accomplished what many in this city would have considered unthinkable. He'd integrated Historic First Church. Or at least for this one service, black and white were going to celebrate the birth of Christ at the same altar. He remembered Chief Sparks' words. *The churches in Falls City are more segregated than the bars.*

The verger approached Steele; he was carrying a white cope trimmed in red and gold. He helped Steele put it on and handed him his biretta to wear. All was in readiness. The smell of incense was now detectable. The acolytes and banner bearers were all in place. The choirs were lined up for the procession. The brightly colored robes worn by Josiah's choir were quite the contrast to the black and white being worn by the First Church choir. Steele made a mental note. Surely there was something we could do to brighten the choir vestments. The organist, brass, and timpani concluded the prelude.

A silent anticipation washed over the congregation. The moment had arrived for the Christ Mass to begin. Steele turned on his lapel microphone and said, *"Behold, I bring good tidings of great joy. For unto us is born this day in the city of David a Savior, Christ the Lord."* Instantly the sound of the timpani drum roll filled the church as the congregation rose to their feet. A trumpet fanfare peeled out over the people as the worshippers turned to watch the procession enter the nave.

A thurifer led the procession, swinging the smoking thurible in figure eights. The lead processional cross and candles followed him. The organist now joined the brass by improvising on the processional hymn, *O Come, All Ye Faithful.* The worshippers bowed their heads as the first cross passed them. A banner to Blessed Joseph followed that cross. Josiah's choir came next. The next banner was to the Blessed Mother, followed by the First Church choir. A second thurifer entered the church; he was leading another cross and torchbearers. The acolytes, layreaders, and chalicebearers followed them. A third thurifer led the clergy cross into the nave. The First Church clergy entered. A verger walked directly in front of Steele. The choir and congregation began singing the first verse of the hymn.

Steele had choreographed the service with all the clergy, music ministers, and vergers. They had agreed to refrain from censing the altar until the congregation had finished all but the last verse of the hymn. The organist would begin a joyful improvisation before the last verse. During that improvisation, Steele would cense the altar. Once the thurifer had censed the congregation, they would sing the last verse of the hymn. Steele took the incense pot from the thurifer and moved around the altar as the organ bellowed the familiar melody. The smoke rose heavenward toward the altar cross. As he finished, a holy cloud had completely enveloped the altar. He handed the thurible to the thurifer. He then blessed Steele, the ministers in the sanctuary, and the choir. The mystical smell of the incense filled the sanctuary. He then moved forward to bless the congregation with the sacred fragrance.

When he returned, Steele waited for the organist and choir to begin the last verse of the hymn, but nothing happened. The organist continued to improvise. Steele gave the verger a confused look, and then he glanced over at the organist. The organist gave Steele a big smile and nodded back towards the verger. Steele gestured to the verger and whispered, "What's going on?" A smiling verger handed Steele a slip of paper. It read simply, *I'm pregnant!* Steele shot another confused look at the verger. He responded, "Not me. Your wife."

Steele turned to look at a glowing Randi, who was smiling and nodding her head. He rushed from the altar and took his wife in his arms. The entire congregation exploded in applause as the organist continued to improvise on *O Come, All Ye Faithful.* Steele asked. "How'd they know?"

Rubidoux showed him a small index card. It read - *Randi is going to surprise Father Austin with an announcement tonight.* The image of two small baby feet, similar to what would be on a birth certificate, was affixed. "One of these was waiting for us on our pew when we arrived."

"When?" Steele asked.

"July." Randi smiled.

"I love you. I am so happy."

"I love you too, but don't you have a service to lead?"

Steele put his arms around her and squeezed her one more time. He returned to the altar as the congregation continued to applaud. The timpani offered a resounding drum roll that literally shook the stained glass windows. The brass exploded with a full fanfare. The organist turned on the zimblestern as its bells added to the festival spirit. The choir and congregation sang the last verse of the hymn at the top of their lungs. *YEAH, LORD WE GREET THEE. BORN THIS HAPPY MORNING.*

The Magnolia Series

Dennis R. Maynard

Epilogue

The South Pacific Ocean surrounding Moorea in the Tahitian Island chain is as pristine as any place on this fragile island planet. The clear turquoise waters off French Polynesia extend three to four hundred yards from the shore. These crystal clear waters are a favorite place for swimming and snorkeling. The brightly colored fish are visible from the surface. They are more clearly seen wearing a mask and snorkel. Beyond the break, the water turns a brilliant blue. The more serious divers prefer the deep water beyond the coral reef.

The people that inhabit these islands are as warm and friendly as the guidebooks suggest. They live off the land. Their lifestyle is slow and relaxed. Shoes are not required, and clothing is often considered optional. There is a quiet spirituality about those that call this tropical paradise home. Music and dance are ever present and bind them together in a tight knit community. Their respect for life and the environment runs deep. As people of the sea, they learn early in life to respect the giant body of water that surrounds them. Not only is it a source of food, but it is their primary arena for recreation.

Gary Hendricks stretched out in the lounge chair on the deck of his over-the-water bungalow. He had bought the beachside hotel and its twelve bungalows. The former owners, also Americans, had resided in the master suite in the main part of the hotel. Gary chose one of the bungalows as his new home. It had a glass floor that afforded him an aquarium that no man could replicate. The slurping waters beneath his house lured him to sleep each night. Gary was at peace.

His hotel remained fully booked most every day of the year. It had a history of being the preferred destination for tourists from France, Australia, and New Zealand. American tourists were occasional residents. Gary had left notice with his desk clerk that any attempted reservations from the State of Georgia, in the United States, were to be immediately rejected.

It had been an interesting journey. When he first arrived, his skin was not used to the South Pacific sun. He had burned easily and often. Now he sported bronze skin that would be the envy of any sunbather. When he arrived in Tahiti, Gary spent several weeks in the city of Papeete. That is where his southern chains first began to loosen. Papeete is an international seaport. It has everything a sailor, or any man, could ever fantasize. Gary owed his liberated self to that city. While there, he'd pierced his ears and gotten a tattoo on his right butt cheek. He'd allowed his hair to grow long, and most days he kept it in a ponytail. Shoes became a foreign object. His sandals were the first thing to be discarded when he entered his new home. Like the natives, he preferred to go barefoot. When he attended the village church, he dressed in a white shirt, as was the custom, but his sandals were left at the door. He honored the native practice of removing one's shoes or sandals when on holy ground.

It now all seemed so natural to him. He was just being the self that he'd always known was inside him. It was a self that he'd rejected over and over again. This free spirit was someone that had scared him. He'd had to keep it contained his entire life in Falls City. Every fiber of his being had been devoted to keeping that unrepressed self under control. It was exhausting. He feared the judgmental eyes and tongues of Falls City. But now, Tahiti was his home.

Thoughts of Falls City, Georgia, occasionally crossed his mind. With the passing of time, they did so with less frequency. The citizens of that mean-spirited town were now light years away. He had struggled to forgive himself for being drawn into their brutish behavior. He regretted the underhanded methods he'd shared with Ned Boone and Tom Barnhardt. Each day, First Church and First Church School were being washed from his memory. They were remote - an illusion. They belonged in a distant past that he had to struggle to remember. It was a life he knew he had lived, but not really. It was as though someone else had invaded his body and lived that part of his life for him. It was more like a dream in which he was both the actor and the spectator. It was all so surreal. He'd allowed himself to live a life that he simply did not want. The battles he'd fought at First Church with Steele Austin now seemed ridiculous, even silly. He had no desire to return. He did not want that life. He wanted to live the remainder of his journey in the paradise surrounding him.

Gary felt water drip onto his face. Soft lips embraced his. Wet hair tickled his cheeks. "Good morning, handsome."

"Where have you been?"

"I woke up early and went for a swim."

Gary put his arm around the slim waist and ran his hand down one of the smooth legs. "God, you're beautiful."

263

"You're not so bad yourself, Lover."

Gary looked into the face that he loved like none he'd ever known. "What do you want to do with the rest of the day?"

"You. I just want to do you. I just might do you until I don't have the energy to do anything else."

Gary smiled. "You know that I love you."

"I know. And I love you so much it hurts. Now, let's get this day started right."

Gary smiled the smile of a man that had finally found the happiness that had always eluded him. He stood. Hand in hand, he walked with Bruce Chance to their marriage bed.

The Magnolia Series

Dennis R. Maynard

ABOUT THE AUTHOR

The Reverend Doctor Dennis R. Maynard is the best selling author of fifteen books. Well over 200,000 Episcopalians have read his book, *Those Episkopols*. 3000 congregations around the United States use *Those Episkopols* in their new member ministries. Several denominational leaders have called it the unofficial handbook for the Episcopal Church. He is also the author of *Forgive and Get Your Life Back*. Another 3,000 clergy have used the forgiveness book and study guide to do forgiveness training in their congregations. Maynard has written a series of novels focusing on life in the typical congregation. These novels have received popular acceptance from both clergy and lay people. The books in *The Magnolia Series* are growing in popularity around the world as readers anxiously await each new chapter.

"The novels give us a chance to look at the underside of parish life. While the story lines are fictional, the readers invariably think they recognize the characters. If not, they know someone just like the folks that attend First Episcopal Church in the town of Falls City, Georgia."

Doctor Maynard's book, *When Sheep Attack*, is based on twenty-five case studies of clergy that were attacked by a small group of antagonists in their congregations. The antagonists successfully removed their senior pastor, leaving the congregations divided and crippled. The book describes how it happened, what could have been done to stop it, and what can be done to prevent it from happening to your pastor and parish. Based on an additional 200 case studies, Doctor Maynard added two more books to the *Sheep Attack Series*. They are *Preventing A Sheep Attack* and **Healing For Pastors And People Following A Sheep Attack**.

Over his thirty-eight years of parish ministry, Doctor Maynard has served some of the largest congregations in the Episcopal Church. His ministry included parishes in Illinois, Oklahoma, South Carolina, Texas, and California. President George H.W. Bush and his family are members of the congregation he served in Houston, Texas, also the largest parish in the Episcopal Church.

He has served other notable leaders that represent the diversity of his ministry. These national leaders include Former Secretary of State, James Baker; Former Secretary of Education, Richard Riley; Supreme Court Nominee, Clement Haynsworth; and the infamous baby doctor, Benjamin Spock, among others.

Doctor Maynard maintains an extensive speaking and travel schedule. He is frequently called upon to speak, lead retreats, or serve as a consultant to parishes, schools and organizations throughout the United States.

He was ordained a priest at the age of twenty-four. His first parish assignments were as the curate at Grace Church, and vicar of Saint Philip's Mission in Muskogee, Oklahoma. The bishop of the diocese charged him with closing Saint Philip's, an African-American congregation, and merging it with Grace Church. At the close of his first year, the merger was realized.

His first parish assignment was to Saint Mark's Mission in Dallas, Texas. In less than a year, the mission achieved parish status. One year later, he successfully led the merger of that parish with nearby Saint Margaret's Parish in Richardson, Texas. The combined congregations chose the name *Church of the Epiphany*. Over the next eight years, they grew to a parish averaging one thousand people in attendance at five Sunday services, including a service in Mandarin. Under his leadership, the congregation held three capital campaigns. One campaign was held to build a new church with a pipe organ, another to remodel the old nave into a parish hall, and one to build a parish life center. The congregation started a counseling center, a bookstore, and a day school. It also became one of the centers for a teen drug abuse program and built a block partnership with an

African-American Congregation in South Dallas. Church of the Epiphany adopted two large Vietnamese Refugee Families, brought them to Dallas, and helped them begin new and productive lives. The parish was recognized for its growth and ministry in a 1978 article in *The Episcopalian*, the national newspaper for The Episcopal Church.

At the age of thirty-four, Maynard was called to Christ Church and School in Greenville, South Carolina. At the time, it was the seventh largest congregation in The Episcopal Church in America. Under his leadership, it grew to be the fourth largest, with six Sunday services. During his fifteen year tenure, the congregation set up four not-for-profit corporations. Each was organized to start a food bank, a soup kitchen, a free medical clinic, and a house for homeless men living with HIV and AIDS. The parish also built four Habitat For Humanity Houses while he was rector. Along with the diocese, the people of Christ Church worked with the Bishop of Haiti on several projects to meet the needs of the people of that diocese.

At the time that Maynard went to Greenville, Christ Church Episcopal School was in decline. The school was being heavily subsidized by the parish budget. This was negatively impacting the growth and ministry programs in the congregation. Conversations were held among the leadership about closing the high school, since more students were withdrawing from the school than were enrolling in it. Maynard and the head of school at the time began an aggressive student recruitment and marketing campaign. Together they established a board of visitors and an annual fund for the school. After five years, the decline was reversed and the school began to grow. Maynard led three multimillion-dollar capital campaigns to expand and improve the facilities for the parish and school at the downtown campus and broke ground for a new middle school building. The campaigns also allowed for the expansion of the downtown campus property. The parish established a bookstore, a preschool, and a counseling center under his leadership. The diocese had made the decision to close one of the mission churches in Greenville. He asked the bishop to make it a chapel of the parish to see if it couldn't be turned around. Saint Andrew's congregation became a self-supporting parish in just three years.

Maynard left Christ Church to become the Vice Rector of the largest congregation in The Episcopal Church, Saint Martin's, in Houston, Texas. While there, he was able to establish T*he Seabury Institute Southwest* as a regional campus for Seabury Theological School in Chicago. Clergy could study for advanced degrees in congregational development through the *Institute*.

Three years later, the bishop and calling committee of Saint James Parish in La Jolla, California, approached him about becoming their rector. The bishop and vestry at the time were particularly concerned about the declining attendance and finances of the parish. The parish was bleeding its endowment for daily operations and was quite literally living from bequest to bequest. Doctor Maynard believed himself called to be their rector. He was instrumental in discovering and convicting a longtime employee of the parish that had been embezzling large sums of money. He worked with the vestry to establish internal controls and audits to prevent a reoccurrence. They established a separate board to safeguard the endowment of the parish. The pledge budget tripled in just three years. During his tenure, the parish also built up an operating reserve to meet projected obligations.

The congregation experienced rapid growth, often filling the four Sunday services. A very successful bookstore and gift shop was established. He also led a capital campaign to address the deferred maintenance issues facing the historic property. The plan included provisions for making the property accessible to persons living with physical disabilities. An international Anglican Magazine carried an article on the turnaround at St. James by the Sea.

After thirty-eight years of parish ministry, Doctor Maynard retired in 2005 to be of service to clergy and congregations in the larger Church. He has worked with the bishops, clergy, schools, and congregations of thirty-two dioceses in the United States and Canada. He has become a best selling author of fifteen books that are being used extensively in the congregations of all denominations in the United States, Canada, and England. Two of his books are currently being utilized as source material for students in theological schools.

Doctor Maynard's ministry has included service on several diocesan boards and committees. These included various diocesan program committees, director of summer camps for boys, diocesan trustee, finance committees, and executive committees. He was elected Dean of various diocesan deaneries on several occasions. He was on the Cursillo secretariat, and he was spiritual director for the Cursillo Movement multiple times. Maynard served as co-chair for two diocesan capital campaigns.

In the National Episcopal Church, Maynard served multiple terms on the board of the National Association of Episcopal Schools, and as a trustee for Seabury Western Theological Seminary. He was named an adjunct professor in congregational development at Seabury. Maynard was the co-coordinator for two national conferences for large congregations with multiple staff ministries.

Doctor Maynard was twice named to *Oxford's Who's Who The Elite Registry of Extraordinary Professionals* and to *Who's Who Among Outstanding Americans.*

Maynard earned an Associate of Arts Degree in psychology, a Bachelor of Arts Degree in the social sciences, a Master's Degree in theology, and a Doctor of Ministry Degree. He currently resides in Rancho Mirage, California.

BOOKS BY
DENNIS R. MAYNARD

THOSE EPISKOPOLS

This is a popular resource for clergy to use in their new member ministries. It seeks to answer the questions most often asked about the Episcopal Church. Questions like: "Can You Get Saved in the Episcopal Church?" "Why Do Episcopalians Reject Biblical Fundamentalism?" "Does God Like All That Ritual?" "Are There Any Episcopalians in Heaven?" And others.

FORGIVEN, HEALED AND RESTORED

This book is devoted to making a distinction between forgiving those who have injured us and making the decision to reconcile with them or restore them to their former place in our lives.

THE MONEY BOOK

The primary goal of this book is to present some practical teachings on money and Christian Stewardship. It also encourages the reader not to confuse their self-worth with their net worth.

FORGIVE AND GET YOUR LIFE BACK

This book teaches the forgiveness process to the reader. It's a popular resource for clergy and counselors to use to do forgiveness training. In this book, a clear distinction is made between forgiving, reconciling, and restoring the penitent person to their former position in our lives.

SHEEP ATTACK SERIES

WHEN SHEEP ATTACK

Your rector is bullied, emotionally abused, and then his ministry is ended. Your parish is left divided. Formerly faithful members no longer attend. This book is based on the case studies of twenty-five clergy who had just such an experience. What could have been done? What can you do to keep it from happening to you and your parish? Discussion questions are included that make it suitable for study groups.

PREVENTING A SHEEP ATTACK

Based on an additional two hundred case studies and reports, this book explains just why a sheep attack necessitates that someone will be ejected from the congregational system. This particular book is written in workbook format to provide a training vehicle for congregational leaders. It is best utilized to educate congregational leaders on the things they need to put into place to prevent a sheep attack.

HEALING FOR PASTORS AND PEOPLE FOLLOWING A SHEEP ATTACK

After experiencing the bullying, intimidation, threats, and blackmail of a sheep attack, the wounds remain with the pastors and parish leaders for the rest of their lives. This book explains why these emotional memories are so devastating. The book is designed to assist with the healing process. It is a must read for all that have been victims of a sheep attack.

THE MAGNOLIA SERIES

BEHIND THE MAGNOLIA TREE (BOOK ONE)

Meet The Reverend Steele Austin. He is a young Episcopal priest who receives an unlikely call to one of the most prestigious congregations in the Southern United States. Soon his idealism conflicts with the secrets of sex, greed, and power at Historic First Church. His efforts to minister to those living with AIDS and HIV bring him face to face with members of the Klu Klux Klan. Then one of the leading members of his congregation seeks his assistance in coming to terms with the double life he's been living. The ongoing ministry of conflict with the bigotry and prejudice that are in the historic fabric of the community turn this book into a real page-turner.

WHEN THE MAGNOLIA BLOOMS (BOOK TWO)

In this, the second book in the Magnolia Series, Steele Austin finds himself in the middle of a murder investigation. In the process, the infidelity of one of his closest priest friends is uncovered. When he brings an African-American priest on the staff, those antagonistic to his ministry find even more creative methods to rid themselves of the young idealist. Then, a most interesting turn of events changes the African priest's standing in the parish. A young associate undermines the rector by preaching a gospel of hate, alienating most of the women in the congregation, and all the gay and lesbian members. The book closes with a cliffhanger that will leave the reader wanting another visit to Falls City, Georgia.

PRUNING THE MAGNOLIA (BOOK THREE)

Steele Austin's vulnerability increases even further when he uncovers a scandal that will shake First Church to its very foundation. In order to expose the criminal, he must first prove his own innocence. This will require him to challenge his very own bishop. The sexual sins of the wives of one of the parish leaders present a most unlikely pastoral opportunity for the rector. In the face of the ongoing attacks of his antagonists, Steele Austin is given the opportunity to leave First Church for a thriving parish in Texas.

THE PINK MAGNOLIA (BOOK FOUR)

The Rector's efforts to meet the needs of gay teenagers that have been rejected by their own families cast a dark cloud over First Church. A pastoral crisis with a former antagonist transforms their relationship into one of friendship. The Vestry agrees to allow the Rector to sell the church owned house and purchase his own, but not all in the congregation approve. The reader is given yet another view of church politics. The book ends with the most suspense filled cliffhanger yet.

THE SWEET SMELL OF MAGNOLIA (BOOK FIVE)

The fifth book in the Magnolia Series follows the Rector's struggle with trust and betrayal in his own marriage. His suspicions about his wife take a heavy toll on his health and his ministry. He brings a woman priest on the staff in face of the congregation's objections to doing so. Some reject her ministry totally. Then the internal politics of the Church are exposed even further with the election of a Bishop. Those with their own agenda manipulate the election itself. Just when you think the tactics of those opposed to the ministry of Steele Austin can't go any lower, they do.

THE MAGNOLIA AT SUNRISE (BOOK SIX)

The lives of The Reverend Steele Austin and the people of First Church face new challenges. Father Austin takes his sabbatical time to examine his life's purpose. Still stinging from the most recent attacks on his wife and himself from the antagonists in his congregation, he wrestles with the decision as to whether or not he wants to return to First Church. He is even uncertain if he wants to remain in the priesthood.

THE CHANGING MAGNOLIA (BOOK SEVEN)

The masters of the great plantations ruled over those they believed to be inferior to them. Their descendants often believe they are entitled to this same position. With divine right, they appeal to their wealth and bloodline, demanding that the unimportant in their world be subservient to them. In Falls City, Georgia, those in positions of superiority utilize intimidation, slander, blackmail, sex, and even murder to get their way. In this seventh visit to Historic First Church, these powerful people have used their influence to destroy the spirit of their own pastor and his family.

All of Doctor Maynard's books can be viewed and ordered on his website.
Discounts on most of his books are available through his website.
www.Episkopols.com
Visit Amazon.com to discover Doctor Maynard's books that are on Kindle.
www.Amazon.com

www.Episkopols.com

Dionysus Publications
Books for clergy and the people they serve.